HEIR OF SHADOWS

SUPERNATURALS OF DAIZLEI ACADEMY
BOOK ONE

KEL CARPENTER

Heir of Shadows

Published by Kel Carpenter

Copyright © 2016, Kel Carpenter LLC

Second Edition

Edited by Analisa Denny

Edited by Danielle Fine

Cover Art by Yocla

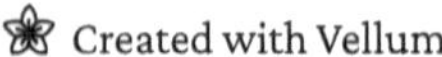 Created with Vellum

About the Author

Kel Carpenter is a master of werdz. When she's not reading or writing, she's traveling the world, lovingly pestering her co-author, and spending time with her family. She is always on the search for good tacos and the best pizza. She resides in Maryland and desperately tries to avoid the traffic.

To keep up with Kel and her books, join her Facebook Group: www.facebook.com/groups/thecrowsnestread-ersguild/

To Greg and Carol
For showing me there's a better world than what I knew. You stood by me through it all.
Thank you.

Of course it is happening inside your head, Harry, but why
on earth should that mean that it is not real?
J.K. Rowling, *Harry Potter and the Deathly Hallows*

THE INCIDENT

The sound of churning gravel cut off our shouting. Our eyes locked as we heard a car door shut, far too faintly for humans to hear. I turned away to hide my grimace as my forty-something, bible-thumping, temporary legal guardian came through the front door like a soldier at war. Alexandra was momentarily silenced by the harsh glare our aunt gave her. A short, plump woman with a ridiculously colorful wardrobe, Carrie had excellent hearing, so we didn't dare continue our conversation; despite being our "parent" at the time, she was also one hundred percent human.

"The principal called, right after *the police*, to tell me you were expelled and couldn't come within a thousand feet of your school." Her dark eyes flashed as she walked toward us.

"I wasn't going to learn anything useful anyway," Alexandra said.

Carrie looked appalled, and her voice rose in direct relation to the disinterest in Alexandra's tone. "You attacked another girl and just got kicked out of school! Don't you realize how serious this is? Don't you care?"

Nope. I doubted she cared in the slightest.

"There's only two weeks left . . ." she muttered.

"Of course, my ungrateful brat of a niece wouldn't care . . . and here I thought I was making an impression."

I nearly choked on suppressed laughter.

No one made an impression on Alexandra. One of the blessings of being a Supernatural with no parents was that you set your own rules, but she took it too far. I might've had a deep-rooted prejudice against humans and a twisted sense of right and wrong, but if there was anything I'd mastered in almost seventeen years, it was self-control. Think before you act, consider the consequences, and never, *ever* reveal our secret.

In my silent ramble, I hadn't heard Alexandra's response. Before I had time to react, my aunt's hand whipped out like a cobra and slapped her across the face. Time stopped as I held my breath. I watched the spark in my sister catch fire. She snapped.

I lunged forward to stop her, but Carrie was too close and Alexandra too fast. Fire erupted from her hand as she grabbed the collar of Carrie's shirt and threw her to the floor, knocking her unconscious. She glowered down at my aunt and the hesitation was all I needed to step between them.

"What the hell are you thinking?" I grabbed her shoulders and pushed her back. The more distance between them, the better.

"Get out of my way, Selena!" she growled, trying to get

around me. Her halo of red hair was covered in flames, making her look like fire incarnate.

"Not until you back off," I said, maintaining my stance.

She lunged for me, and I grabbed her swinging fist. Twisting her arm so hard she hunched over, I stepped behind her and pinned her other arm behind her back. Within moments, I had her secured by her wrists and on the ground.

"She's human. Get it through your damn head that no matter what she does, you can't behave like this!" I was nearly shouting. I had to stop myself from pulling her back so I could smash her into the ground again; she was my sister, after all.

"What *are* you?" a voice hissed.

My eyes snapped up to see Carrie staring, wide-eyed. She was by the front door and holding herself protectively. Her shirt collar was charred, and red burn welts nearly wrapped around her neck.

Great. Collateral damage.

The front door started to open behind Carrie, and she jumped back, terrified.

Sunny blond hair peeked through before the door swung open. My sister Lily was home. It took her no time at all to assess the situation, and her smile dropped into a grimace. She did a once-over of Carrie's expression and looked away; her mind now closed to any excuses Alexandra would undoubtedly give.

"I'll go pack," she said dryly.

CHAPTER I

Tick.

Tock.

Tick.

Tock.

Tick.

Tock.

Three hours and fifty-two minutes ago, they'd closed the plane doors. I'd checked my watch seventy-eight times since then. We still had half an hour, and my anxiety was building.

I wiggled out from between my sisters. Alexandra cast me a tired look before narrowing her eyes at Lily's sleeping figure. It's amazing how at sixteen years old they still argue over who gets the window seat.

I ran my hand over Lily's forehead to clear the wrinkles away, but the troubled frown remained, and she mumbled in her sleep. I didn't have to hear her to know what she was dreaming; it'd been the same for five years. Her fitful sleep wasn't the only consequence of our parents' deaths, but it *was* the only one there was no help for. The only one beyond my control. I frowned, shaking my head as I squeezed past Alexandra into the aisle.

Leering male gazes followed me as I breezed past. I set my jaw as I headed toward the rear of the plane, trying to pay no attention to the visual pedophiles.

I slipped into the tiny bathroom. The fluorescent light was awful, and the mirror smudged with lipstick. I waved my hands under the faucet, scooping up cold water and splashing it on my face, letting it run down my neck. It helped clear my mind, but not my unease.

My long black hair fell forward into the sink, soaking my shirt as I sighed unhappily and shifted to sitting on the toilet seat. I hadn't slept in three nights. Not since Carrie threw plane tickets at us and she kicked us out of her house. But ever since, I'd been up thinking. Planning. This was it— our very last option before foster care. I wouldn't let that happen. I couldn't. If this didn't work out, we'd go some- where. San Francisco, Las Vegas, maybe New York . . . I didn't know yet, but somewhere. It would be so much easier if Alexandra could just get her act together.

We could stay put till we turned eighteen then go off to college. Lily could grow up and meet a nice, pathetic human boy. Alexandra could become a model or something equally outlandish that would get her both attention and men . . .

But what about you?

The thought rang like a bell in the eerie silence. What *about* me? My defenses were falling more every week. The threat of insanity loomed just out of sight, like a shadow, always there. Waiting. I'm not normal, but I'm not crazy . . . yet.

I was growing restless, impatient. My temper was shorter, with just as big a bang. If I said yes to the insanity, to the darkness, to my disease . . . Selena would be no more. The monster would reign. And once I let it out, there would be no going back.

If I let it out, people would die. People I cared about much more than myself. I had to hold it together—for them. Had to remember the things this world would do to them as justice for my actions . . . I could never release the monster, not for anything less than the world. I grimaced at my black boots. The laces were falling apart, like the seams of my life, but somehow they survived. Worn and walked on, they remained.

I tapped my feet impatiently as I glanced at the time. Twenty-five more minutes. Could it go any slower?

"Good evening, ladies and gentlemen, this is your captain speaking—"

I jerked my head up sharply. "Great. Just flipping great . . ." I muttered, not even listening to what he had to say.

I stood, stumbling as the plane rocked sideways. Turbulence. The door flung open and the frame rattled, but whether it was from me or the shaking, I didn't know. Before I'd even made it out into the aisle, a greasy man with awful breath fell onto me, pushing me back into the wall. I flattened like a sheet to escape his touch.

Stop.

"Well, hello, darlin'." His gaze traveled to my disheveled shirt, which had been pulled down in the commotion. He smelled of alcohol and stale smoke. My eyes glazed over as the violent calm took over.

"Get the fuck off me if you want to keep that hand," I spat, pushing him into the counter.

"Don't be like that, sugar." He made the mistake of reaching for me.

Before his hand even made contact with my skin, I grabbed it and sidestepped behind him. I thrust my palm into his elbow, snapping the bone.

"Fuck!" He cried out in pain, surely not prepared for— nor accustomed to—having his ass handed to him by a hundred-and-twenty-five-pound girl. I twisted his arm sharply behind his back and threw him into the wall.

I turned to leave and almost ran into two blond Amazonian flight attendants who were staring in horror.

Shit.

CHAPTER 2

"So you're saying this man tried to sexually assault you?"

"Yes. I've said yes the last five times. My answer's not changing, so yes, yes, and wait—yes again," I snapped.

The policeman looked me over. He was an older man—maybe forty. He was utterly normal with an average face and forgettable features. To the very core, this man was nothing but human. Which meant he was nothing.

"Where are your parents? I'm reading the report and it says here you're sixteen."

I narrowed my eyes and opened my mouth—

"That would be me," a voice said behind me.

I didn't have to turn to know who it was. Her heels on the tile were almost inaudible, her pitch authoritative, and the light hand on my shoulder too firm.

"Are you aware of the charges brought against your daughter, Mrs. Foster?" he asked, interrupting my train of thought.

I scowled. "I'm not her daughter."

"Mariana Stormer, and I *am* her guardian. Yes, I'm well aware, and it's been squared away already. You can release her now," she said, all too sweetly. There was definitely something off about her.

"I have to run it past my superior—" His cellphone went off. My aunt squeezed my shoulder gently. "Yes . . . but . . . okay . . . yes, sir." He looked up from the phone. Dumbstruck.

A shadow of a smirk crossed my lips.

"You're released," he said with apprehension. He came around to uncuff me. "The assault charges are being dropped. Consider this a warning."

I smirked in his direction as I walked out.

He met my gaze with a suspicious look that transformed as I came closer. Uneasiness—as if he could sense the danger I presented—and confusion. Subconsciously, he knew I was different. I wasn't like him. I wasn't human.

"Mrs. Stormer, will you please sign the release papers?" He beckoned from the desk, but his gaze didn't stray from me.

"Wait outside. We're going to have a talk when we get home," she said in a hushed voice intended for my ears only.

I looked back one last time before leaving. Mariana was tall and arrogant with a beauty very different from my mother's—hard, and colder than most, but it was beauty, nonetheless.

That wasn't what I saw in her. I saw something else, something darker. Instead of her velvety voice or carefully placed smile, I saw the strain behind it. The harshness in her eyes that hinted at a different woman. Was there more to her?

Perhaps.

Or perhaps I was closer to crazy than even I knew.

~.~.~

It was silent for about ten seconds. I was grateful for that, at least. It gave me a chance to compose myself into the unreadable figure I was supposed to be. The mask I couldn't take off. It gave me ten seconds to find an excuse. A lie.

"Honestly, Selena. You're the one with self-control. If you can't keep it together, how am I supposed to expect her to?" My Aunt Mariana thrust her chin toward the rearview mirror that reflected my ill-tempered sister. If I hadn't known better, I would've said she knew something. Something she shouldn't. Something dangerous.

"What?" My stomach flipped.

She sighed and closed her eyes. "I really didn't want to spring this on you. I told them you wouldn't take it well, but I only have a limited amount of time here." She sighed.

Terror gripped me, aided by adrenaline. Fight or flight. I stiffened.

"What are you talking about?" I don't know which of us said it, but somehow one of us managed to say the words we'd rehearsed so many times. They weren't for a cover-up this time; they were meant to buy time. The problem was, here on the road to nowhere, we had nothing but time.

"You know what I'm talking about. All of you do, and the longer you pretend you don't, the harder this is going to be." Her voice was solid, strong, but her hands gripped the wheel, and her gaze was glued to the road, unblinking. She was nervous. Which meant she wasn't stupid. To approach three unknowns in a car alone was suicide.

"You're one of us," I whispered.

"Yes."

CHAPTER 3

I hadn't seen a Supernatural in five years. They'd abandoned us. Forgotten us. Yet here sat one of my closest remaining relatives, unveiling not only her secret, but also our own. What was I supposed to think? Feel?

"But the rest of your family's human."

There was no point denying it now. She knew. I was lost, though. Confused. Conflicted. Confined. As emotions raged through my system, anger came out on top.

"Yes."

"How?" I demanded.

"We were adopted, your mother and I."

Speechless.

Five years ago, our parents died. Five years, we've spent in the human world. Five years, we've struggled to keep our identity under wraps. Five years, she'd waited. In those years, we lived with humans not even remotely related to us, and yet Mariana still waited. I'd always assumed my mother was a bastard child by the woman I called grandmother, but 'adopted' opened a whole new can of worms.

Which begged the question: why? Why had they done this to us? Why hadn't Mariana taken us? Why had it happened like this?

Too many questions and not enough answers.

"Why are we only coming to live with you now?" Alexandra spoke up from behind me. Her voice was hard, like my own. This wasn't some heartfelt family reunion; it was an interrogation.

"My daughters are both Supernaturals. I had to be sure you were as well before I could take custody of you," Mariana said dismissively.

"The signs have been there since the first house burned down." Alexandra rolled her eyes.

"Outside factors sometimes have a bigger impact than you would think, dear." She shrugged. I didn't buy the passive nonchalance she was trying to sell.

"And what the hell is that supposed to mean?" Alexandra raised her voice, unyielding.

"It means I'm not explaining myself to a sixteen-year-old. I understand that you're angry, Alexandra, but I need you to trust me right now. There are things going on that you don't know about; things that require you to believe I have your best interests at heart. Can you do that?"

"Give me one reason I should."

"Because you don't exactly have a lot of options at the moment. I'm the last person before foster care, and I think you know that," she snapped.

In the mirror I saw the glare Alexandra was giving her. I had to rein this in.

"You wouldn't dare," she said.

A single look over my shoulder conveyed the message to my sister.

Shut the hell up.

Mariana must have her reasons. She wouldn't do this to her own flesh and blood otherwise. She wouldn't wait five years without one.

You have secrets too—terrible and destructive, another voice whispered dangerously. *Things that would make her turn this car around in a heartbeat. Who are you to judge?*

I stared glumly out the window. The shock was wearing off, replaced by even harder questions that I didn't know how to answer. Who *was* I to judge? Mariana didn't know all of it; that much was obvious. She'd only skimmed the surface. So where did that leave us? Did we trust her? Did I trust her?

Can I?

She said she had our best interests at heart, but people seldom did. She was family . . . but not really. She hadn't been there once in the last sixteen years. So what was her motivation? Why did she want us? Why now? Perhaps she felt guilt about what happened to our parents. She would've taken us five years ago if that were the case. Either way, she was Supernatural, and that counted for something. Or did it?

The way I was raised, being Supernatural meant every-thing. Anything less wasn't anything at all. Humans and dogs, they were all the same to my kind. Surely the people who'd taught me that would've wanted this. They would've wanted us to go with her. Wouldn't they?

I pushed away the unsure voice. My mind was made up, regardless of where this path took us—or how I felt about it. They would've wanted this, and I owed it to them to see it through.

Only one question remained.

"What happens now?"

I could feel Alexandra's incredulous gawk, and Lily's bewildered stare. They didn't understand my line of thought—not yet, anyway. All they could see was what was right here in front of them. That was my job, my life. I could see what needed to happen and do what needed to be done. I would ensure we survived. No matter the costs.

"My dear, dear niece. Now it's time for your life to really begin," she said softly, turning her eyes to the road. There was sadness in them, behind the gray, so similar in color to my own.

I wasn't sure what she meant, but I had a feeling we were about to find out.

~.~.~

I didn't speak after that, and my aunt didn't push it. She seemed to know that my cooperation—and by extension, my sisters—was limited and coming to an end. I understood her predicament, but I also knew the risk I was taking by going into a situation with so little information. We were both out of options.

Alexandra resorted to throwing me filthy looks from the backseat. I didn't know what to tell her; I knew as little as she did. Mariana was being intentionally vague, and we all had more questions than answers. I wasn't in a place to challenge our aunt, and neither was she. Her audacity, as always, astounded me. Why couldn't she understand?

"It's beautiful," Lily whispered.

The mansion looming in front of us was weathered, seemingly abandoned, and vastly eerie despite the sunset painting it in a soft glow. Back in the day, it might've been beautiful. Now . . . not so much. I glanced at Mariana. How could someone with her polished looks and sterile car live *here*? The driveway was new; stylish and attractive, but subtle enough most wouldn't notice it when they looked at the house. Perhaps it was all a façade.

"We're late. Leave your things. Fiona will get them during dinner," she said.

I followed her as we approached the house.

Ivy wove in and out between the steps and through the walkway. It climbed the stone and encroached on the roof. The only things left unscathed were the dark mahogany doors. Embellished carvings spanned from one door to the next—beautiful despite the chips and nicks from age. Brass handles shone like gold, completing the vintage home that —in its better days—could've belonged to Gatsby.

The picture was one-sided. When Mariana opened the door, the aged wood gave way to marble floors and modern styling. Everything was stark white—floors, walls, couches—aside from a blood-red rug. A staircase with no railing wrapped around the room, starting at my left and ending at my right. There was a brief hallway leading to the kitchen; stainless steel dominating the hanging lights and modern appliances. Black cabinets with glass panels showcased iron kitchenware, while a grand island displayed a buffet that could've fed an army. The most striking thing of all was the entire back wall made of glass. I let out a low whistle. We came from Carrie's shabby, mismatched furniture and plastic plates, not gold spoons and Lamborghinis.

"In here, dears."

I followed her through the door to my left. My feet came to an immediate halt. Blood-red walls and archaic chandeliers dragged me back in time, to a memory of sitting at a table very similar to this one. Blood. I could remember the blood. I saw it everywhere, even though it wasn't real. The sickly omen threatened to drown me, and stumbling forward, I grabbed for the only solid thing within my reach —the table. Panic fought to take over. I knew it was there, but the memory was a distant thing. Like looking through a haze only to find nothing.

Someone reached for me, and my body reacted on instinct. I swiped the encroaching arm away then stepped in to throw the attacker back. I wrapped my hand around her throat and moved to slam her head into the wall. Inches before impact, I saw my error and hesitated. Lily. My attacker was Lily. I snatched my hand away, and stepped back to put distance between us.

"I'm sorry," I muttered, looking away.

Everyone's eyes turned to me.

"Damn it, Selena. Seriously?" Alexandra said.

I cut my eyes her way and glared. After everything that had happened in the last week, the last thing I wanted to deal with was her attitude.

"It's okay. I'm fine," Lily choked.

Was I really that on edge that I couldn't tell the difference between my sister and my demons? The unwelcome thought crept into my mind as I averted my eyes.

She knows not to touch me.

Especially during an episode. I turn volatile.

"Those are quite the reflexes," a blonde with gray eyes said.

"Yes," I said, turning to the blonde.

She was a dead ringer for Lily, with long, wavy blond hair and pale skin—though not as pale as mine. From a distance, they could've easily been confused, but those eyes . . . I couldn't get past them. So like my own, cold and ruthless.

What perplexed me was that she wasn't the only one with them, just the only one who made me think of myself. Mariana's were similar, but when I looked at her, I saw a broken woman. Everyone said she'd slipped a little after Mom died, but maybe there was more to it. Then there was the matter of the Hot Topic brunette sitting at the opposite head of the table. She was pretty, but not outstandingly so. Her face was as forgettable as her bored expression as she sat with her legs thrown over the arm of the chair. She may have had my eyes, but they were also singularly her own. They held no malice, cruelty, or dispassion. On the contrary, she was an open book. She didn't guard her emotions. It was so very strange to look at her and see a complete and total stranger staring back without a shadow of unease. How could she sit at a table with three unknown Supernaturals but not have a care in the world?

Several moments of tense silence had already passed, and my calculating stare was only making it worse. "Forgive me. It's been a very long day, given the circumstances. I think I should go lie down."

"Of course. Follow the stairs up to the third floor. I'll

have Fiona bring your things . . . " Mariana trailed off, looking at the bag slung over my shoulder.

"Thanks, but no thanks," I said, leaving the room without sparing my sisters a glance. They would have to deal without me for half an hour.

I took the stairs two at a time then walked through the matching double doors. On the other side, I came to a spiral staircase. Wanting to put as much distance between myself and everyone downstairs, I climbed.

I was expecting more ominous colors on the third floor, not that it really mattered. We moved so much I rarely bothered with painting a bedroom. Bright and sunny yellow wasn't expected. The bright egg yolk color was an eyesore.

I threw my bag on the bed as I paced. A headache was coming on, courtesy of the events of the day. I'd almost been arrested in the airport. My extended family of Super-naturals had shown up out of nowhere. Now my episode in the dining room. What the hell was going on with me? I reached into the side of my bag for Tylenol and downed four pills.

Does that make twelve today? Sixteen?

I didn't even know anymore. In any case, my metabolism worked so fast I would probably burn through them in an hour.

The darkness crept in on me. I wanted to bang my head on the wall so hard I couldn't feel it anymore. Couldn't feel anything. But I had responsibilities. Things more important than losing my fucking mind. We were living in a house with three unknown Supernaturals. Not to mention the more pressing issue of keeping my ability hidden. I was dormant now, but my demons wouldn't be suppressed so easily. I was going to need a cover, and I hadn't the slightest idea how I would find one.

I could hear voices coming from downstairs. Even with my hearing, they were still only the smallest of whispers. Warning bells were already starting to go off as I approached the spiral staircase in the center of our room.

"They're hiding something," Alexandra whispered.

Dinner's over already?

Mariana must keep it short and to the point.

"You think I don't know that?" Lily whispered back.

I heard her soft thudding steps as they ascended the stairs. Alexandra was far stealthier. It helped that she didn't walk like a caveman.

I didn't bother moving as they rounded the final curve and came into view. The look on Alexandra's face instantly turned hostile.

"Who the hell do you think you are?" she whispered.

At least she had the decency to keep her voice down. I put a finger to my lips and cut my eyes to the bathroom. She got the hint and went with me while Lily followed behind.

The bathroom was huge with white tiles and porcelain surfaces covering the space, giving it a distinctly feminine feel. I flipped the bathtub on, allowing the water to drown out our voices as I turned to my sister.

"I don't know where you got the idea that I'm the enemy here, but I'm getting sick of you second-guessing everything I do. Obviously, I have my reasons, and I've more than proven myself to you a hundred times over." I was ice, and my voice reflected the distance I'd put between myself and any type of emotion.

"Selena, it's been a long day . . . " Lily murmured. She sat on the counter with her legs dangling over, watching the fight. Usually, it was the other way around, and I had to play referee.

"You know what I'm getting sick of? You acting like you're my parent. They might be dead, but no one appointed your ass as queen! Why do you get to make all the decisions?" She kept raising her voice until she was shouting. Where I lacked in emotion, she was nothing but. Fire was in my sister's very core.

"That's why. You're too immature. Did you ever stop to think when you were running your mouth like a fool today? Regardless of why Mariana brought us here, this is our last stop before foster care. What are the odds that someone would be willing to take triplets with a record like ours? Huh? Fighting. Drugs. Three counts of arson. Who the hell would be dumb enough to take us on?"

Oh, she'd pissed me off this time. I was going to rip her a new one that would make my usual reprimands look pale in comparison. She was going to remember this a year from now and then some.

"So, please tell me—because I'm just dying to hear— why you would act like a demanding little bitch to Mariana, who knows damn well the power she holds? She's a Super- natural, Alexandra! Did it never occur to you that maybe there's a legitimate reason we ended up here finally? I don't think it's a coincidence that she's the last stop." I paused, and took a shaky breath. I gripped the leash, forcing the monster to heel. "Did you seriously believe I hadn't consid- ered *why*? That I didn't see how sketchy this situation is— magical fairy godmother pops up after five years to save triplets from foster care?" Sarcasm rolled off me in waves. The leash I kept my monster on felt too tight. The disease. My disease. Insanity. They couldn't know. They couldn't find out just how much of a battle it was for control.

"Selena . . . " Lily said gently. It was an unspoken warning to watch myself. I'd already been to the brink of crazy once today; twice was testing it.

I took a step back, putting a foot of distance between my hotheaded sister and myself. Taking a deep breath, I walked around her to regain my self-control. I paused as I grasped the door handle. "I'm your sister, and I'm sorry you feel like this is a dictatorship. I've done everything in my power to make it up to you the past five years. I can't change who or what I am, Alexandra. I've always had your best interests at heart, and the fact that you still question that . . . frankly, it pisses me off. I didn't choose to be the strong one. I was born that way. I'm going to make you a promise, sister. If you pull shit like this again, I'll give you a reminder why this isn't a democracy."

Though the water was running, there was no doubt she could hear me. Her entire body went still; she knew what I was talking about. With her memories from that night resurfacing along with mine, I walked out, letting her decide for herself if she believed my threat, or if she was going to call my bluff.

CHAPTER 4

Even though Mariana's house was miles from civilization, it was hard to get a moment of privacy with five other Supernaturals under the same roof. That was what had driven the three of us out onto the deserted road—a chance to speak openly. I hadn't really missed Alexandra's input on things in the last week, but I supposed it was necessary if we were to decide what to do. In all my grandest plans, I'd never considered boarding school . . . until my aunt announced that she was shipping us off with her brats.

I didn't know what bothered me more: that she'd waited five years to remove us from the human world, or the thought of this boarding school—Daizlei Academy for the Prodigies of Tomorrow and Home of the Gifted. 'Gifted.' That was what they were calling us nowadays. I'd laughed when I first heard it. My aunt had avoided going into the details, but we all knew what she meant. We were going to a school for Supernaturals. The thought should've thrilled me. I wanted nothing more than to be done with humankind, the parasite on our planet. But even now, at the end of the week, it was the *why* that still bothered me. Why wait five years? Why now?

I'd manifested long before my parents' deaths. Hell, even Alexandra had manifested years before. There had to be a reason. Something I was missing. My parents knew where we would go in the event of their deaths. They knew we were unstable. All Supernatural children are, to a certain degree. Physically and mentally unprepared to live undetected in the human world. The three of us together? I shook my head in disbelief. They had to have known the consequences. We should've gone to Mariana first, no questions asked. So why hadn't we? Unless . . . they hadn't wanted us to. Why wouldn't they want us to, then? I sighed.

"What?" Lily asked.

"This is just all so confusing," I said, more calmly than I felt.

"Tell me about it . . . " Alexandra mumbled.

"It could be worse," Lily said.

Normally, I agreed with her, but not this time. "Not really," I said quietly.

"Oh, don't you start too. Look, I know this is confusing, but we'll get through it. We always do," she continued, her stubbornness setting in. Lily was the sun that would not be eclipsed if only from her sheer willpower. Her voice was too high, and it gave away that she wasn't nearly as optimistic as she tried to pretend.

"How? Lily, I can't control my temper. I don't care what that bitch says, we all know what's going to happen when I lose it," Alexandra said.

"Seriously? You're going with that same old excuse? Grow up," Lily retorted.

Her tone was so cold she sounded both dead and alive. Alexandra's escapades had cost her dearly, and it seemed she was tired of rolling over. She was ready to fight for something. If only that something wasn't a boarding school that made my hair stand on end.

"Grow up? Really? You're one to talk. You still cry yourself to sleep every night. Grow some balls, Lily. Maybe take a step outside your books every now and then, and you'll see that the world isn't all rainbows and butterflies." She sneered.

"Rainbows and butterflies? Are you really that ignorant, or is it your arrogance? I take three different medications so that I don't slip into severe depression. Every time I close my eyes, I see coffins and cliffs, and you want to judge me?" The color drained from Lily's face as she gritted her teeth.

"Stop," I said, stepping between them. "This is ridiculous. Are you guys really going to sit here and argue about whose vices are worse? That's hardly the issue at hand." I glared at them.

"You're right. It's not her issues that are the problem. It's her." Alexandra scowled down at her.

"Me? You're the reason we're here in the first place!" Lily cried, throwing her hands up in anger.

"And you're defending every word that lying bitch says!"

"I'm not defending her, you idiot. I . . . I agree with her." Lily looked down, staring at her hands.

Alexandra stared open-mouthed at her. "You seriously believe all that bull—"

"No. I know she's not telling us everything, and I know you both have your little conspiracy theories, but . . . but I think she's right." She met my eyes, pleading. "We won't be roomed together, and we probably won't have the same exact schedules, but I think it's best for us. Honestly, I need some space from you. From all of this." She waved her hands at the air around her. "And you need to get your attitude in check. I know you can't ignore everything, but you go off at every other thing. I don't know how Selena does it."

I rolled my eyes. *Self-control.*

"How very self-righteous of you," Alexandra said.

"Self-righteous? Do you even know what that means?" Lily said.

"Probably not," I said dryly.

Lily snickered.

"Don't even start with me," Alexandra shot at me.

I raised my eyebrow, daring her to do something.

"Or what? You'll flip out and burn her alive?" Lily motioned to me, letting out a cold laugh. "Did you ever think that she's given up everything for us? Every time you make a mistake, she fixes it. Every time I wake up screaming, she's there. Every time. I know you have your reservations about us going to Daizlei, but if not for yourself, do it for her."

I held up my hand to stop her there. "Those are beautiful words, but I'm fine, thank you. And I think you've made your case." My tone was short. I didn't leave room for argument, and yet she continued.

"See? You don't even know how to handle normal human interaction. If someone says something you don't want to hear, you just dismiss them . . . " Lily faltered slightly in a tirade that was coming far too close to the truth.

"Firstly, we're not human. Secondly, when did you become a psychologist? I think we're done here," I said.

Lily snorted and turned to Alexandra for help.

"She has a point, " Alexandra muttered under her breath.

I turned on my heel, fed up with the bullshit.

"There you go again!" Lily called.

"What do you want me to say?" I snapped. "I'm not this way because I take care of you two. I'm this way because of what I am. Maintaining control has never been more important." I pointed at Alexandra.

"Case in point." Lily nodded, crossing her arms over her chest.

"Hey—"

"If you want to go there, that's great. I'm happy for you. I don't. I've already got enough shit to deal with, so forgive me for not sharing your enthusiasm. We're going because we have to. We have no other option at the moment." My chest started to constrict, my frustration getting the better of me. I inhaled deeply and closed my eyes, feeling the earth beneath my feet, and the wind in my hair. Only when I was calm did I open my eyes and turn to Lily.

"I have no choice. So I'd really appreciate it if you would back off." There was a warning in my tone. Silence that spoke of danger and an edge that was almost desperate. It wasn't the kind of lapse in control that would kill someone, but it stirred something in me.

Control and power are two very separate things that

dance on a fine line. Sort of like love and hate. Having one without the other is useless; having both or neither can lead to self-destruction. The key is balance. I'd spent over a decade perfecting the scale. Yet, as I stood there, I felt the scale tip. Slightly—oh so slightly—but it did, and I knew in my heart that there was no coming back. It was only a matter of time now.

"If something happens, will you move us again?" Lily asked suddenly.

I flexed my fingers, contemplating my answer.

Would I? If I did something, we would have no choice, but even getting out of boarding school wouldn't be enough to make me come undone. Life or death. Nothing less would draw it out of me. Nothing.

"I don't know," I answered, turning to face them.

"Can you do it again?" she continued.

I frowned a little and looked past her at the horizon. "I don't know," I said.

She nodded twice.

"I think if it really came down to it, or if you guys really wanted it . . . I could," I said quietly, turning back toward the house. I was tired, and this conversation was going nowhere.

"You do realize you may not have to move us again. I could, like, end up burning down the school before it came to that," Alexandra said, and my lips curved up in a half-smile. If there was one thing we shared, it was our twisted sense of humor.

"Yep. I'm banking on it."

CHAPTER 5

"I trust you talked it over." It wasn't a question.

I took a seat across from my aunt in her medieval dining room. My sisters took their seats, and Alexandra eyed our cousins with suspicion. Red walls and that godawful chandelier set the mood for a very disagreeable conversation. I silently hoped I was wrong. I'd dealt with too much this week. I didn't think I could take any more surprises.

"We came to a mutual understanding," Lily responded stiffly.

"I believe the term is impasse," I said.

Lily shot me a glare before stabbing her lasagna.

I sighed. I knew how badly she wanted to go—to get away. She always had. At what price? I couldn't blame her for wanting friends, but then, by the same token, she couldn't be angry with me for my reservations.

"Impasse?" Mariana's voice curled around the word like a snake. "I must say, I am mildly curious. Might I ask what you're disagreeing about?" Her haunting, familiar gray eyes never left my face.

I stiffened almost imperceptibly as a chill ran down my back. "Your school."

Mild surprise and immediate interest danced in her eyes. I pushed the lasagna around, suddenly not hungry. "Hmmm. What about it?"

"She's concerned with the safety aspect," Lily cut in.

"Ah. Well, you can rest assured that you will be completely safe there. I understand your hesitance, but the campus is in a very secure and remote location."

She'd misunderstood. Of course, most Supernaturals would be concerned with attacks from the outside, not within. I should've been thinking the same thing, and yet . . . the need to protect my secrets overrode my distrust of the human species.

"And what about from within?" I asked tentatively. I didn't want to give anything away, but I had to know.

"What exactly are you asking?" She cocked her head, examining me.

"Are the students safe from each other?" I said, choosing to be blunt as I leaned forward and returned her gaze.

A smirk played on her lips. "Of course. Students are heavily supervised at all times. Especially when using their abilities." She laughed, and my cousin Blair joined her.

"What kind of abilities are we dealing with here?" I continued, ignoring the snort that came from Alexandra two seats down.

"That's a complex question, dear. You may as well ask how many kinds of flowers are out back. Every ability is different. They can be physical or mental. Weak or strong. It all depends on the individual. Daizlei has over three thousand students . . . so your guess is as good as mine." She smiled, but I suddenly felt very, very sick. Three thousand Supernaturals . . .

I could barely manage the five people at the table. Three thousand was incomprehensible. It would be physically impossible for me to shield myself from that many people. I'd go crazy just trying.

"That does bring up a very good point. What are your abilities? I should let the headmaster know before your arrival," she went on, unaware of my silent breakdown.

My heart skipped a beat. I still hadn't found an excuse —not a respectable one anyway.

"I can heal people," Lily spoke up beside me.

"Really? That's a very unique gift. Can you heal yourself also?" She looked fascinated.

"No." She shook her head delicately. Her soft blond hair swished back and forth, light as a feather.

"Shame . . . " she murmured.

Lily frowned in surprise at her disapproval, but didn't speak.

"And you?" She turned to Alexandra.

A wicked grin spread across her face as she did something I should've expected. Opening her hand palm up, she allowed a small flame to dance across her skin. Safe. Contained. Until she lifted it to her lips as if she were blowing a kiss. It fanned eight feet high and arced over the already burning candles, melting them to stubs as they splattered all over the food.

Mariana jumped back as part of the white tablecloth caught fire.

"Alexandra!" Lily and I admonished in unison.

She giggled like a four-year-old with her hand in the cookie jar.

I scowled at the fire as it spread.

"Blair," Mariana commanded.

My cousin stood, lifting her hand the way Alexandra had when commanding the fire. She wasn't a fire user, however; she was ice. Her fingers turned an unreal blue as frozen flakes blew from her hand and settled on the fire until it died out.

Blair turned an icy glare on my hotheaded sister, who looked rather pissed off that someone had stolen her thunder. "You're arrogant and foolish. Just because you have power doesn't mean you should abuse it like a parlor trick. Maybe Daizlei will do you some good. You obviously need it more than we need you." She turned on her heel and strode out the room. I listened to her walk away until she reached the second floor and silence overshadowed the table.

A sharp clap pierced my ears as the brunette stood, applauding slowly. "Well, this has been the most interesting family dinner we've ever had. I'm going to head out now, but we should do this again some time. Thanks for the entertainment, cousin." Elizabeth made a grand bow with a sweep of her hand. It was comical in a way, and amusement danced in her eyes.

"And, Mother, I told you to get rid of that ugly chandelier three years ago. You can blame yourself. I do." She smiled sarcastically as she looked up at the chandelier, shaking her head. Her cocky grin was admirable, and I appreciated the easygoing tone in her voice that was a warm contrast to those icy stares and clipped voices. When she swaggered out of the dining room with an arrogance so like my own, I couldn't help smiling.

"Well, I'll be going now. It's about time I turn in for the night." I got to my feet and started to leave.

"Not so fast," Mariana said harshly, moving to block the door.

I raised an eyebrow, but remained where I was. Alexandra stood to follow me, and Lily sighed. "Yes?"

"I don't know who you think you are, but you will not turn my house upside down. You may think you're something special, and you might be, but you're in for a rude awakening in three days." She looked from Alexandra to me, and I rolled my eyes. "While you may know how to use your enhanced senses, I doubt you're even a level three. I suggest you drop the attitude before you get to Daizlei." She looked at me like I was filth on the bottom of her shoe. That would've pissed me off if she hadn't just been my saving grace.

Without realizing it, she'd provided me with the perfect alibi to hide what I was. Enhanced senses. Strength. Speed. Reflexes. Due to my real ability, mine were far greater than most Supernaturals, but she didn't know that. We could really do this.

I could do this.

If I didn't go crazy first.

CHAPTER 6

Sunrise. I loved to see it. When I was a kid, my dad would take me out on the roof to watch it every morning—we were always early risers—and even five years after he died, I'd never missed one. I used to think of him when I saw it. The time we spent together, and the talks we had. I would think about boxing, living, my promise . . .

But not today.

Not now.

I had too much on my plate. Too many things depended on me not screwing up. How was I going to handle a school full of Supernaturals? I may be able to pretend I had enhanced senses, but I couldn't ignore the situation Mariana had put me in. What she was asking for could ruin me, and my sisters. It could ruin their shot at a better life. My parents' dying wish wouldn't be fulfilled.

Normal? I tested the word. No, we would never be normal. I could hope for happiness—for them, at least. Would they be happy there? Lily wanted it so badly she could taste it, but Alexandra didn't know what she wanted. Who was to say they wouldn't hate it?

A sharp tap on the window startled me back to reality. Alexandra's red head peeked out before she scrambled on top of the roof next to me with the grace of a baby giraffe.

"What are you thinking?" she said after several minutes of sitting there.

"If we stay here, we have no choice. We'll be walking into an unknown situation where I can't control the outcome." That was the part that scared me.

"I know. I know that's what worries you. It's the reason you froze at dinner and take three hour-long showers . . . I know. You have to let it go." She sounded so wise for someone who, not twelve hours ago, had set fire to the dining room table.

"I can't," I whispered.

"It's going to destroy you if you don't," she said quietly, taking my hand.

"Alexandra, I don't know how. Control is everything. It's all I know. If I let that go . . . I don't know what will happen," I said, choking on my own words.

"That's life. There are no guarantees, remember? You taught me that," she said with a sad smile.

I didn't respond. Instead, we sat in silence until the sun was nearly on the horizon.

"You know, if we do this, there's no going back. Like it or not, when we get there, we're stuck. If we leave for any reason, there are no relatives left. It will be us on our own, for good." I could only hope that the path we were taking led us to a future together, whether it was alone or among three thousand. The odds were never in our favor.

"What choice do we have? It ends the same, so why not try it?" she said finally, and there it was. She'd made up her mind. Silence expanded between us, and my options weren't good.

"You want to go?" I asked softly. It sounded more like a statement.

"Yes."

I didn't like it. We were already going, but, hearing her now, I was surer than ever that we were on the cusp of something. It was terrifying, exciting, foreboding, and reckless. I didn't know if I wanted whatever this something was, but like it or not, I had a duty.

CHAPTER 7

Fear. It's a tactic in war, and a feeling I was very well acquainted with. I'd used it for years to clean up the messes my sisters left behind, but what did you do when others stopped fearing you?

The more time that passed, the more confusion set in. Lily was gaining a backbone as we grew older. Alexandra was gaining an edge. And me?

I didn't even remember what it felt like to be alive anymore.

I was so far gone that the lines of reality were blurring, and my glasses were nowhere to be found. It was moments like these when I could feel myself sinking deeper, retreating more, crawling so far under my skin that it was a wonder I was still here.

Why would the world fear me? I was a hollow shell of the girl I'd once been.

Three sharp knocks startled me.

"What?" I spluttered under the shower. Burning hot water ran down my skin like the tears I would never shed.

"We're leaving in an hour, Selena. You can't hide in there forever." Alexandra spoke as quietly as if we were talking face-to-face—my unnaturally good hearing was the only reason I could even make her out over the thundering water.

"I'll be out in five. Is your stuff packed?" I already knew the answer, but anxiety made me double check.

"Yes, for the fifth time. I'll be downstairs if you need me."

Her footsteps faded as I switched the faucet off.

I sighed, wrapping my hair in a towel. I'd spent all yesterday up on the roof like a hermit, calculating everything. Anything. I counted down the seconds for eighteen hours until I fell into a disturbed sleep. I dreamed of a funeral where I died a thousand deaths because I've relived it a thousand times. Three little girls in matching black dresses laid roses on a grave. Then I woke up, only to lie in bed for six hours, counting down the time. Always counting.

I wrapped myself in a plush orange towel and brushed my teeth for the second time. I tried to look away from the eight-foot mirror of cleanliness. Yet, standing in a room made of porcelain it was impossible not to see my reflection. I looked different today—too pale, even for me. My hair was so dark against my ghastly white features. Purple bruises surrounded my eyes, and my lids refused to completely open. My cheekbones were far too prominent, the skin stretched so tight across my face it might split. I looked more ghoul than girl.

I flung the door open and cringed when it went through the wall.

"Shit." I pulled it out again.

I walked into the closet and jumped to grab a stylishly frayed pair of jeans off the top shelf. Half the stack fell on me, and the orange towel was nowhere to be seen underneath the pile of clothes.

I cursed, flinging them to the side as I tugged a pair on. I had to open eight different drawers before I finally found t-shirts, and even then, they were all emblazoned *Daizlei Academy for the Prodigies of Tomorrow and Home of the Gifted*. I rolled my eyes and threw on a blood-red shirt with Daizlei written in black, gothic letters.

"Well, look at you, all Daizlei'd up, and you aren't even there yet. I must say, I thought it would take longer."

I spun around and came face-to-face with my brunette cousin. "You," I said by way of greeting.

"I go by Elizabeth." She gave me her characteristic smirk.

"Elizabeth," I corrected with a tight smile.

She laughed. "Cheer up, cousin. It's not half as bad as the t-shirts." She motioned to the one that said *Home of the Gifted*.

"Very reassuring," I responded dryly.

"I like you. You're not all stuck up Blair's ass and buying into the bull my mother preaches. Lighten up a little, and we can have some fun," she said, offering a wicked smile.

"You're very flamboyant for someone raised in your sister's shadow," I said.

"You're very observant for someone with nothing to hide," she quipped back with flashing gray eyes. So there was a spark of something in her. Maybe it was her nonchalance that was misleading.

"Touché."

"I'm not here to unearth your secrets, cousin. My mother wants to do a final run-through to make sure we all have everything before we leave." She rolled her eyes at the mention of Mariana.

"Okay."

She looked me up and down once before turning to lead the way. "Are you nervous?"

I didn't need to ask to know what she was talking about. "No," I said. *What a lie*, my subconscious mocked me.

"I would be, if I were in your position." She shrugged.

"There's no reason to be nervous. We're going whether I like or not. I'm prepared."

"I can see that. What are you going to do about your sister?"

"Hope that she can get her act under control." Even thinking about Alexandra made me apprehensive. She was the joker in a stack of cards.

"You'd be surprised what the school does to you. I can't really explain it, but it changes you. Have a little faith." She sounded optimistic.

I released my hold on my hair and let my hands fall to my sides. Why was I talking about this with her? I hardly knew her . . . and yet, it felt like we were friends. I'd never had a friend before, apart from my sisters. Most days I was more like their parent than their sister. I couldn't always share my concerns with them. Maybe I could with her. Not all of them, by any means, but some—the safer ones.

"You're such a smartass, I don't know when to take you seriously," I said.

"That's the beauty of it, Selena. Neither do I." She smiled cheerfully.

Against my better judgment, a chuckle escaped my lips before I heard footsteps behind me.

"Mom wants to talk to you in the kitchen," Blair said to me through gritted teeth.

I looked over at Elizabeth, who shrugged it off. Figured she wouldn't know anything. I picked up the pace downstairs.

"You wanted to talk to me," I said, rounding the corner of the kitchen.

"Yes, I wanted to give you these." Mariana motioned to the three phones on the counter. Each was a new iPhone with different colored cases.

"Why?" I asked, dumbfounded.

"You're going two thousand miles away, you're in high school, and I would like to have a way to get hold of you if I need to. Besides, I am your guardian, and both my daughters already have one, so you should too," she said.

"Thank you," I said with hesitation and picked up the one with a purple case.

"You're welcome. Where are your sisters?" She sounded impatient and even a bit flustered compared to her usual self.

"Alexandra's in the car. I'll give her hers." I tried to keep the sour note out of my voice as I picked up the red one.

"Thank—Ah, Lillian! There you are. This is for you." She beamed as she handed Lily the last one. *Really?*

"Really?" She echoed my thoughts.

"Yes. Blair insisted I get you one so that you can stay in touch." She smiled fondly.

My mouth dropped open before I turned on my heel. "I'll be in the car," I muttered. Elizabeth's carefree laugh followed me all the way.

~.~.~

"Goodbye, girls. I'll see you in a few months. I love you!" Mariana was still calling to her daughters as we went through security.

"Walk through," the woman ordered.

I stepped through the metal detector, barefoot.

"Clear." She allowed me to pass with a wave of her wand.

I grabbed my shoes and phone from the conveyer belt. "What gate?" I asked Blair.

"89A," she said as she handed us our tickets. Amusingly, half her daring attitude had disappeared along with Mariana.

I glanced over mine. "That can't be right . . ." I murmured.

"What?" She didn't look up, clearly not caring in the slightest.

"89A is on the other side of the airport, and our flight leaves in ten minutes."

Her head shot up, turning to the departure board. "Goddammit."

I'd never heard her curse, and judging by Elizabeth's expression, she didn't do it often.

"Our flight has been bumped. We have to run," she breathed, grabbing her purse.

"Which way?" I asked.

"Left," the sisters said at once.

I took off down the hall, careful to keep it at a humanly possible speed. 16A . . . 34B . . . 49A . . . 61C . . . 74B . . .

"Final call for flight 89A to Denver. Final call for flight 89A to Denver," the overhead speaker cracked shrilly as I ran right up to the desk.

"Here's my ticket." I handed it to the girl.

She pursed her lips and gave me a look but scanned it anyway. "Your plane leaves in five minutes. I'd advise you to hurry, miss," she said with a smile so fake she could've been a Barbie. "You really should be going, ma'am," she continued when I didn't leave.

"I'm waiting for—"

"Here! We're here!" Blair called, running up to the counter with her ticket in hand and the other three girls trailing after her.

She rolled her eyes as she took their tickets. "You have three minutes to be seated before the door closes," she said, handing Lily back her ticket.

I hurried down the stairs and outside to the runway where our plane waited.

"Welcome. Thank you for flying Delta." The captain greeted us far more nicely than the harpy flight attendant had.

I stepped into the cabin and looked over our seats.

"Blair and Lily can take the two seats on the left, and the three of us can sit on the right," I instructed, without asking for their opinions.

"Window seat!" Alexandra called, slipping by like the Leaning Tower of Pisa in her four-inch wedges.

"Why on earth are you wearing heels?" I demanded.

"Because she's an attention-seeking whore," Blair breathed.

I stepped forward to block the blow as Alexandra turned and swung. It caught me square on my left eye, and I had to take a step back to absorb the impact. "Fuck." That was going to leave a bruise. "Sit your ass down," I said, pushing her back two feet.

She glared viciously over my shoulder but did what she was told.

I turned around. "Keep your comments to yourself, or next time I'll let you play punching bag, and I won't stop her," I hissed under my breath.

She looked utterly shocked as she nodded once and took her seat.

I sat in the aisle seat and leaned back into the chair.

"That was quite a hit you took there," Elizabeth said quietly.

"Better me than her," I muttered, closing my eyes as we started to move.

This was going to be a long flight.

~.~.~

There was only one word to describe a plane trip that was five hours long, with four other girls, three dead cell-phones, Blair and Alexandra on the verge of killing each other, and one outrageous migraine. Depressing.

My terrible attitude kept Blair and Lily quiet on their side of the cabin, and Alexandra was just smart enough to keep her mouth shut. Once, when Alexandra got up to get her bag out of the overhead compartment and "accidentally" dropped something on Blair, I had to straighten it out. When the flight attendant came around, Alexandra's drink was frozen solid. In turn, Blair's started boiling. I swear they were going to start World War III right there. My death glare managed to keep us all intact until Denver, but landing couldn't have come soon enough.

I was the first off the plane and had to wait ten minutes for them, which I did without being impatient . . . mostly. When we bought lunch, we all sat at the same table and they didn't talk to each other.

Our plane to the school was on a back runway with no official schedule or destination. As it turned out, Daizlei Academy was nestled in a valley in the mountains of southern Montana. I'd missed Montana, but this wasn't what I'd had in mind.

On the way there, I played cards with my sisters and Elizabeth. Alexandra paid me twenty dollars to keep my mouth shut about her gambling habits. Unbeknownst to Elizabeth, my sister was quite good at counting cards, and she never lost. It cost Elizabeth one hundred and eighty dollars.

As much as I wanted to stay on this plane, people came and went, as did the time.

~.~.~

I was standing in the middle of a train station. Around me, everything was either going by in fast forward, or I was in slow motion. Maybe both. My parents were there; my sisters, cousins, everyone I've ever known. I tried to speak, to call out to them, but they just kept walking past me as if I weren't even there. The train was loading. They were leaving. My parents and sisters were leaving me again. Where were they going? I ran after them, but with every step I took, it seemed they were two ahead of me. I screamed for them, but no one heard. Why couldn't they hear me? Did they not see me? My parents boarded the train. Sweat trickled down my back as I tried to catch up to them before it was too late. I was going to be too late. Even as I reached the loading platform, the train was already pulling them away. Far away from me, where I would never find them. I screamed in rage, and slammed my fists into the ground. They were gone. They'd left me. Cracks of light burst from my fists as the ground shattered. Consuming the train station, my vision, me. My blood pounded in my veins, sweat coated my skin, and my body trembled. A voice called to me, telling me to wake up, wake up, wake up . . .

I jumped to my feet before I was even awake.

"What?" On high alert, I looked around the cabin, but all I saw were bewildered stares.

"Whoa, there. I was just waking you up. We're almost there," Elizabeth said calmly.

I glanced out the window as I settled back into my seat.

We were flying low in an open valley and crossed over a town in the middle of nowhere. The town was small and on a crossroads in the mountains. We didn't stop there and continued flying farther north and to the west until I saw it.

Reconstructed Victorian buildings greeted me with dramatic gothic architecture. Tall and majestic. They were protected by a stone wall. Black metal ran through it and formed spikes at the top. Despite its lethal intent, it was beautiful. The largest building was in the center: the clock tower. Displayed there in the tower was a stained-glass clock so huge it could've easily been the size of two of my aunt's SUVs. As we got closer, I could see people walking along the stone pathways and waving from the balconies. We were here.

The jet landed inside the stone walls, coming steadily to a halt. The stairs lowered, but I stood waiting until the very end, with Elizabeth on my left and Alexandra on my right. Even Lily left Blair's side to squeeze between my cousin and me, taking my hand. I didn't have to look to know she was absolutely terrified.

People poured out of the buildings onto the sidewalk around us. The crowd was growing as people came to say their hellos, and the sheer number was staggering. It wasn't just my claustrophobia this time. Lily's social anxiety had to be having a field day right now, and even Alexandra looked tense. The crowd continued to grow louder and louder as people swarmed the campus . . . then we stepped out.

CHAPTER 8

Everyone stared, and a hush fell over the student body. I could sense the curiosity of a few. Many looked on challengingly, and I met their stares with a cold gaze of my own. I squared my shoulders. This was a test, just like any other. We were with our own kind now, and it was about time we started acting like it. I gave Lily's hand a gentle squeeze before dropping it as we faced the masses.

Girls looked on with envy while boys gawked with predatory gazes. Unintentional or not, it was repulsive. Little did they know who the real predator was. My redheaded sister basked in the spotlight. Which of these weak-minded fools would fall prey to her charms? My pride made me smile. I would not look weak. I would not show my slightly shaking hands. I would show them the animal inside. The one whose gaze inspired fear in grown men.

I walked fluidly down the steps with my head held high, my sisters on either side of me. Blair and Elizabeth trailed behind, something that didn't go unnoticed. We were the outsiders here, and anyone who said differently was a fool. I waded through the parting crowd of whispers, thankful for the breathing space when we broke free of the crowd. I took a deep breath, and relished the cool mountain air I'd missed so much. Perhaps being back in Montana wouldn't be so bad.

"Thanks for the warning," I murmured to Elizabeth.

"You did fine, cousin. Just fine," she responded quietly.

"Headmaster Daizlei was unable to meet with you. He asked that I give you this," a short girl with glasses and curly red hair informed Blair, handing her a white envelope.

"Thank you, Darcy," Blair said, dismissing her.

If I hadn't known any better, I would've said that Blair was the ringleader of this circus.

"What's that?" I asked her as we strolled down the brick pathway.

"Your room numbers," she answered as she glanced through the papers.

"What building?" Elizabeth asked.

"Two."

She frowned. "The main? That's strange . . . those rooms are usually first come, first serve."

It was so bizarre to see my cousins in their element, and not under Mariana's thumb.

"Tell me about it," Blair muttered. "I only got in this year, and I've been here four years."

Only four years . . . Now that was an interesting piece of information. Why hadn't she come sooner? I would have to file that away for later.

"This is a beautiful campus," Lily said.

"It ought to be. Millions of dollars were wasted building it," Elizabeth said.

I cracked a smile at the dirty look Blair gave her.

"It looks hundreds of years old. Was it rebuilt?" Lily asked.

"Actually, it's only a hundred and fifty years old. It's constantly being remodeled," Blair said proudly, apparently taking over as tour guide.

"Well, it's amazing," she told Blair as they strolled side by side.

"Not half as amazing as what's inside," Blair boasted, then giggled like the schoolgirl she was.

"No one cares," I muttered under my breath, blocking them out. I fell back next to Elizabeth and Alexandra as I attempted to mute everyone's voices. My migraine was getting worse.

"Are they irritating you, dear sister?" Alexandra snickered, nudging me.

"Slightly." I flashed her a don't-mess-with-me look.

"Cheer up. You promised her you'd be good," Alexandra said sarcastically.

"Oh please, I'm always good. Even if I'm not always nice." I sneered just as someone twice my size bumped into me. I stumbled a little, but my strength was nothing to be trifled with.

"Excuse yo—" I turned to see my attacker, and the earth stood still. Gravity shifted, and I was unprepared.

"Sorry. That was my fault," he managed.

His eyes held me in a trance. They were so vividly green and alive—it awoke something in my dying soul. A shiver ran through me. A yank on my arm brought me back to myself.

"Hellooo! Anyone in there?" Alexandra waved her hand in front of my face.

"Rude much?" I muttered, turning my back on him. *Strange.* I shook my head, clearing him from my thoughts.

"Who was that? Talk about hot . . ." she said and ogled.

"I have no clue." I glanced behind me, but he was gone.

"I'm going to be taking off now, cousin. Catch ya later," Elizabeth called as she ditched us for a group of Goth kids across campus.

Figures. I thought of her all-black ensemble and studded belt.

"Welcome to Building Two," Blair said from a few feet ahead of us.

We stood in front of a Victorian mansion with a giant *Welcome Back* sign hanging from one balcony to another. Inside, there were multiple halls and stairs. At least the doors had numbers on them.

"Okay, so if you just walk around, you'll find your hall. Alexandra, your room is one-oh-one, Lily's is two-nineteen, and, Selena, you're two-twelve. I'm going to take care of some things. Dinner's at seven. I'll see you later." She disappeared into a hallway.

Great, now we'd been dropped by the only two people we knew in this forsaken place.

"Glad she's gone. I mean who does she think she is—" Alexandra started.

"Not now," I told her. "Look, you should be in the front here somewhere. Lily, I think you and I are on the next level."

"We'll catch up with you later, 'kay?" Lily told her.

"Yeah, I need to go find out what people I'm living with

for the next year, so . . . bye." She gripped the backpack strap a little too tightly as she walked through the door, and then she was gone.

I followed my gut and went up the stairs on the right. My room was the second on the left and Lily's was the fourth down. I hugged her and watched her close the door before I turned the handle on room two-twelve.

Two girls looked up in surprise.

The closest to me was a brunette with shoulder-length curly hair and golden eyes. She was lying on a bright red, twin-sized bed, open-mouthed as if I'd disturbed her conversation. "Who are you?"

"Uh . . . I'm Selena," I said. Was I in the right room? It *was* built for three, and there *was* an empty bed . . . but the blond girl with dark emerald eyes seemed very confused.

"Oh, *you're* the new roommate. I remember now," the brunette said.

"New roommate? You didn't tell me anythin' about a new roommate, Amber!" The blonde had a country twang.

Oh great. Hillbillies.

"I forgot. God, Tori, give me a break," Amber said, throwing her hands up in frustration and giving the girl a look.

"You forgot? You forget your homework, you don't forget a person," Tori said, motioning to me. She stood from her bed and made her way to Amber.

"Well, I'm sorry, but I can't do anything about it now," Amber shot back, rather rudely. She jumped to her feet, and the height difference was almost laughable. Amber was short. Possibly under five feet kind-of-short.

"Wait. She's one of the new girls they told us about

before summer vacation?" Tori asked, again motioning to me.

We didn't move until a week ago . . .

"I don't know. Why don't you ask her?" Amber snapped, waving a hand in my direction just like Mariana did when she motioned at something she thought wasn't worth her time.

"How would she know?" Tori rolled her eyes.

"You know I'm standing right here," I said.

"Sorry, it's just, we've never had anyone start late, ever," she said, putting her hand to her forehead and sighing.

"Well, I guess I'm an exception. Yay, me . . ." I threw my stuff on the bed in the corner and unthinkingly played with the ring on my left pinky finger.

"But you are, actually. You must be really powerful or somethin'. They've never done this before."

Truthfully? I was, and they had no idea. Of course, they never would either. My sisters and I were the only ones *alive* who knew about me. I shrugged.

"Amber, did they tell you anythin' else to do with her?"

"Look, if you think I'm incompetent, read the letter Professor Clearwater gave me a while back." Amber dug a letter out of her backpack on the floor and thrust it at her.

Tori just huffed as she opened the crumpled piece of paper.

"In the unlikely event that Miss Johnson delivers this letter, I would like to let you know about the new roommate you will be receivin'. Her name is Selena, and this is quite a transition for her. I hope you will welcome her and make your parents proud. She will be attendin' all the same classes as you. Please show her around and answer any questions she has. I'm countin' on you, Victoria. Don't let me down," Tori read aloud.

"Oh wow, big surprise. I'm Miss Johnson, and you're teacher's pet Victoria," Amber whined.

She muttered, "Well, you ain't the most respectful—"

Huh, could've fooled me.

"And? This girl is what? Sixteen, maybe seventeen? She hasn't earned respect! No offense," she added, and I just smiled to myself. "Respect isn't something you give to everyone, only those who earn it. So Clearwater can go and—"

"I agree," I said. I strolled into the bathroom and took in the amount of styling products covering the sink and shower, and spilling out of the medicine cabinet. I ran my fingers across the fixtures before returning to the room.

"Agree with what?" she said in her annoying voice.

"I agree that people should have to earn respect. I *don't* agree that you should be disrespectful when they haven't yet been given an opportunity," I told her in a flat, cold voice.

"Excuse me?"

I stifled laughter. God, how amusing this little girl was.

Like a flash of lightning, she was in my face. She was *fast*. Unbelievably fast. If she'd been hoping to startle me, she was about to be disappointed.

I kept my critical gaze leveled at her. "No offense," I said, echoing her earlier comment.

"Of course," she said tightly and sat down again.

The other girl I might be able to get along with, but this one, whoa. She was a piece of work—a rude, annoying, outspoken . . . I stopped myself before I sounded childish, even if it was only in my thoughts. Especially *here*, where there were no limits to what we could do. Even my thoughts had to be guarded.

"Umm . . . it says this is new to you? Have you actually, you know . . . ?" Tori asked, clearly trying her hardest not to offend me.

I nodded once.

When she looked unsure about whether to ask her next question or not, I decided now was probably the best time to tell them how this year was going to go.

"I've known all my life, and I don't need anyone's help adjusting. I can find my own way around. I'll keep to myself, and I expect you to do the same. You can continue living your lives just as you did before I came here. I'm your roommate, not your friend. Oh, and one last thing, don't ask questions and don't borrow my stuff. I take it personally."

The country bumpkin's mouth dropped into a perfect O, and Amber stared like I'd grown two heads before turning away.

After that, they didn't say a word to me, or I to them. Amber took a nap, and Tori put up photos from summer vacation. When an alarm went off at 6:55 pm, my torment ended. For the time being.

~.~.~

When I stepped into the hall, someone crashed into me hard, and we both fell to the ground. I looked up to see Lily's smiling face on top of me.

I groaned. "Lily, I've told you more than a million times not to do that." I sighed and pushed her off me.

"Selena, this place is amazing! I can't wait for you to meet my roommates, Devon and Bella. They're so nice and—"

I got up off the hard, wooden floor. "Lily, do you think I care?" I said but regretted it right away when her eyes watered.

Two girls came up behind her—the redhead I'd seen earlier, except without glasses, and a small brunette with large brown eyes.

"I thought your name was Darcy," I told the redhead.

"No, my sister's Darcy. I'm Devon. We're twins," she said with much more confidence than Darcy had shown.

I nodded once then proceeded down the hallway, with Lily giving me a rundown of every other moment between when we'd parted and now. I pretended to listen, occasionally catching a word and nodding. That was, until I spotted my other sister.

"How was it?" Lily asked her before I could speak.

"Like, great. Duh." Alexandra rolled her eyes.

"No, really. Tell me all about it." On one hand, I was happy that they were enjoying themselves, for the first time in a very long time. On the other hand, I needed fresh air.

"How about we chat over dinner?" I prodded them out the door.

Outside, the warm August air hit me. It was a little over an hour after we'd arrived, but the sun was already setting.

"Selena, did you hear me?" Alexandra bellowed from a few feet away.

"No. What do you need?" I said pointedly.

"I asked you what you think so far."

"Honestly? I'm bored." I yawned. It was more for show than exhaustion, but I didn't want to tell them how I actually felt about being here.

"Bored. That's the best you can come up with?" She rolled her eyes again.

"Would you like me to lie to your face instead?" I asked, falsely cheerful.

"Ugh, never mind." She waved me off. "Just stick to your sulking, okay?"

"Gladly," I said.

We strolled across the ground while they swapped stories and I stared off into the sunset. Only when we got to the cafeteria did I notice my sisters' friends waiting for them.

"We're not sitting together, are we?" I asked them as it dawned on me.

"Umm . . . sorry. I told Blair and Bella I'd sit with them." Lily shrugged as Bella came over and dragged Lily into the cafeteria with her.

I looked at Alexandra.

"I kinda told Hannah I'd eat with her. Sorry, sis. You're on your own." She patted my shoulder awkwardly for a second before walking away.

I sighed and followed. Being by myself never bothered me anyway.

I walked through the doors to a room of three thousand seated individuals. Eyes fell on me from every direction, including the multiple balconies that hosted tables. I looked up to the second floor where only a single man stood. His dark features were ageless, and I could tell he was both tall and strong, as were all Supernatural males.

"Ahh, just the person I was waiting for," he said in a deep, but kind voice.

Me? What would he want with me?

I made my way through the crowd of chairs and took the only available seat I could see.

"First, I would like to say welcome. For all of you who are returning, and those of you who are just beginning." His voice echoed as murmurs rippled through the crowd. "As many of you have heard, this year is going to hold many surprises. We're welcoming three new students into our sophomore class. I hope you will all embrace them. They aren't outsiders, after all." He paused, and the crowd chuckled. "Which brings me to the subject of classes. Your schedules will be handed out in a few minutes, and many of you will notice a new name. I would like to personally welcome our new Battle Simulation instructor, Professor Vonlowsky."

He motioned to one of the teachers sitting at the head table behind him—a young man with pale skin and cold features. His aloofness immediately drew my interest.

"Students, this will be a hard year, no doubt about it. Many of you will be dealing with even more changes, which can, at times, be a great struggle. Do not let this discourage you. All of you are up to this. You wouldn't be here if you weren't." He paused again. "And now, before we all die of starvation, I bid you a very good night, and wish you the best of luck this school year. You'll need it." And with that, he took his seat and the room broke into a dull roar.

Everyone got up and went to get in line for dinner, but I just sat there, pondering.

"Stop thinking. You do that too much," a voice behind me said—a voice I would've known anywhere.

"What would you *like* me to do?"

"Look, I told Hannah you're gonna eat with us tonight, so come get in line with me," Alexandra told me. I rolled my eyes but didn't object.

"This is my sister, Selena. Selena, this is Hannah."

Hannah was tall, like her, with deep eyes and brown hair that framed her face. Very pretty, of course—all my sister's friends were pretty. I think she had an aversion to ugly people or something, because it was like this everywhere we went.

"Nice to meet you," Hannah said.

"And you." I flashed a polite smile and turned as a boy walked up.

"Are you the Foster girls?"

We nodded.

"Names?" he said in an irritated voice.

"Selena and Alexandra," I answered, just as irritated.

He looked up at me and shrank away, handing me two pieces of paper as he went.

"What was that about?" Alexandra asked me, taking the one that had her name on it from me.

"Oh, they're just the middle schoolers who hand out schedules while everyone's in line. It forces them to learn names and meet people," Hannah answered before I could speak.

I looked down at the paper in my hand. I was in class from 7am to 4:30pm.

"Why does my schedule have a bunch of human classes if this is a school for Supernaturals?" I asked Hannah. The only class that stood out was Battle Simulation, and I hadn't the slightest clue what that was about.

"For sophomores, the half before lunch is what we would take in a regular high school and the half after is the Supernatural curriculum," she explained.

"Let me see yours," Alexandra said, taking it out of my hand to compare as we reached the counter.

As we walked back to the table, I spotted Lily across the room eating with her new friends. These roles seemed to be reversed at the moment. Alexandra was taking it upon herself to sit with me, since they both seemed to think they needed to look out for me. Which was both bizarre and oddly entertaining. I was the one who took care of them, picked up the pieces of their lives every time something happened. Yet they thought I couldn't eat dinner alone. I smiled to myself. It was endearing.

"Okay, we have first, fourth, fifth, and seventh together. That's good. We have more together than not," she pointed out, marking an "S" on her schedule next to our shared classes.

"So you said that our Supernatural classes are after lunch?" I asked Hannah, taking my schedule back from Alexandra.

"Mm hmm," she mumbled.

"How are Health and P.E Supernatural classes?" I asked her.

"P.E. is really hard. Lots of physical stuff with our abilities and everything, and health is, like, how we became this way, or something? I don't know," she said vaguely.

So . . . she was a pretty bobble-head, not a brain. That was why Alexandra had chosen her—this girl was her first step to power and alliances in this school. The mind games had already begun.

"What if you can't use your ability?" I asked, feigning nonchalance.

Her eyes widened. "You haven't—"

"No, I have. I just mean, what if you can't use it? Like, you have it, but can't use it," I said, trying to get it through her thick skull.

"Oh, I don't know. I've only been taking Supernatural classes since last year. The middle school only does preparation classes for what to do when you manifest."

"What if you manifest earlier?"

"No one does," she shrugged. "Manifesting by twelve is rare enough, and no one's ever manifested before that as far as I'm aware."

I paused.

My eyes flashed to Alexandra, who was looking pale and tense as she stared at her food.

We'd all manifested *before* middle school. Alexandra was nine, and Lily ten. They were so jealous of me growing up because I was only five years old when fate decided to screw me. It suddenly made sense why I hadn't seen any children here. That Blair had only been here four years. If nothing happened before puberty, there was no point in bringing them in sooner.

"Something wrong?" the idiot girl asked me.

I had no time for her. "Nothing. I'll be right back. I have to use the restroom." The words fell out of my mouth too sloppily to be a proper lie, but I hoped she still bought it. I stood up so fast that several kids looked over from their conversations as I hurried to get out of there.

"Uh, so do I. We'll be back in a minute," Alexandra said apologetically as she followed me.

I pulled my cellphone out and hit two to speed dial Lily. She picked up on the second ring as I pushed the door open to autumn air.

"What are you calling me for? You're right across the"—she paused, and a chair scraped in the background. "Where are you two?" she demanded. "Don't tell me she's already done—"

"Stand up and tell your friends you need to take this call. Walk outside to the front of the cafeteria. Don't ask why, just do it."

It was risky for all three of us to leave abruptly—it could cause questions—but for now let them ask. I had bigger problems than high school gossip.

Lily burst through the door, looking more pissed off than I'd ever seen her. "What's wrong? Why did you just interrupt our first dinner here? I mean—"

"Shut the hell up, Lily," Alexandra scolded.

Lily's face flamed as she whirled on Alexandra, and glared at her. "What is your—"

"Just be quiet for a minute, and let me explain." I started pacing. We'd been through worse. At least they didn't know . . . *yet*. Right? And they wouldn't find out if I could pull this off—I just had to get through to her. "We were talking at dinner, and this girl said that middle schoolers didn't have supernatural classes, only classes to *prepare* them for manifesting." My voice was deadly quiet.

"But I was—"

"I know. But here . . . no one has ever manifested before twelve. It's considered a safe age so that our secret is never discovered. Even manifesting at eleven and twelve is regarded as rare."

The night wind slapped our faces and chilled our bones. The reality of the game we were playing set in.

"How . . . how is that possible?" she choked out as she struggled to breathe.

"I don't know." I lifted my fingertips to her cheek and tried to comfort her. "I knew I was early, Lily, but I had no idea how early. I didn't know that the average kid manifested at thirteen or fourteen." I so desperately wanted to apologize for how things had turned out. If our parents had never died, we would've known this by now, and we wouldn't have been here.

"Well, I like it here, and we don't fit in anywhere else. I know we're not exactly like everyone else, but it's close enough. If they all find out about this . . . I don't know what they would do. Shun us, maybe? I don't want to take that chance. I don't want to be different anymore." Though she was talking to me, Lily sounded more like she was trying to calm herself. I could feel her hysteria building and decided not to mention my revelation.

This was why we were never sent to Mariana. This was what our parents were trying to hide. Me. Me and my ability. I was the reason that my parents' must have believed we'd be safer with humans than our own kind. I was the reason we'd suffered all along. This was all my fault.

"Okay, that's what we're thinking. God, you're, like, so slow if you just came to that realization." Alexandra threw her hands up in exasperation.

"You know what—"

"Enough, both of you." I pushed them apart. "Here's the deal. Now that we're all on the same page, this is what's going to happen. We're going to go back in there and act like nothing happened. While we're here, not a word about this comes out. If somehow it comes up, lie. Say you both were thirteen like everyone else. Lily, if you want to stay here, you can't slip up or tell anyone the truth. None of us can."

Lily nodded desperately.

"Alexandra and I will go back in first—once you see us seated, you come in but don't look at us. If anyone asks where you were, say our aunt called to check on how you were doing. Keep it vague."

I disappeared into the cafeteria with Alexandra following close behind me.

I made sure there was no hint of our recent discussion on my face as we took our seats. Out of the corner of my eye, I saw Lily enter, and hoped she could handle this little lie compared to the big secret she had to keep. If anyone found out and learned the truth about our abilities . . .

I shook my head.

No one would learn the truth. We were the only three people alive that knew it.

"Your sister disappeared after you went to the bathroom. Everything good?" Hannah asked us.

"I don't know. We didn't see her." I shrugged and fake-smiled.

"Huh. Oh well. So where do you guys come from?" She smiled back, taking the hint and moving on.

I was prepared to tell her it was none of her damn business, but Alexandra quickly answered. "We move around a lot, but we're originally from Montana." She was telling the truth, for the first time in a long time. It used to be hard for any of us to talk about our time here, which had made lying easier. When had she gotten past that and decided to move on?

"It must be nice to be back up here in the mountains, then," Hannah said.

It would've been nice if it didn't remind me so much of what I'd lost here, or the guilt that threatened to suffocate me. Once again, I'd cost my sisters a better life.

"It's okay," Alexandra lied, probably thinking along the same lines. She was so convincing. I wouldn't have known she was lying if she hadn't been playing with her hair. She always did that. It was her tell.

"What about you? Where are you from?" I asked, only to get the attention off us.

It ended up turning into an hour-long conversation about Washington D.C., her hometown, and how she'd landed modeling jobs that led to her discovering that she was a Supernatural, along with a bunch of other stuff I didn't care about. She and Alexandra were still talking when I excused myself for the night.

Outside, the air was cool and felt good against my skin. The night was lit up by the full moon, which looked so close I could've almost plucked it from the sky. I strolled down the pathway until I reached my building and sighed as I walked into the still-crowded hallway. I made my way upstairs and went to my room, thinking about Lily, who was probably still up and would be the demon sister from hell tomorrow if she didn't go to bed at a decent hour.

My stuff had finally arrived and was set up in my corner, so sparse in comparison to the abundance of crap my roommates had brought. Amber was sitting on Tori's bed, and from the sound of it, talking about boys. I stifled my groan. I quietly made my bed and slipped into sweatpants before retreating to my music for the night—or, at least, until they went to sleep. Hours later, on Tori's nightstand, a bright red 3:57am glinted in the dark of the room. Forcing myself to relax, I started to drift off into an unknown place.

My toes sank into the dirt. There was no wind or sound, only a cold that chilled my bones. The trees in this forest were scattered, but the fog was so thick I couldn't see my feet. I looked in every direction for another living being, but was only met with silence, and the never-ending woods. So I walked, and my unease grew. There had to be catch. There always was.

It was quiet. Too quiet. I scanned the forest for someone, anyone. I waited—for the paranoia to go away, to wake up . . . but I didn't. A shadow moved in my periphery, and I panicked. I needed to get the hell out of here.

Something was watching me.

It wasn't until I heard a twig snap that I knew I wasn't imagining things. It was following me, hunting me like prey. I screamed, but there was no one to hear it. Closer. It was closing in. I ran away from my nightmare. Away from problems. My fears. Away from myself.

CHAPTER 9

I bolted straight up.

Tori's alarm clock was making a godawful sound. I slipped out of bed and flipped the light on.

"Turn the damn light off," Amber groaned, chucking her pillow at me.

"Get up, and it won't bother you."

"Tori!" she yelled.

"I got it," she muttered, and the annoying beeping stopped.

I went over to my suitcase and looked at my uniform: a pair of loose-fitting black slacks and a white button-up blouse with cuffs that went to my elbows. I carried it into the bathroom, shutting the door behind me. I turned the shower on and groaned when I caught my reflection in the mirror. My hair was chaotic and puffed up like an eighties hairdo gone bad. I would need a lot of conditioner for this mess.

I stepped into the shower, trying not to fall over all the crap in the bathroom. There were multiple shampoos and conditioners, gels, creams, sprays, and anything else you could think of. I'd forgotten to buy shampoo, so I just used theirs. I mean, they wouldn't notice, would they?

I let the water do its work as it pounded into my back, easing another rough night of sleep from my muscles. Banging on the shower door made my eyes narrow, and I had a good idea who it was.

"What is taking you so long? It's six-twenty. We only have twenty minutes before breakfast, and other people have to use the bathroom. Hurry up!" Amber yelled.

"Get out! I'll be done in a minute," I yelled back. I would need to remember to lock the door from now on.

Once the door shut, I turned the faucet off and climbed out. Hastily dressing for my first day of school, I ran a comb through my hair while I tried to wipe the condensation off the mirror and brush my teeth.

"Selena, if you don't hurry up—" Amber shrieked through the door.

"I'm almost done," I shouted as I tried to quickly blow-dry my hair. When I thought I wouldn't freeze to death, I opened the door and stepped into the room.

"Finally," Amber said in her irritating voice. She was wearing a very short, black plaid skirt with a peter pan blouse and heels. I doubted the uniform was supposed to be taken that route, but whatever. She looked completely ready, so I didn't see what the big fuss was about. Nonetheless, she walked into the bathroom and started primping.

I rolled my eyes and turned my back on her.

"Uh, Amber, we only got two minutes before we go. You might wanna hurry up with that," Tori said as Amber came out with her makeup and hair done. I guess being super-fast had its advantages. I hurried out the door, leaving the other two behind.

This morning, there were no screaming girls running around, and I slipped quickly through the silent hallway, down the stairs, and out onto the grounds. The sun was just starting to rise, but the sky was still dark. I hurried across the grass to the pavement and found my way to the cafeteria. When I opened the door, the room was full of surprisingly alert teenagers. I mean, it was the first day of school and everything, but it wasn't even seven yet.

I made my way across the cafeteria to my sisters, who were actually sitting together. Well, Alexandra was sitting; Lily was half-asleep on the table. I took my usual place between them.

Just how it should be.

"Hey, Selena. Wanna go get us some breakfast?" Alexandra said as she lounged back in her chair.

"Not particularly," I told her.

"Please? I need brain food. Heck, I just need food," Lily begged.

"Lazy much?" I told them but got up to get it anyway.

"Thank you," Alexandra said as I walked away.

"Love you," Lily called.

"I'm sure," I muttered as I stepped into line.

I picked up a tray then just started piling on food—bacon, yogurt, fruit, juice, an extra helping of eggs and toast. If it was there, it was on my tray. I walked back to the table, and set the tray in front of them. Lily glanced up, and I swear you could see her eyes come alive. I took an apple then let them have at it.

"How late did you guys stay up?" I asked nonchalantly a few minutes later.

"Three in the morning," Lily croaked.

"Like, four," Alexandra said as she closed her eyes.

"Hmm . . . you know better. Both of you." I scolded them in my own way—most of the time, my sheer disapproval was enough.

"We'll be fine. Food makes up for lack of sleep." Lily smiled languidly at the tray.

"I'll settle for cold water," Alexandra murmured and sipped from one of the bottles.

A bell rang as we grabbed our things to leave. Lily finished off her toast and followed us.

"Who do you have first?" I asked Lily as we reached the pavement.

"Ummm . . ." She shuffled through some papers. "Brighton. Professor Brighton in Building One," she proclaimed in the middle of the path.

"Well, what a coincidence," I said. "So do we."

"Yeah, great. Like, who cares? It won't matter if we don't know how to find the damn building." Alexandra sneered.

"Excuse me, I couldn't help hearing. Are you lost?" a cute boy with blond hair and dimples asked.

We nodded.

"Where are you looking for?" he asked, falling into step between me and Alexandra.

"Professor Brighton, for languages . . ." Alexandra smiled and batted her eyelashes at him.

"Well, that's perfect, because that's exactly where I'm headed." He grinned.

"What a coincidence that you just happened to show up, then," I muttered sarcastically, but only Lily heard me.

"I'm Michael. And you are?" he asked Alexandra.

"Oh, give him a break. He seems like one of the nicer ones," Lily whispered.

"They all seem nice until they get you alone," I said.

"Alexandra." She gave him a smile that said, *hello, new boyfriend*, and he gave her one back that said, *marry me*.

"Ew, Selena, don't go there," she almost screeched.

"I'm just saying." I smirked.

Foreign languages wasn't exactly boring, like normal classes, but it wasn't great either. Professor Brighton wasn't that awful. He was extremely strict and sarcastic, but he had a sense of humor—even if it was slightly twisted.

We each had to choose between Russian, Spanish, French, German, and Mandarin. Alexandra and I chose Russian since our mother had been fluent, and we'd been bilingual since birth. Lily decided to be an overachiever with her friend Bella and take Mandarin—a choice that came with a lecture about cheating by taking a language you already knew. Fortunately for me, she didn't get to finish it thanks to the professor. Brighton caught Alexandra in the middle of a response twice, and he wasn't too pleased. She kept her mouth shut for the rest of his introduction and didn't respond to his taunting, like a good girl, which led to us being partners for the next year in what would now be considered Russian Class. Unfortunately, Alexandra couldn't keep her mouth shut for the entirety of the class and got us both afterschool detention at 4:30. I mentally slapped her for that one.

My next class was different again. Neither of my sisters

were there, but I didn't mind. Professor Anderson was the
—and I'm not exaggerating when I say this—epitome of
boring. He looked like he was in his forties, with thinning
hair and glasses so thick I could've used a ruler to measure
them. His face was plain and his features dull, just like his
voice. After he called roll, he started a lesson I couldn't even
hear because of all the noise. He shut them up eventually,
but by the time anyone could hear, it was already time for
my third period.

Science had never been a favorite of mine, but I'd never
disliked it either. It was just there. Professor Monroe
changed that. She was the meanest, most spiteful teacher
I'd ever known, with beady eyes and a rude attitude. It was
almost like she was only teaching to punish kids. If you
answered a question wrong, it was detention, and speaking
out at any time was at least a week's worth. By the time
lunch rolled around, at least half the class had detention,
and I was relieved not to be part of that half. Skipping
detention on the first day probably wouldn't go over so
well.

When the bell rang, I was the first out of there, not
wanting to get stuck in the mob of students. Despite my
attempts to stay ahead and avoid people, some were very
persistent. Two boys asked me on a date, a group of girls
wanted me to sit with them, and I was given an invitation
to join equestrian studies, tennis, and cheerleading. All of
which I declined without a second thought and continued
toward the cafeteria. Only a few tables were occupied, but
people were filing in rapidly. After grabbing a salad for
lunch, I took a seat at one of the empty tables and pulled
out my science assignment—I had a feeling my sisters

would be eating with their friends today. I'd only completed half a page of annotated notes before I was interrupted.

"Why are we sitting here?" asked a godawful, movie-worthy, bitch voice a few feet away from me.

"Look, Aaron, if your girl's gonna complain, she can move, and you can follow after her like a little puppy dog. It's your choice."

The chair next to me dragged across the tile, and after an audible sigh, the rest followed.

Just how many people were sitting here?

I refused to acknowledge them and just continued with my homework until someone tapped my shoulder.

Without looking up, I said, "Yes?"

"Umm, hi. I'm Jack." I didn't say anything and tried to continue writing. "And your name is?"

"Selena."

"Wait a minute. You're Alexandra's sister, right?" I recognized that voice.

I looked up. It was the blond boy with dimples from this morning.

"Yes, and Lily's." I smirked. I almost felt bad for the poor kid. He wasn't even a player, and my lovely sister was going to break his spirit in two.

"I don't know if you remember, but I'm—"

"Michael." I make a point of learning about people my sisters get involved with.

"Wait, you know each other?" one of them asked.

"Sort of." I shrugged.

"I escorted her to foreign languages this morning," he said, without taking his eyes off me.

"Then why haven't you introduced us?" a boy with a devilish look to him asked.

"Selena, this is Jack," he said, motioning to the one who'd already introduced himself.

"April." The irritating girl.

"Amy." A follower of the irritating girl.

"Will." A boy with light brown hair and blue eyes.

"And Aaron." He finished with the player with devilish looks.

"Nice to meet you," I lied, already bored with the conversation.

"Pleasure's all mine." Aaron grinned, and April slapped his arm.

"Quit flirting with my boyfriend," she said to me, then muttered "tramp" under her breath.

Strike one.

I narrowed my eyes and looked down at my paper. *Breathe. In. Out. In. Contain the temper. She's a child. She's beneath you. Let it go.*

"Is something funny, bitch? Do I look like I'm joking?"

Strike two.

Breathe, I repeated. *Let it go.* My knuckles were white from clenching my pencil so hard.

"Aaron, your girl," Jack said.

"Answer me!" she nearly shouted.

Strike three.

The pencil snapped.

"Let me clue you in on something before you make another mistake by talking to me like that." My voice was clipped and detached as I snapped my notebook closed and looked her straight in the eye.

"You should rethink who you're calling a tramp, or a bitch. Especially given that little *reunion* you and your boyfriend had last night." Her eyes widened slightly. "Thought that was between the two of you, did you? I bet he promised to love you forever. And now he's flirting with the new girl." I kept my eyes locked on her, refusing to break contact even when I could see Aaron's smoldering gaze in my periphery. "I'm not to blame here. Your ignorance isn't even to blame here. You want to get pissed? Look at him." I pointed directly at him as I looked her in the eye. I waited for her to say something, but she faltered. Looking between me and him, unsure what to believe.

"You want to know how I know? Your boyfriend is in my third period, and he likes to run his mouth to all his buddies. I don't give a damn what you do, or what happens to either of your reputations. Leave me out of it, and next time, maybe lay off the hypocrisy a little when you were on your back less than twenty-four hours ago." I walked away. A slap rang in my ears, and I hoped she made the right choice and dumped his ass.

I hadn't even said the worse part, about her being on her period. That definitely didn't need repeating. I still remember when Alexandra had been in a similar situation with a human boy.

She gave the other girl third degree burns.

If only they'd realized what happened when you played with fire.

~.~.~.~

I was strolling along the wide-open pathway about

fifteen minutes later when Lily came striding up to me. "Why?" she demanded, falling into step with me.

"Why what?" I asked, even though I already knew.

"Don't play dumb with me, Selena. You're the talk of the school right now. Why?" Her voice was rising.

"If I'm the talk of the school, you should already know."

She glared at me. "I don't believe it. I want to hear it from you." Her voice trembled slightly. This was the first time she'd ever demanded anything from me. I would make sure it was the last.

"You want to hear it from me? The girl's boyfriend flirted with me, and before I could respond, she went after me for it. *Me.* I gave her three chances. Honestly, I think I did her a favor." I kept calm as I started to walk away.

"So that's it? What happened to my sister who let everything go because it wasn't worth her time? Where'd she go?" Lily called.

I stopped. "Lily, I don't care if you think I made the wrong choice. At the end of the day, I remember what happened to Alexandra and I wish someone had done that for her." I didn't look at her.

"What are you talking about? I heard—"

"I don't care what you heard. Clearly, you think you have the full story," I said harshly. My hands balled into fists.

Breathe, I repeated. *In. Out.*

She huffed and stomped away from me.

I could not curse this place enough.

CHAPTER 10

When I got to my next class, Alexandra greeted me at the door, and we walked into the gym together, staying at the edge of a large group. This was supposed to be my first actual Supernatural class. I was scanning the faces, remembering one here and there when Alexandra said, "So, I talked to Lily today . . ."

"Mhmm," I said casually, keeping myself composed.

"She, like, told me about your little umm . . . fight." She watched me closely.

"I didn't get into a fight, but go on." I sighed.

"Okay, that's what I said. A fight is, like, when two people actually do something," she agreed as if it were obvious.

"Then why are we discussing this?" I stared at the door, not believing my luck—or lack thereof.

Aaron had just entered the gym with three of his friends from lunch, but his eyes locked on mine.

"Because it's still not like—"

Someone blew a whistle, and everything went quiet.

My gaze broke from his, and I turned toward the noise.

"My name is Coach Boreguard, Coach B, or Coach," a tall, thick man wearing sweats and a ball cap said. "You may not call me by my first name or any other name. I will give you detention if you do."

He raised his clipboard. "Now, when I call your name say here and don't give me any lip. Anderson!" he barked, and the process began.

"Now, what were you saying?" I asked Alexandra quietly.

"That it's still not like you to act like that," she said.

"And yet, it's so like you to listen to gossip without knowing the full story."

"But, Sel—"

"Foster!" Coach yelled.

"Here," she said, glancing over at him.

"Foster!" he repeated.

"Here."

"But, Selena, we were talking." She paused. "And we think it might be a side effect from, you know . . . "

Oh my god. I was going to kill her for even going there. How dare she? I refused to apologize for what had happened in that cafeteria. I could've been so much worse. But I wasn't.

Because of her.

"It doesn't matter. Even if it is, what can I do about it? You guys wanted to come here, so here we are. You knew that sacrifices were going to be made this year." I turned on her.

"That's not fair. We know you don't want to be here, and we accepted your terms, but why can't you do sports or something to release some of it? I know they have boxing." Her voice rose slightly.

"It doesn't work like that," I lied. Truthfully, if they were right and I really was losing it . . . I didn't belong anywhere near a mat.

"Okay. I know it doesn't, like, fix it, but it helps," she insisted.

There were things going on that she didn't know about. On one hand, she was right; boxing would help release it. To truly feel the release, someone had to feel pain. I was already so close to the edge . . . I was terrified it would tip.

"Okay, I see what this is about," she said, her temper clearly rising. "You're trying to wait long enough so that when something happens, you have an excuse to leave, for all of us to leave."

My pulse picked up again, and my temper rose. She was being pigheaded and ignorant, not necessarily in that order.

"You don't understand," I said calmly.

"I don't understand?" She snorted. "Wrong answer. *You* don't understand. We're here because we need to be. We're tired of playing hide and seek. Somehow, Mariana found us when no one else could. I get that you've been taking care of us for five years. You've done your best. You put Lily back to sleep every night and promised it would all be okay, that one day it would work out. Well, now it has. Now you can have friends and give it a try. Why are you so against this?"

Rather than accepting the truth, she'd rather believe that I was so against this place that I'd do something I'd vowed would happen over my dead body. She couldn't grasp that I had real reasons, that someone could very well end up dead if I wasn't careful. My training wasn't in boxing, not originally. My father had taught me to kill. To cause pain. To torture. While our mother was baking with them in the kitchen, I was being honed into a weapon. Perhaps she couldn't grasp that because she had only started her training the year before they died.

"You wouldn't understand," I said to her coldly, and then the whistle sounded again.

"Now, seeing as the class got to a late start, I don't think we'll be able to do what I had planned. Instead, I'll put you in pairs for an exercise, and we'll see how you do."

Alexandra and I kept glaring at each other, neither willing to give.

"You and your partner will come to the center of the gym, stand across from each other, and begin the Contest of Deception. If you're too stupid to understand this, it means that you'll dual. Hard. I want to see what you guys are made of. What I don't want is a bunch of ballerinas out there. I don't want to see a bunch of circling and dancing. I want to see a fight. Now, any volunteers?"

Only one hand went up, and I knew then that I was screwed because I was too frustrated not to take up her challenge.

"Name?" he asked her.

"Foster. Alexandra Foster," she said, not taking her eyes off mine.

"Any challengers for Ms. Foster? Anyone daring enough to try?" he called.

"I will." My voice rang high and clear.

"Name?"

"Selena Foster," I said without breaking eye contact.

"You girls related?" He looked back and forth between us.

"Sisters," we said in unison.

"All right. Get to the center."

I swaggered to the center of the room and faced my sister with a mischievous grin. If people were placing bets on who would win, Alexandra was probably in the lead—she had a good four inches on me, plus her temper was far more obvious. After today, they would think twice.

"Are you girls ready?" He put his hand between us.

"Are there any rules?" Alexandra asked.

"Anything goes. You guys are sophomores. It's not like you can do anything." He shrugged then laughed.

Alexandra and I locked eyes.

"The Contest of Deception. Ladies, fight!" he shouted.

I knew her style as well as I knew my own, and way better than she knew mine. That would cost her a lesson on picking a fight.

We circled, and I was aware of the room watching, surrounding us so quietly you could've heard a pen drop.

Her gaze started at my eyes, skimmed my chest then flitted back to my face. The second her hand twitched, I dropped and kicked her legs out from underneath her. Fire fanned the room, as she fell and her control on it loosened.

She caught herself and spun, trying to knock me to the ground, but I jumped and missed her kick by a long shot. It gave her time to recover, and we circled each other again. I watched her closely, never taking my eyes off her, and her greatest flaw cost her. She looked out of the corner of her eye just long enough to see the cute guy watching her, and didn't notice my hand. I wasn't throwing with even a tenth of the force I could've used, but I was going to hit her, and it was going to *hurt.* My fist made contact, there was a *pop*, and she gasped. I'd dislocated her shoulder. So much for *sophomores can't do anything.*

It got her attention, and now she was mad. Fire burned in her eyes as the last of her self-control left her. Her fists ignited, and *oooohs* and *ahhhs* sounded throughout the room. She tried to throw a punch at me with her other hand, but it fell short. With a dislocated shoulder, she was at a severe disadvantage in range. I sidestepped and grabbed her wrist, twisting so that she involuntarily turned, and I had her good arm pinned. I swept her feet out from under her again, and threw my knee into her back as she came down. I put my free hand on her bad shoulder, and she cringed at the touch.

Leaning forward, I whispered in her ear, "Pick your battles. That's what dad used to tell us. Obviously, you still need someone to take care of you if you can't do that."

She sighed, but her body remained tight.

"Time," he called from the edge of the crowd.

I lifted myself off her without putting my weight on her and helped her up. She could barely move. I needed to pop it back into place soon.

"Very nice, ladies," he said while writing something down on his clipboard.

"Great," Alexandra said sarcastically.

"Next volunteers?" he called.

A few hands went up this time; some were very timid.

We went to the edge of the group to pop her shoulder back into place without an audience.

She was still glaring at me, but now it was because I'd won. "You were asking for it," I told her.

"You dislocated my shoulder," she accused.

"Hold still." I put a hand on each side of her shoulder, and with a snap of my wrist, and a sharp pop, it was good as new. That didn't stop her from gasping in pain. She should've been used to it by now; we'd boxed together on and off for the last five years.

"Thanks," she said, though I could tell it pained her to say it.

"You're welcome."

"Of course, if you hadn't done it in the first place, we wouldn't be having this issue, but okay," she scoffed.

"You started it," I said coolly.

"No! You did, okay? By going on this insane . . . exercise strike that's going to do more damage to you than good. You can't see it, but we can. Every single day you're getting worse. It's not like when we were eight and nine. We're almost seventeen."

She wasn't wrong. I could feel it pushing every second, dragging me toward insanity. My veins pumped with power every time I took a breath. You can't have power like I do and not know it, not feel the pull. The danger. Yet I refused.

"Okay, here's the deal. I'll talk to you about it later when I see you." Her pushiness was bringing on a headache.

"I'll be waiting," she promised.

The class ended soon after, and I was on my way out the door when Coach Boreguard called, "Ms. Foster, can I see you for a moment?"

"Coach?" I was ready for this day to end.

"You're new here, correct?" Of course, he already knew the answer.

"Correct," I said, humoring him.

"Today in the exercise, you had the most skill, by far. More, even, than students in my junior and senior classes."

I stayed silent, taking the compliment but not wanting to encourage any questions. Still, if he thought that was impressive, he hadn't seen anything yet.

"How, though? Do you have a past in some type of contact fighting? Perhaps your parents taught you some?"

I knew I had to give an answer. "Boxing. My family encouraged boxing when I was younger. They said I had natural talent." Not a lie, but not the truth either.

"Yes . . . " He thought for a moment. "Well, that was all. Get to class, Foster."

I left the gym before he could think of anything else to ask me.

When I got outside, it was almost time for my next class, which was all the way across campus. Uhhh . . . crap.

I walked quickly, trying to retrace my steps, and when the bell rang, I was sitting in the last open seat in health class. I sighed and put my head on the desk. I had to face Alexandra later, which was going to be a nightmare.

A teacher with long brown hair and milky irises was shuffling papers at the front of the class with an odd kind of grace. "Good afternoon, class."

"Good afternoon, Professor Clearwater," some of the class responded.

"Love the enthusiasm," she mumbled sarcastically. "So, since it's the first day, I thought I'd open by getting to know each of you. So, when I call your name, tell me something about yourself and what you know about health and being a Supernatural, if anything." She sat at her desk and began taking roll.

Most of them answered with simple things like, "I like to . . ." or "Sometimes, I . . .", but occasionally someone would say their ability or say something they *thought* about Supernaturals.

Amateurs. No one cares what you like to do or who you are.

"Foster," she called.

I blinked. *Crap.*

"Foster," she repeated.

"Here," I said.

She looked up from the roster with a curious look. "Is there anything I should know about you?"

"No." Yes.

"I'm the best boxer in the state," Aaron said from the seat behind me.

"Very impressive, Mr. White. And do you know anything about Supernaturals?" Professor Whatever-her-name-was said.

"Not a thing," Aaron said, but I could tell by his voice that he was lying. All of them were. They'd been raised by mothers and fathers of our kind. Unlike human children, Supernaturals were raised to a standard. Part of a parent's job was to teach them about themselves and their past. These children were liars. And I was their queen.

"Okay, well, after today, you will. Now, this is the syllabus for this semester . . ." She walked down the rows, handing out pieces of paper. I glanced at the sheet. It covered everything, starting with Supernaturals and how they manifested, from a genetic perspective, and going on to well-being, daily precautions, and coping with it. Coping with it? What the hell? She practically talked about it like a disease. We were the greatest beings on this earth. If you couldn't have pride in that, you didn't deserve to be a Supernatural.

"Now, we'll be starting with the section on genes and genetics. This week, we'll specifically cover how you gain the genes to be a Supernatural. But before we talk about that, does anyone know what being a Supernatural even means?"

No one raised their hand.

"No one has any idea what they are, or wants to take a guess?" She strode across the classroom until she stopped next to my desk. "Ms. Foster, how would you classify yourself?"

"A Supernatural is a person with inherited genes that enable them to manifest abilities when they reach maturity," I said, giving her the definition I'd just read in the syllabus.

"Very good, Ms. Foster, you can read. Supernaturals are people, yes. However, they are not humans—we are not human. Some of us appear human, but others don't. We are a species of our own. We may share many superficial similarities with humans, but don't be fooled; we are very, very different.

"Not only is our species set apart by our abilities—although that's the biggest known difference—but many of us also have qualities and traits stemming from our unique genes. Any ideas what they are?"

No hands went up right away, but, finally, one crept up.

"Yes, Ms. Hunter," the teacher said.

"The lifespan of a Supernatural is twice as long as a human's," Tori said.

"True. Humans only live to be eighty, on average, and Supernaturals live to be one hundred and sixty-five."

"Different DNA," someone said.

"Yes, but I already said that." She scanned the class, but no one else raised their hands. "What about appearances, personalities, and general health?"

Still no hands went up.

"So, other than your lifespan, genes, and abilities, you have no idea what separates you from humans?" she asked in astonishment.

She turned and went to the blackboard, where she wrote something, while the class started talking. When she finished, she turned around and waited for us to stop. "Well, if you have enough time to talk, you have enough time to do an essay. So, I will be choosing your partner at random, and you and that person will have to write an essay together. This essay will cover defining Supernaturals and the differences between humans and us. It is due on Friday. You'll find my guidelines for essays in your syllabus. Now, let's see . . . " She looked around the classroom then grabbed the roster and started pairing people off.

"Ms. Foster and . . . " I silently prayed, if there were a god, that I'd get some loser I wouldn't even have to talk to and who'd do all the work. "Mr. White."

My heart skipped a beat. I wanted to shatter her into a billion pieces. Aaron was the very last person I wanted to be paired with. I looked at my phone to see how much of this class I had left, and when it was only 2:04, I sighed and put my head on my desk. This just kept getting worse and worse.

"Now, onto class." She launched into a speech about what we'd be learning this semester and explaining each of the parts of health and how it related to our well-being.

After about five minutes, I got bored and put my earbuds in, cranking up the sound of "It's My Life" by Bon Jovi, and letting my mind wander. It wasn't long before I was considering all the ways I could break out of this godforsaken school.

I wanted out. My entire life, I'd always put them first. *Their* safety. *Their* happiness. What about me? I hated being here, but there was no way to leave without them—and I'd sworn I wouldn't do that to them. How could staying be the right choice? How long could I make it? I had to protect them, but nobody here could know what I was.

I was jerked back into reality by the sound of the bell. I took my earbuds out and was grabbing my stuff when someone came up to me and slipped a note into my book. I took it out.

Meet me at 5 in front of the clock
-A.

WHEN I LOOKED UP, all I saw was the door closing—but I knew who it was. Balling up the piece of paper, I threw it in the trash as I walked out of class. Outside, I pulled out my schedule and looked at my last class: Battle Simulation.

Whatever that was. I'd just started walking when someone called my name.

"Selena!" Lily yelled. "Selena!" I turned to face her as she came running up to me. "What's your next class?" she said as she tried in vain to stop herself.

"Battle Simulation," I said as I caught her.

"Me too!" she nearly screamed, and I dragged her away from the staring people.

"How was your day?" I asked politely. Her earlier frustrations seemed to have dissipated.

"Well, it was good until I heard about my sister starting a fight."

"I didn't start a fight."

"Call it what you want, Selena, but it was a fight. And very unlike you, I might add." She sounded disapproving, and I could tell she'd rehearsed this little speech.

"You're obsessing," I said without emotion.

"You're losing your grip," she said as we approached a metal door with no handle.

"Name," an electronic voice said from somewhere.

"Selena Foster," I said, looking at Lily.

"Lily Foster," she said, returning my gaze.

"Alexandra Foster," a voice from behind us said.

The door clicked and opened, and the three of us entered together. It was like a classroom, with desks and a teacher, but behind the desk was a window to another room that looked large and white and empty. A padded room for crazy people. How fitting. My breathing picked up.

The classroom was crowded with students. Only three desks remained, and I headed for the one in the front, hoping to dodge my sisters for another hour. When I got there, I almost wished I'd taken one of the middle ones.

"Why are you late?" the teacher asked, leaning back against the desk.

"We didn't know where the building was," I said in a bored voice.

"Ah, you must be the . . . Foster girls?" He looked down at his roster.

"Mm hmm," I said, like it was obvious.

"Names?" he asked, not looking up. Was that a slight Russian accent I heard behind his words? His name certainly was, but he could've been from any of the countries surrounding the federation.

"I'm Selena. The redhead's Alexandra, and the short one's Lily."

He glanced at me and wrote something down then turned his attention back to the class.

"Now that everyone's here, let's continue. I am Professor Vonlowsky, and this is Battle Simulation. Who knows what that is?" He pointed behind me. "You."

"Fighting," a girl said.

"Yes and no," Vonlowsky replied. "Can anyone tell me why it is yes and no?"

No one answered.

"So you're telling me no one in here has any idea what this class is about, and I am wasting my time asking?" He looked around for another moment, but the class remained silent. "Okay, everybody pull out a piece of paper." He waited until the rustling died down. "I can't believe out of thirty-seven kids none of you know what you're doing here."

It shouldn't have been a surprise. These kids were clueless about everything. They thought the world revolved around high school and drama, yet no matter how much they tried, they would never be normal. It was sad, in a way, that these people had recreated a high school atmosphere to make the kids feel normal while trying to teach them about themselves. Pitiful was the word.

"Take ten minutes and write a syllabus for this class," he said. No explanation, no seeing if there were any questions, nothing.

I glanced at the paper, not sure what to write. So I left it blank and waited ten minutes while the whispering of pencils counted down the time.

Vonlowsky paced the room, watching us with frustration on his face. His walk was precise, like a predator hunting prey. It almost seemed as if he were looking for something . . . and then he found it.

"Foster," he said suddenly. I was already watching him, and it wasn't me he was referring to. "Bring me your paper."

There was a flash of red hair when Alexandra appeared.

"Why is there nothing written?"

"Because, like, I don't know any of it."

"So you're not going to try at all?"

"Nope. I'm new here. I don't know any of this shit." She popped her gum obnoxiously.

"So you don't know anything. You're not going to try. You're speaking like an illiterate, and completely ignoring my authority?"

"Look, you're not teaching me anything, so why would I try?" I hated it, but I kind of agreed with her.

He looked at her for a moment with an odd expression then started pacing around the room. "Name?"

She looked at him like he was dumb but responded, nonetheless. "Alexandra Foster." She rolled her eyes.

"Species?" he continued, though we all knew the answer.

"Supernatural."

"Ability?"

I tensed.

"Fire," she said, but now there was uncertainty in her voice.

"Level?" he asked.

"Unknown." The uncertainty was replaced by irritation.

"Potential?" he continued, brushing it off.

"Unknown," she said grudgingly and flipped her flaming red hair behind her.

"Energy source? Fighting techniques? Specialization classes? Manifestation periods?" This was starting to sound like an interrogation.

"I don't know. Why are you asking me all this crap anyway?" She rolled her eyes again.

"Because this *crap* is what battle simulation is. This is the only class you'll take all three years, and this is the only class that focuses on you, what you can do, and what you're capable of." He motioned for her to sit down. "Your abilities are who you are, not just what you can do. When you graduate and leave here, you will have to be prepared. Some of you might go back to the human world and try to continue living in hiding, but most of you will take your place in our society. Battle Simulation is a class meant to prepare you for that, for yourself," he declared like the charlatan he was.

This guy was an imposter. There was no way he was an actual teacher. The only thing he knew how to teach was arrogance.

The bell overhead rang to let school out.

"And that concludes our lesson for today," Vonlowsky said.

The class filed out, chatting away. As I packed up my things, my sisters approached me.

"You looked very productive up here doing nothing," Alexandra snapped at me, still fuming from being patronized.

"Could've been worse . . . " I said.

"Sure, you could've actually gotten mad and hurt someone," Lily said, though clearly it wasn't her place to say so.

"I find it amusing that you can grasp that and not my reasons for not wanting to get back into boxing." I walked away briskly with a purpose in my step and fire in my eyes.

The metal door was still open, and when I stepped outside, the wind caught my hair and cold brushed against my face. I continued walking until I was almost at my door.

"If you want to continue being a bitch, I have detention to get to, but if you actually want to talk, I have my phone on me," I said to Lily.

She stood speechless.

"I'll see you at detention, since you couldn't keep your mouth shut," I said to Alexandra.

She just glared at me then smiled spitefully.

I gave her a bitter smile in return before turning my back on them and their judgments.

Screw them. They could be judgmental ingrates together.

CHAPTER 11

When I got back to my room, it looked like a tornado had come through. Clothes, makeup, and shoes were scattered everywhere. I grabbed my suitcase and rifled through it for something comfy and non-uniform for detention since what I would be doing there was unknown. I pulled out a pair of loose black sweats and a tank top. I changed swiftly and glanced at the clock. I still had time, but if I left now, maybe he'd let me out early.

I pulled on a sweatshirt and headed back to Building One to serve detention with Professor Brighton. My skin warmed as a slight breeze went past. I could feel eyes on me as I walked, but I refused to look. Let the gossipers think what they wanted. I was above that. I knocked when I reached his classroom and entered without waiting for a response.

"You're early," he said to me without looking up. "The other one, however, is not."

I walked up to his desk. "What do you want me to do?"

He appraised me. "Seeing that you're dressed to work,

I'll give you a choice. You can scrape gum off the bottom of the desks in this room or wash all the windows in the building." He smiled smugly, and I knew there was some kind of catch.

"Anything else?" I asked.

"Nope," he said. I looked around the room. That was a lot of desks.

"Windows," I said after a minute.

"Good choice. There are only six in the entire building." He got up and gave me a rag and cleaning spray.

"How many desks are there in here?" I asked.

"Sixty." He chuckled.

Alexandra walked in behind me. She'd also had changed, except it wasn't into something appropriate for what we were doing. She wore white skinny jeans with black boots and a sequin tank top. She never learned.

I grabbed the bottle of cleaner, went to the first window I saw, and started cleaning.

"You can use this to clean the gum off the desks." In the reflection in the window, I saw him hand her a scraper and bucket. I choked on my laughter at the horror on her face.

"You're, like, kidding . . . right?" she asked him, completely bewildered.

"Nope. I guess you should've, like, done what you were supposed to, right?" He went back to his desk.

"Ugh . . . " She groaned, got on her knees, and started scraping.

I hurried through the windows in a rush to get out of there. Around 5:00, I finished and left the building while Alexandra was still scraping. On my way out, she glared at me, but I just kept walking. After I left Building One, I felt like I could breathe again. The sun was setting, and the campus was alive.

Girls gathered around the fountain to watch the water user as he manipulated it to his will, clearly happy with the attention he was getting. People strolled down the pathways, hand in hand, ignoring the occasional couple that was mercilessly making out. Teachers watched from their rooms for any sign of trouble or mischief. The lamps kept the campus lit, but the fireflies made it glow. People were living and enjoying life, while my world crumbled around me.

Lily was right. I was losing my grip. I looked more hellish with each day that passed. It didn't even compare to the hollowness I felt with my growing isolation. My sisters no longer needed me. At least they didn't feel they did, and for now, I was inclined to agree.

I put a hand to my right temple, massaging my head in a poor attempt at getting rid of the migraine. After walking stiffly back to my room, I raided our bathroom for painkillers. Clearly one of my roommates was a pill popper because there were also stimulants, antibiotics, and prescription meds. I downed four Tylenol and stumbled into bed, not even bothering to turn the light off as I got some much-needed sleep.

~.~.~.~

Wake up . . .

The haze of sleep eased as I slowly came back to awareness. The room was too bright. I groaned and rolled over to look at the clock, but fell out of bed and landed on the floor with a thud. My head banged against something hard, and there was a flash of pain that faded as quickly as it had come. I dragged myself off the ground, getting a good grip on my bed to pull myself up. This was pretty pathetic. I was stumbling around like a drunk person, but I wasn't inebriated in the slightest.

Outside my window, complete darkness had replaced the full moon. Stars were just starting to appear, and my headache wasn't any better, likely from banging it. I grimaced. The cafeteria lights were on, and I remembered Alexandra, who would probably still be working until late tonight. I was going to do something nice for her—maybe then she would lay off.

I walked out of the building and took off at a sprint toward the cafeteria, hoping to get rid of the ache. The wind on my face was blissful. Exhilarating. I needed this. At the very least, it would help me stay in control tonight while I was with Alexandra. The distance between the cafeteria and me closed far too soon. I slowed to a stop and strolled in.

The overhead lights were so bright I winced. Hurrying, I grabbed a salad and a slice of pizza. As I was getting two waters, someone bumped into me. The plate of pizza toppled off my tray. A hand swiped it out of the air.

"Thank you—"

Aaron. His black eyes studied me for a second before he set the food on the tray and let me pass. I suppressed the shiver that fought to run through me. I felt him watching me as I swerved through the cafeteria and walked swiftly across campus. The lights in Building One were still on and the door was unlocked.

I went inside and found Alexandra crouched on the ground, working in silence. Her white jeans had black marks all over them, and she'd kicked her boots over into a corner. She wasn't even halfway done.

"Hungry?" I asked, setting the tray down next to her.

"Starving." She snatched the pizza off the tray.

I plopped down on the floor and started into my salad. Picking at the lettuce, I looked up. Something was changing. She was changing. Being here . . . it was maturing her. Alexandra didn't do work. Especially not the physical sort. She usually just outright refused, despite the repercussions, and occasionally resorted to having a lackey do it. Yet here she was, on her hands and knees with a gum scraper and bucket. I smiled, but my joy was short-lived. I needed to tell her the truth; that was the real reason I'd come back. The pizza was just to butter her up.

I sighed.

"I didn't want to box because I'm scared of losing control. To actually get the release I need, I would have to beat those boys to a pulp. As you've said, I'm not eight anymore, and the stakes are higher. It takes more than it ever has to keep myself under control." I looked away, not sure I was ready to see what was in her eyes.

She put her hand over mine and squeezed. "I knew you weren't telling us everything. I did know more than you've given me credit for. I know what it will cost you and your morals to keep your sanity. I get that. You don't want to be a monster. If you don't do this, you will go insane. If you don't do this . . . I don't think you have even a year left."

I turned to look her in the eye. She was serious.

"I can't lose my sister."

If I were capable of crying, it would've brought tears to my eyes. As it was, all I could do was grip her hand.

"I know what I'm asking, even if Lily doesn't. We can't lose you." Her eyes watered, and I gave her a sad smile. We both knew what she was asking.

"So, I need you to do this. Box again. Please. We'll worry about the rest later." Her eyes were pleading, and though she would never know how much it would kill me if I lost control and ended someone—I would do *anything* for them.

They come first.

My mantra rang true.

"I'll start tomorrow," I promised.

CHAPTER 12

"Meet me today at, like, five, and we can go together, okay?" Alexandra told me as we were walking out of Russian.

"No, I want to do this alone."

She tore her eyes away from the upperclassmen boys walking out of the gym. I waited for her response. I didn't want to hurt her feelings, but if I was going to do this, it would be on my terms.

"It's your decision, sister. You know I'd rather do nothing if I can get away with it."

I liked the twinkle in her eye I'd been seeing since we got here, since she'd used her ability without fear of repercussions.

"I'll see you later. Relay the message to Lily so she gets off my case, will you?" I rolled my eyes.

"I'll deal with Lily. You worry about tonight." She laughed, walking away only to be surrounded by admirers almost instantly.

I took a deep breath. This was just the beginning of another very long day.

Professor Anderson's class went about as slowly as expected, and by the time the bell rang, I was already out the door. My third period was awful in comparison. Professor Monroe paid abnormal attention to students, and what they did during class. With eyes like a rat, she was the only teacher I'd ever met who could enforce silence without saying a word. Of course, that came in handy when Aaron sat next to me and brought his whole crew along, surrounding me in testosterone. I wasn't going to let him think he made me nervous; I wouldn't flatter him like that. So, I did the opposite: I leaned back, relaxed, and enjoyed the ride. He slipped me a note when Monroe's back was to us, but I didn't touch it. I didn't even look at it until she turned around and was staring in my direction. Then I stretched my arm forward and opened it silently.

Before I could read it, Monroe snatched it off my desk. "Passing notes, Foster?"

"Actually, I didn't get to respond yet." I smirked, thinking of a smart-ass quip.

"Well, let me read it for you, and you can tell me what your response is. 'Meet me in the library at five today. We have a health project to work on, and I don't want to wait until the last minute. Signed A.'" Even for her, she sounded abnormally bitter.

"Well, Professor, I would say that I have plans, and that if he's hitting on me, he really needs to stop. He's not my type, and I do hope his girlfriend gave him hell for being a douche bag," I said, without taking my eyes off the board, even though she was standing next to me. I smirked at the snickers that broke the silence. I hoped he hated me.

"Language, Foster," she scolded as the bell rang.

I stood in one swift movement, my stuff already in hand. Aaron was still watching me as I walked out the door. It seemed to be happening a lot lately. I hope he didn't make a habit of it for much longer. Creepy bastard.

After lunch, Alexandra and I walked to P.E. together, and she told me that Michael had asked her out. I asked questions when needed, but paid as little attention as possible without letting her figure out she was basically boring me to death. When Coach Boreguard told us we were running today, it was a relief. I already needed a break from her.

I pulled my hair back into a ponytail and changed into the unbelievably short shorts they provided for gym. All around me, girls were applying makeup, fixing each other's hair, and taking selfies. Gag. I left the locker room immediately.

"Outside!" Boreguard grunted when everyone was there.

"I don't wanna run," Alexandra complained, coming up on my left side.

"Well, I guess it sucks to be you," I said unsympathetically.

"We'll see," she said and disappeared.

We walked for another five or so minutes before we got to the track. It looked almost new with the freshly cut grass, fresh coat of paint, and security cameras partially concealed on the edge of the woods.

"Coach, I just had lunch and I really don't feel like

running today, so could I, like, do it another day maybe?" Alexandra piped up next to him.

"Ha, you think you're different and deserve special treatment, do you?"

She just looked at him. The funny thing was she did believe that.

"Well, just for that, princess, you earned yourself another mile. And while I'm making a point here, since you aren't actually any different, I think you should all run another mile. Make that two." He raised his voice as if daring anybody to complain, but the worst they did was mutter under their breaths or glare at her.

She groaned, but didn't say anything as she got in line next to me.

"When I blow this whistle, your time starts," he said to the line of thirty kids.

I watched the others prepare to try to sprint it. Foolish children. Here, their Supernatural abilities were hardly what I would've called mature.

Enhanced senses.

Hmmm . . . maybe now was the time to use that to my advantage.

At first, I stayed in the middle of the front group, which was sprinting, but one by one, they faded in the first lap. I was only getting started. When I hit the marker for the second lap, only four others were with me. Amber was one, which didn't surprise me with how fast she'd been on my first day. Aaron was another, which did—I'd expected him to be all talk. We were also joined by Michael and Jack, but they were both losing speed.

It was then that I fell into a trance-like state.

Faster ...

Instinctively, I raised the level and lost Jack and Michael instantly. I was halfway through my third lap when I heard it again.

Faster ...

My heart beat with a steady thrum like a hummingbird's wings as I began truly running. I didn't notice who I was with anymore, who was behind me, or even what lap I was on. I was just going ... *faster, faster, faster.* The whisper continued until I was practically gliding. I felt weightless.

It stopped. In my head, I counted the laps as I rounded the corner to where the coach was standing. Eight. I was done, and I wasn't even sweating.

I looked around. Only Amber had finished before me. I searched for Alexandra; it wasn't too hard to find her with her bright red hair like a flame in the sunlight. She was running steadily, but her skin was all pink and she'd already broken a sweat. There was no way she could go to her next class without a shower.

I waited patiently as kids came and went. Slowly, people finished their laps, and when every last person was done, we waited for Coach's next order.

"You princesses have got a long way to go this year." He looked over his clipboard. "Out of thirty students, eighteen of you run under the average, nine of you are barely making the cut, and only three of you are above." He glowered down at us, but I refused to buckle. I had no reason to.

"That's not that bad," Alexandra muttered under her breath. She'd been one of the average runners.

"Not that bad? You're right, that wouldn't be *that* bad if I weren't grading by human standards."

How could eighteen Supernaturals be slow by human standards? We are superior, mentally and physically.

"By Supernatural standards, twenty-seven of you are below average, one of you is passable, and two of you are above average. You know what that means, right?"

Silence followed.

"It means that from now on, we're running four miles a day. You kids are lazy. Entitled. A bunch of spoiled brats used to having everything handed to you. Not in this class. If you plan on passing, you're going to work for it. It's going to hurt. If it doesn't, you should be worried."

This undoubtedly would've brought a more emotional person to tears or pumped them up for the year. I was just disappointed. I'd expected better from my race, from my sister, from those who shared my DNA.

After the talk, I showered and changed. My hair was still damp and felt heavy on my neck as it drenched my clothes. I cursed myself for not cutting it when I had the chance.

I still had to figure out that project. I was going to have to work with him on it sometime. Sighing, I took a seat in the back and waited for the rest of my class to trickle in. Professor Clearwater and her milky irises zoned in on me all through class as I listened to my music, but she didn't say anything. It was bizarre how often my teachers stared. The students were one thing—I was new—but the professors should've been more professional. Unless . . . were they watching for something? Paranoia made its way into my mind, but I quickly quelled it by reminding myself that no one had said anything. Perhaps it was all my imagination. Or . . . perhaps I *was* actually losing it.

Battle Simulation went off without a hitch. Professor Vonlowsky gave a lesson that was . . . intriguing.

He spent the entire class asking us questions, but no one could answer them. Not correctly, at least, and he made sure you knew it. No explanation. No answer. Just wrong. It was madness. How could a teacher expect you to learn when all he ever did was tell you 'wrong answer?' By the end of class, he'd offended nearly everyone, and they were all waiting for someone to get something right, so that maybe he would shut up. That never happened.

"So tell me, students, did you enjoy today's lesson?"

No one answered. Prick.

"Or maybe you found it frustrating. Some of you look a bit put out after that. The lack of respect is hard to handle, isn't it?"

Most of the class instantly looked down, as if their hands were suddenly extremely interesting.

"I hope you take today as a lesson. From now on, I want respect, and I want it always, whether you're in this class or not. I want it quiet in here from the first bell to the next. Lastly, make sure you get this 'I don't care' attitude fixed because I won't put up with the rest of the school year like this."

The bell rang. Time to box.

CHAPTER 13

I'D GROWN TO EXPECT BIZARRE SCENES AND BAD ATTITUDES IN MY dorm, but chaos?

Clothes had been strewn everywhere as Amber tried to decide which leotard to wear for gymnastics. How that was difficult was beyond me, but apparently it was. Tori stood appraising herself in the bathroom with her cowboy boots and a flannel shirt. She looked like she'd walked out of an old western movie, and was that a cowboy hat in her hand? I snickered to myself. Hillbilly.

I dug out a clean pair of spandex shorts and a white tank then cursed under my breath when I realized that these were all I had. I now lived in Montana where it got down to twenty degrees outside during the winter—on a good day. Shorts just weren't going to cut it when the snow came. If only I'd prepared for situations like this instead of spending forty-eight hours harping on something I couldn't change.

It's your own fault, my subconscious mouthed.

I snatched the clothes off the bed and changed quickly

before I could find something else to be pissed about. In truth, the clothes were nothing. I would survive. It was everything else that was getting to me. Insanity. Scheming dead parents trying to protect me, even in the afterlife. Which wouldn't be so bad if it hadn't cost their other two daughters dearly. I stopped myself there. I didn't need to add self-pity to the list on top of everything else.

Pushing aside all other thoughts, I dug under my bed for my gray workout shoes and hand wraps, getting caught in the cobwebs under my bed in the progress.

"Ugh," I groaned then sneezed from the half-inch of dust.

"What are you doing?" Amber asked.

I looked up from the shoe I was tying to read her expression. "Boxing." Wasn't it obvious? I glanced at the wraps beside me. Maybe not . . .

"Really?" She sounded surprised.

Without looking up, I nodded.

"Are you any good?"

I laughed lightly for the first time since I'd been here. "You could say that." Oh yes. I was very, very good. I left it at that. We may have been able to do small talk at the moment, but I hadn't changed my mind. No friends. No attachments.

They come first.

Without another word, I took off down the stairs and across campus. As I entered the gym, I went to the last door on the right where I'd seen the boxing ring earlier. The second I went through the door, I was engulfed in loud rap music and the smell of sweat mixed with testosterone. It felt like coming home. In the five years since my parents died, it was the only thing I'd taken joy in.

The ring was to my left, and two boys were already going at it. To my right, there was a wall of mirrors with weights lined in front of it.

Eyes followed me with every step I took.

The back area was a lot larger than I'd thought it would be. Four punching bags hung off the right corner of the room while a speed bag was mounted on the back wall. There was a small table in the left corner with stopwatches and timers scattered across the laminated top and jump ropes in a pile to the side. The entire floor was matte blue. Probably more for the effect when blood splattered across it.

Moving quickly, I dropped my wraps and rewound them tight around my hands. The guy facing away from me in the ring seemed familiar, somehow, but I couldn't see his face. There was also something unusual about his reflexes, the way he moved . . .

The guy he was fighting was tall and tanned with hair as black as mine. His chiseled features reminded me of paintings of Greek gods, and muscles rippled under his shirt . . . but that was all trivial compared to one thing. Green. Eyes so green. So alive. So vivid.

It was him. The boy from my first day. The one with the green eyes.

They parried back and forth, occasionally exchanging punches. By the time they made a complete half-circle, I could see the other boxer's face. Aaron. His concentration broke when his gaze left the ring for a moment and met mine. It was only a second, but I shook my head with a small smile. He was making the same mistake I'd seen so many times. It would've cost him if I'd been in the ring.

Apparently, I wasn't the only one who'd noticed. A hand flashed out of nowhere and plowed into his stomach. Aaron doubled over from the impact, and the green-eyed boy hit him so hard his head snapped around. A streak of blood slapped his cheek, and the whistle signaled a win.

Turning away from the ring, I walked over to a clear spot on the mat and dropped into a split. Placing my palms on the ground in front of me, I took a deep breath and began lifting myself. I had to be patient with my body as I lifted slowly. This exercise was all about strength of body and mind. I closed my legs so that I was in a handstand. The second it was solid, I knew it was time to go upright before I got lightheaded. Kicking my legs forward, I landed facing a man.

He was tall and broad with chestnut-brown hair. His eyes were light brown and his face told me he was no student. I took in the jeans and loose red shirt. He had to be the coach.

"That was impressive, but you're distracting my boys," he said, motioning to Aaron, who was now climbing out of the ring.

"It's more like your boys are letting themselves get distracted," I countered.

"And you think you could do better?" he asked.

"I know I can," I said without hesitation.

"This is a private gym. You only get to practice here if you're one of my own." Amusement touched his lips, and a grin was fighting its way through.

"You're only telling me that because I'm a girl," I

argued, but kept my tone amused. Men didn't take well to women telling them what to do.

"No, I'm telling you that because you're not strong or fast enough. We're invitation only."

It was obvious he honestly believed that, which completely infuriated me. But I'd made a promise. If fulfilling it meant I needed a coach, then I had to earn his respect, and arguing wouldn't do it.

"If this isn't about me being a girl then let me earn my place," I said after a moment.

He considered this for several seconds before speaking. "How do you plan on doing that?" he asked, humored.

"The only fair way there is. A fight."

He grinned at me and shook his head as if he couldn't believe what he was hearing. "If you can actually get one of my boys to fight you, and you win? I'll train you. Deal?" He held out his hand.

"Deal." I took a step forward, and put my dainty hand into his. His eyes widened when my grip tightened and my hand was like ice, cold and unmoving.

When I released him, he turned to his boys and explained my proposition. Most of them refused, saying I had no business being there. My blood boiled when they started laughing. This was humiliating.

"Can I say something?" I asked from behind him.

Their eyes turned toward me, and the coach motioned me forward.

"You guys are arguing because I'm a girl. You think I'm wasting my time, and yours, and it's impossible for me to win. If all this is true, wouldn't it make sense to let me have one fight and get it over with?" I said, smiling in what

I hoped was a charming way. Underneath it, I was writhing.

"Just pick your opponent." The coach rolled his eyes, already knowing where I was going with this.

A cocky smile slipped onto my lips. I knew who I wanted. "You," I said, walking up to the green-eyed boy.

The coach sighed and motioned for him to come over. Without a word, he walked away, eyes never leaving mine. They started whispering in hushed tones, and I could tell they were arguing.

"He won't fight you," a voice said behind me. I turned to see Michael standing next to me.

"What makes you say that?" I asked, examining my sister's new boyfriend.

"He's the best, and he knows it. He could *kill* you," he warned.

Please. This boy didn't know me, and he didn't know what *I* was capable of. I wasn't the one who needed to be warned.

"Mm hmm . . . we'll see about that," I whispered.

They were walking back over to us, and I had a feeling I was going to get my way.

"He'll fight you on one condition," the coach said.

I smirked a little at Michael, who appeared bewildered by the decision.

"Name it," I said.

"You only get ten minutes to put him on the ground," he said. He thought it was impossible. He thought I'd never win. He had another thing coming.

"Okay." It wouldn't take me half that time to make my point. A wicked grin spread across my face. I needed to prove myself, but at the same time their incompetence would cost *him*.

When I turned back, they were all talking again, exchanging glances and whispers. I knew the reason for the time limit: they figured I couldn't do anything in ten minutes, and if he just stood there and parried, I would lose.

"Do you need any time to warm up?" the coach asked, and I shook my head. "Okay then, let's get started. You know, I admire your guts," he whispered quietly to me as I passed.

I smiled slightly without stopping.

"Do you need any help up?" one of the boys called from the side of the ring.

I laughed sarcastically and pulled myself onto the outer edge. Without hesitation, I slipped between the ropes and turned to face my opponent. "No thanks," I called over my shoulder.

"When you hear the whistle, the match is over. Begin," he announced.

Show time.

I watched him carefully, looking for an opening, but he was well-guarded. However, there was something different about his style. He was sloppier because he underestimated me. This was it, my one chance, and he was barely taking me seriously. I ground my teeth.

He studied my face, his eyes widening when my emotions changed, not even noticing my hands. It was like he was relying on my eyes to tell him my next move. And the look on his face . . . I'd only seen it on one other person in my life. I let anger cloud my other emotions, take hold of my thoughts. A slightly confused look crossed his face, and I knew I was right. I had him.

Cheater.

I'd just found a way to win this fight without even fighting. Using anger as my shield, I had the upper hand. While he was still confused, I went for it. Without thinking, I pivoted to the left and aimed for his stomach. He blocked it like I'd known he would, but he was behind. I exchanged light punches, biding my time.

"Cheater," I muttered to him.

"How am I cheating?" he asked under his breath, blocking another blow.

"Mind games won't work on me. Nice try."

He fumbled for a moment and glanced at my face as if it were the first time he was really taking me in since that first day. Then I struck, hitting a spot right below the ribs you would only know to aim for if you were trained.

A look of shock came over his face, and I smiled a little. I knew it was demented, but to see others in pain because of their own ignorance "fed" me when I was the one causing it. It was the very reason I was in this ring. Before he could recover, I took a step back. Without worrying about the implications afterward, I swung.

When my skin made contact with his face, there was a sickening crunch and snap. He fell to the ground immediately, and I couldn't help thinking that he'd just lost the same way he'd won not ten minutes earlier. The dull pain spreading through my fingers and wrist told me it wasn't just his jaw I'd broken.

Looking down at him, I almost felt pity and even a little guilt for pulling that on him, but it was the only way to get in. I was exhausted now, and this mental shield was drawing more energy by the second, sapping my body of its remaining strength. This was the first time in years I'd had to put it up, and I'd forgotten how draining it could be. I'd let myself grow weak over time and was now putting myself at risk. I was going to have to practice; get my strength up. I stared down at his unconscious figure and made a split-second decision to let the shield down. How much harm could he do lying there?

Around me, it was silent—not a word spoken, not a syllable uttered. I knew why. The damage I'd just done should've been impossible for someone as little and charming as me. Especially with their supposed best boxer. Where did that put them? More importantly, where did that put me?

The whistle sounded.

Pulling my shoulders back so that I was standing at full height, I allowed my fists to drop to my sides, but kept my face away from the rest of the gym. Out of nowhere came a slow clapping. I turned, and the coach was standing in front of them and applauding me. He had a smile on his face despite the boy at my feet. That was Supernaturals for you.

"What's your name?" he asked in awe.

"Selena Foster," I said quietly. The sound of my name was like an omen. Foreboding. Dark.

"Well, Ms. Foster, I'm Coach Avery, and you're my newest recruit, whether you like it or not." He made no attempt to hide his admiration, but looking down at the boy in front of me, I was uncertain about this path I was on. Could I do this? The feeling was . . . unsettling.

Before I even realized what I was doing, I knelt on one knee, tilting his head so that I could see his face. My black fist was printed across his jaw, my knuckles clearly outlined. If he were to get it x-rayed, I already knew what it would show—his jaw completely unhinged and broken, his cheekbone cracked. The kind of wound I'd given him would take weeks to heal, even for a strong Supernatural, and it still might not come out properly.

Coach Avery crouched next to me, examining it. Undoubtedly noticing the swelling that wasn't stopping, he reached forward like I had. Anyone with two eyes could see he needed help, and quickly.

"You taught me a lesson today, Ms. Foster." He paused. "Never underestimate the opponent."

"I have a feeling you're not the only one who's learned it," I murmured so that no one else heard me.

"Even with surgery and shots, it's going to take him weeks to heal," he said, mirroring my thoughts.

Now I really did feel bad. If I hadn't taken my emotions out on him, he wouldn't have been in this state. I had to fix this.

We'll worry about the rest later . . . Alexandra's words replayed in my mind. It was later.

"Michael," I said, loud enough for him to hear me.

There was a thump as he entered the ring and crouched on my other side. I didn't trust any of the people here, but he was the closest I came to it.

"Listen to me very carefully. I need you to find Alexandra and tell her to get Lily and bring her here. If she asks why, tell her I slipped up, but nothing else, okay?"

He nodded once and left my side.

It was strange for me to care about someone else—especially someone other than my sisters.

I must be spending too much time with Lily. Caring was her thing, not mine.

"We need to get him to Melony. She'll know what to do," he said at last.

"Just wait a few more minutes," I told him.

"For all we know, he could have a concussion or internal bleeding, and he's already passed out," Coach Avery said.

I could tell he didn't blame me—in boxing, this was always a possibility—but it *was* my fault.

Even if it was what I'd come here to do.

"Just give me a couple more minutes. I know someone who can help," I told him.

He didn't seem to hear me. His voice was too loud, already giving orders to get help. I stayed silently with the boy for what was surely only a minute or two, but felt longer.

He was an enigma. Puzzling beyond compare, and yet, the simple fact of what he could do made me feel like I knew him. A part of him, at least, with the rest a mystery. Who was this green-eyed boy?

The door slammed behind me.

I looked over my shoulder to see Alexandra and Lily walking with Michael.

"Lily, can you come here for a second?" I asked softly.

Lily bounded up to the ring and wiggled her way up onto it. When she reached us, I heard her gasp, and Alexandra followed.

"I know this is going to sound unusual for me . . . but can you heal him?"

"I . . . I haven't healed anyone in a long time, Selena, you know that," she whispered.

"Can you try? I've never asked before, but this was my fault."

She seemed to consider it for a moment before kneeling before him and placing her hands on his face.

"Who is this?" Coach Avery asked.

"This is Lily, my sister. She's a healer. Since I did this to him, I figured I should find a way to fix it."

Coach Avery nodded, not seeming to question Lily's presence any longer.

She took a deep breath and closed her eyes. Her hands glowed where they were touching the boy's skin. The reaction was almost immediate. His bones popped back into place, his jaw reconnected, the cracks sealed, and even his bruise was disappearing. She took another deep breath then lifted her hands, and his face was the same as before. You could almost pretend he was sleeping. Almost.

"Thank you," I told her.

"Selena, I need a word with you," Alexandra said from behind me.

I turned and nodded once. "Why don't you guys wait outside for me? I'll be there in minute."

I waited for them to leave before turning to Coach Avery. "When he wakes up, he's going to have a headache and he'll probably want to sleep, but he'll be fine."

I glanced at the green-eyed boy. He looked peaceful lying there. I reached forward to brush the hair off his closed eyes but stopped myself an inch from his face, pulling back. What was it with me tonight?

"That was a nice thing you did for him," he told me.

I rolled back onto the balls of my feet and stood up, turning away from him. I took a shaky breath.

"Yeah, don't remind me. I have stuff to take care of, but I'll be back." My words hung in the air as I walked out.

Outside, it was a lot warmer than I'd expected. The pain of my hand suddenly came back to me, and I mentally cursed myself. Alexandra and Lily were waiting right outside the door.

"You have thirty seconds to explain," Alexandra demanded.

I quickly recounted everything, starting when the coach approached me all the way down to when they'd come in, only leaving out the part where I'd discovered his ability unintentionally. The entire time Alexandra tapped her feet impatiently.

"When I said we'll worry about the rest later, I'll admit, this wasn't what I intended." Alexandra sighed.

"If you both think about it, it wasn't really that bad. We knew when we suggested that you start boxing again that we would have this problem. You've just never felt bad about it before. I can understand," Lily offered.

"I was frustrated. It won't happen again. At least not with someone here."

Alexandra looked at me for a second before nodding; she understood what I meant.

"You know, Selena—" Lily gasped. "You broke your hand?"

I continued unwrapping my hand, letting it free of the

pressure of the wraps. In their full glory, my knuckles were black and purple, and my wrist wasn't much better.

"I've had worse." I shrugged.

"Give me your hand." Lily rolled her eyes, taking my hand without waiting for my response. White light appeared under her fingertips, and heat flooded me, chasing away the cold that had chilled my bones now that the adrenaline had left me. When she pulled away, I flexed my wrist and fingers.

"So are you sure you didn't feel bad because you didn't want your fist to ruin that boy's very handsome face?" Alexandra smirked.

"Very funny," I scoffed as I walked past her, knowing they would follow.

"So apart from bashing a pretty boy's face in, you had a good time?" Alexandra continued.

I knew what she was getting at; she wanted to know if it was working. Was I more stable?

"Yes, I'm already feeling more at home," I said.

She gave a subtle nod, and squeezed my now healed hand.

"Really? That's so great! Why don't we go get—"

"Thank you, for everything. Not tonight, though. I'm tired." I smiled by way of apology.

Lily smiled and shrugged. I could tell she was proud that, for once, she'd gotten to help me when it was usually the other way around.

"Okay, why don't we just make plans for Friday?" Alexandra suggested.

We agreed on that, and I said goodnight, leaving them in front of the dorm.

As I made my way back to my room, I couldn't help thinking of the green-eyed boy. The way he'd boxed mercilessly with Aaron, but had restraint. Something I still struggled with every day. It wasn't only that; it was how I'd let my control slip. Would I see him tomorrow? Would he say anything about it? Only time would tell.

In any case, I had to let these trivial things go. They didn't matter. I was here to protect and look after my sisters. This was for them. For my promise.

That was all.

CHAPTER 14

On the way, I was asked out yet again, and I declined, yet again. That put me on a total of seven guys in the last three days, half of whom had been sitting at lunch with me that first day when I'd met Aaron and his ex. It was startling how many boys had approached me since I'd started here. Supernatural males were unafraid in the traditional sense of fear, but how did that play into rejection? It couldn't have hurt too badly since they kept coming.

I breezed through the door to find the gym much the same as yesterday, with matches going on and boys paying a bit too much attention to me. Walking to the back, I did my usual warm up, because it was the only thing I could do to clear my head.

"Foster."

My tranquility snapped, and my arm twitched. I lost my balance and toppled onto the ground, hitting my head.

"Damn it," I said, a little too loudly.

A hand appeared out of nowhere and, without thinking, I took it. Once I was standing on my own two feet, I turned to thank the person. I stared at Aaron, my eyes narrowed, but I thanked him, nonetheless. Without waiting for a response, I walked over to Coach Avery.

"Have you ever boxed in the Supernatural world before?" he asked me, completely ignoring my little screw-up.

I shook my head.

"There are a few things you need to know then. The first is that this is a brutal sport. Show no mercy. After yesterday, I have a feeling that won't be your problem." He paused. "Second, there are no points. You fight until someone hits the ground. There are no time limits, and no out-of-bound calls."

"You're telling me that a match could go on for hours as long as no one hits the ground? And almost any move is legal—"

"That's exactly what I'm telling you, which is why this final rule is going to be the one that affects you most." The look he cut me shut me up instantly. "The third is that there are no weight classes or differentiation between men and women. When our first match comes up, it will be completely based on your level."

"Which means I could end up with some six-foot-eight guy who's a spitting image of Lou Ferrigno?" I asked sarcastically.

"Basically," he agreed.

There was a short silence between us as I contemplated this.

"Which is why the main things I'm going to work on

with you are your speed and endurance, along with a little weightlifting. Maybe some rounds in the not-so-distant future once we know your level." He gestured to the bench.

"Okay. What are you proposing I start with?" I asked him. I didn't want to be stuck lifting weights and jumping rope for the next three months, but to keep my promise, I had to play by his rules.

"I haven't dec—"

There was a sudden commotion behind me.

I whirled around to see Aaron deck someone. After the less-experienced fighter fell, he didn't waste any time advancing on him. There was something fascinating about the animalistic urge that drove him further and further from civilized. The way he fought—the way he hit him— was so raw. Untamed. Out of control.

War spun in his eyes as he gave way to a darker side—a side of him that didn't answer to morality, or any sense of right and wrong. It was a part I doubted he recognized. As blood covered his hands, it was increasingly familiar to me.

Avery grabbed the back of his shirt and ripped him backwards. Aaron lunged once more, but Coach was fast— faster than Amber. He grabbed him in a headlock with power I'd scarcely seen before.

Aaron instantly went slack as the anger that had pushed him to fight left as fast as it had come. The boy on the ground wasn't faring quite as well.

"This is my gym, and you two are replaceable. How about instead of acting like chest-banging gorillas, you actually do something beneficial before I kick both of you out!" Avery roared. "White, I want you with Foster on weights. Show her what to do and spot her while I deal with this moron over here." He grunted, releasing Aaron.

Aaron turned to me and wiped a trickle of blood from his mouth. With dark eyes flashing and the whole after-fight-vengeance thing going on, he looked kind of hot. I still couldn't stand him—solely based on his man-whoring attitude and pain-in-the-ass arrogance—but there wasn't any denying that he was more than just a little easy on the eyes. I laughed quietly to myself as he crossed the distance between us and came to stand in front of me.

"What was that about?" I asked, only minimally curious.

"Nothing, just John not knowing his place," he replied, though his glance toward me said otherwise. "Have you ever bench pressed before?" he asked in a blatant attempt to change the subject.

I shook my head.

"Okay, well, what you're going to do is lie back on the bench, plant your feet firmly, and hold the bar about here," he said, motioning to his chest.

"I gathered that much," I said.

He shot me a look before continuing. "And when you lift it, you want to go straight up until your arms lock then come back down." He got on the bench and demonstrated before motioning for me to try.

I got on the bench and copied his posture. He handed me the bar, and I held it precisely where he'd told me, going through the motions. "This isn't exactly difficult," I said.

"Let me see it." He took the bar out of my hands and set it on the rack.

I wasn't paying attention to exactly how much weight

he added, but when he gave it back, I could feel the difference immediately.

"Try that," he said smugly.

I started lifting again, but after several reps, I couldn't ignore how heavy my arms were. They seemed to weigh a hundred pounds each, and they were only getting heavier.

"How much weight did you put on here?" I complained.

"Forty pounds. Why, too heavy?" He smirked.

"Not at all," I lied. I continued for a few more minutes in sweet silence before he broke it.

"Can I ask you something?"

"You just did," I said.

"What did I do to piss you off?"

I thought about my answer before responding. "How do you know this isn't just my personality? That I'm not just a bitch?" I countered.

"You're not a bitch, you just don't put up with bullshit, but I can tell you have a problem with me," he insisted. For a cocky, self-centered fool, he actually didn't sound too stupid right now.

"Who said I have a problem with you?"

"It's obvious." The note of seriousness in his voice struck me.

I thought for a moment. "I don't particularly like you, but I wouldn't say that I have a problem with you."

"But what did I do?" he asked as if he needed to know the answer.

"You want to know what you did?" I said, handing him the bar and sitting up. "Nothing. You did absolutely nothing. You were yourself, and I just don't like you. I think you're obscenely arrogant and shallow. It's nothing personal, really, and it shouldn't bother you, but it obviously does. Now, if you'll excuse me, I have work to get done."

His mouth popped open in disbelief, and anger flared in his dark eyes. I was tired of this conversation. If he didn't want the truth, he shouldn't have asked.

"We still have a project due Friday. Will you at least meet me at lunch tomorrow in the library to get it done?" This time it seemed like he'd honestly gotten the clue. He spoke deceptively soft, but his eyes were elsewhere, looking everywhere but at me.

"Sure," I said, walking away without even looking back.

Which was when it dawned on me: the green-eyed boy hadn't even shown up for practice.

~.~.~

"How are we going to do this?"

I was sitting in a library, wasting my time with one of the most uninteresting Supernaturals on campus. Needless to say, my opinion of Aaron hadn't improved overnight.

"Do you actually know anything about Supernaturals?" he asked me.

I watched the way he examined me, looking for deceptions or clues. He was the same as everyone here, trying to unravel the mystery of Selena Foster. I stayed silent for a minute, challenging his gaze. Truthfully, I knew a lot—a lot more than I was letting on, anyway.

"Nope," I lied.

He scratched some things down on a piece of paper and slid it across the table to me.

"What's this?" I asked.

"This is the layout for our project."

I pushed it back toward him. "I've got a better idea. You tell me what you need, and I'll go find it," I suggested with a smirk.

He rolled his eyes. Apparently, he found my idea of partnering aggravating.

"I need you to find a book on the differences between humans and Supernaturals." He sighed.

I got up and left the table to look for the librarian. After a few minutes of walking up and down numerous aisles, I stumbled across her. She was a short, dark-haired woman who seemed rather flustered.

"I was wondering if you could point me in the right direction?" I asked her, trying to put on my most charming attitude.

"What are you looking for?"

"Something about the differences between humans and Supernaturals. I have a report due in health . . . "

She considered my request for a minute then her arm, as if it weren't part of her body, stretched. It was as if she didn't have any bones. It snaked down the row and around the corner. A few seconds later, it came back with a book and shrank back into her arm.

"Try this. I think you'll find it useful." She flashed me a smile.

"Thank you, Miss . . . ?"

"Rivas," she answered warmly.

"Miss Rivas, thank you." I smiled and tried to find my way back to Aaron. I wandered for another minute or two before coming across our table. He was writing something.

I walked up behind him silently and looked over his shoulder. He already had a page written, and I hadn't even given him the book. I got the impression he hadn't really needed it, but it had given me something to do.

"If you want to know what I'm doing, just ask."

"How did you know I was behind you?"

"I heard you," he said.

"How did you—?"

"I can hear a pin drop a mile away. I can smell a girl's perfume from across campus. I can even see every single hair on your head right now. My ability isn't something you can see, but I have enhanced senses."

I froze.

Literally. Stopped. Breathing.

Enhanced senses. The ability I supposedly had. The ability to be better than average at all the trademark characteristics but not specialized in anything that counted. It seemed fitting for him, but I was an imposter. I might've had better senses then most, but I was by no means as developed as he was. I excelled in strength, speed, and reflexes. Things that were physical and could be improved through effort—sight, sound, and smell weren't in that mix. I stayed completely still for the two-point-five seconds it took me to analyze that. Two-point-five seconds that I simply stared. Two-point-five seconds that he misunderstood, while staring back.

Two-point-five seconds before he moved.

He stood and turned toward me until he loomed over me. His lips parted, and he leaned in . . . and then he was on the ground. He clutched his face gingerly. Splayed across the right side of it was a bright red and purple handprint where I'd slapped him.

"You can finish the project on your own," I spat, dropping the book.

I walked out of the library and tried not to break the door when I slammed it behind me.

CHAPTER 15

"So who's your admirer?" Alexandra pestered.

It was Friday, and I was having dinner with them like I'd promised.

"Huh?" I said as I picked at the lettuce in my salad.

"The guy you skipped lunch with yesterday, in the library?" she said encouragingly. It sounded more like an interrogation. Fancy that.

"How did you know that?" I asked, raising an eyebrow at her.

"Not important. Who is he?"

"No one."

"I don't believe that for a se—"

I cut her off with a gesture. "Believe me when I say he's no one," I said, ending the subject.

"So did I tell you guys I started horseback riding with Bella?" Lily said.

"Why?" we said in unison.

"A lot of kids ride horses here." She shrugged.

"But you hate horses," I pointed out.

"I don't hate them. I just never really cared for them," she said in self-defense.

"No, I'm pretty sure you hate them. You have since you were four," I said, and she glared at me.

"She's just trying to fit in, not be a loser for once." Alexandra yawned for effect.

"Oh, shut up, Alexandra," I snapped.

"What? If she wants to make herself miserable in exchange for not being a total loser, let her." She rolled her eyes.

"I'm not a total loser, and I'm not miserable," she argued feebly, throwing a nasty glare at Alexandra.

"Then what are you?"

Lily didn't answer.

"Pathetic, that's what you are—"

"Stop it. I don't want to hear your bickering. Do neither of you get that?"

Now it was their turn to stay quiet.

"I agreed to have dinner, not to listen to you two arguing nonstop or be questioned about what I do in my spare time," I said, eyeing Alexandra.

"Okay, like, what is your problem, Selena?" Alexandra said. "Fighting is supposed to make it so that you're not—"

"My problem is that I'm sick of listening to you two going at each other every time you're together for more than five minutes—and, no, Alexandra, boxing doesn't fix everything. It makes it better. It doesn't *fix* it," I hissed. She *thought* she knew. As if she could actually understand how I felt. What it was like to be me. She was sadly mistaken.

"We don't argue every time we're together for more than five minutes," Lily piped up.

What? I wanted to scream, but thinking of my self-control, I shot her an annoyed look instead. They'd just been arguing, and now she was defending her? This was just—

I am losing my fucking mind.

"You know, maybe Alexandra's right . . . Boxing used to help, but maybe—" Lily went on.

No. *You can't seriously be saying—you wouldn't dare. Not after what I am doing for you—for both of you.*

I was so infuriated; I didn't trust myself not to react. To snap. It would be so easy . . . so easy. To let go.

"I'm not listening to this," I growled. Fury had me, and I wasn't listening to *anything* anymore. I stood to leave before I did something I would regret.

"Selena—" Lily pleaded.

"No." They didn't know what it was like to be different. *Truly* different. When you were so powerful that it could put you on the edge of losing control. *Losing your mind.*

"Just forget it, Lily. If she wants to—"

I left before I could hear the rest. I couldn't believe them. After all we'd been through . . . We'd even talked about this. I told them I had it under control, and I did. They didn't believe me. They didn't trust me. I wanted to scream. It was one thing for them to bicker, and another to think I was losing it. And not just that, but letting it control me. I wasn't. I wouldn't. They were naïve children to think it. I was better than that; smarter. I would beat the chaos that raged inside me. Somehow.

Outside near the fountain, I sat down and sighed, looking up at the stars.

"Why did you do this to me?" I whispered, but no answer came.

CHAPTER 16

It was Monday. A week and a half had passed without me talking to my sisters, and for the first time in my life, I didn't feel the need to. I didn't want to. I'd thought they understood me, or at least tried to, but they didn't understand a damn thing. Besides, they had their own lives now. Lives that didn't involve me.

I had a life too now—one where I spent every waking hour at the gym, even when no one was there. I went before and after school, skipped dinner, and stayed until two or three in the morning. It didn't matter—if I was awake, I was there.

Nothing had changed in the last week and a half. Aaron stared at me half the time, and avoided me the other half. I preferred the latter. Avery still hadn't let me in the ring since that first match, and I was beginning to wonder if he was nervous about what I might do. Since starting, it had become increasingly clear that I was leagues ahead of most boxers, even here. I was the fastest, and my reflexes were as good as Aaron's—maybe even better. But I was a wild card in Coach Avery's eyes. Unleash me, and there was no telling what I might do. Images of the green-eyed boy flashed through my mind.

He still hadn't come back. Word around the gym was that he was taking a break, but I wondered how many nights he was spending replaying that to himself. Probably twice as many as I was. I hated that I'd let him get to me, get under my skin, but his eyes . . . they were all I could see at night. He was such a puzzle to me, unlike other men. He was different. I could feel it. I didn't know what *different* meant. Was it just his ability or was there more?

You punched him, I reminded myself. *Knocked him out stone cold, to be accurate. That fleeting conversation in the ring is probably the only conversation you'll ever have. I doubt he'll even look at you after that little stunt*, I reassured myself.

I wasn't supposed to be distracted by anyone. The sooner he realized I was bad news, the better.

I walked through the door of the gym, and the sound of familiar rap lyrics filled my head. Without even thinking about it, the guys cleared me a spot on the mat. They knew my routine by now. None of them gave me cautious looks, or made jokes anymore—I'd beat them as blue as the mat if they did.

I dropped into a split, doing my usual warmup. Afterward, I got a jump rope and started the timer. I fell into step with the beat as I jumped. Jumping rope had never been my favorite exercise, but if doing more of these got me off the bench, I was all for it. I was still thinking about it when the timer went off, and I knew I couldn't avoid it anymore. I put the rope and timer away before walking over to the bench.

"Foster," Coach Avery called.

I smiled to myself and turned to walk over. Finally. He was going to take me off the bench and actually let me do something productive.

I hesitated for a second, and by hesitated, I mean stopped dead in my tracks. He was there. The green-eyed boy was standing there, watching me intently. I made my feet move again and crossed the space between us.

"I want you to increase the weight to one-ten. It's getting too easy for you."

I tried to keep the grimace off my face as I turned to go. I was strong, strong enough to knock a man twice my weight unconscious—I didn't understand the need to lift weights. But, without a word, I piled on the weights, straining to hear their conversation.

"Is she any good?" the guy asked.

"Good enough to knock you cold," Avery grunted.

"You know I wasn't actually fighting her. How the hell was I supposed to know she was the real deal? I've fought guys twice her size who couldn't hit that hard."

"She's good," he said, and I smiled to myself. I might've been here because of a promise, but I took pride in myself. To the point of arrogance, occasionally.

There was silence for a few seconds, and I realized I was standing there, just staring at the weights.

"So where'd she come from?" he asked when I started lifting.

"I don't know. She's not much of a talker."

I could tell they were still watching me.

"She have a name?" Why was he so interested?

You have no room to talk, my subconscious criticized. I glared at the bar in my hand.

"Selena Foster." My head instinctively turned toward them, and they stopped talking as they moved across the room out of earshot. I turned my head back to face the ceiling and kept working.

I lifted my arms again and again, refusing to stop. If I stopped, I might not start again. My arms ached and my hands were already trembling. Any longer and I might drop it, but I wouldn't stop. I had to go through it; I had to do this. I refused to show weakness in a place where it was unacceptable.

The trembling got worse, and the bar shook in the air. Sweat coated my hands from a too-tight grip, and the bar slid. Before I could stop it, my other hand lost its grip, and the bar was falling, crashing, tumbling through space . . . A steady hand swiped it from out of the air and placed it on the rack.

My hands were still shaking when they fell to my sides. I took a deep breath before trying to lift them. I couldn't. Physically, I just couldn't move them anymore. I slumped back onto the bench.

"It's called muscle fatigue, Selena. You pushed yourself too hard," Coach told me. He crouched down next to me.

"Nonsense," I muttered.

His chuckle filled my ears, and I tried to slow my pounding heart. "I watched you keep going when you knew you shouldn't," he replied, but he didn't sound angry.

"I don't have limits," I explained.

"Everyone has limits, and you pushed yourself past them." He sounded . . . admiring.

"I. Don't. Have. Limits," I insisted, pushing myself up so that I was sitting. "I never have, and I never will."

We were face-to-face now, and my resolve was unwavering. He didn't understand. He didn't know. My body could take far more than a few weights; the kind of power I channeled wasn't even comparable.

"I admire your strength," he said out of nowhere. "But you're headstrong. Ignorant, even, of what your body tells you. You're an amazing boxer, Selena, but I can't use you if you run yourself into the ground. You need to listen to your body. Okay?"

"I don't have limits." I paused, thinking of how to phrase this.

"Foster—"

"But, perhaps, I have minor setbacks," I conceded before he could reprimand me. This argument was a lost cause and would get me absolutely nowhere.

"I think we should start setting a timer when you're on weights, to prevent this from happening again."

"Okay." I sighed. He wouldn't let me have my way regardless of what I thought, and I was too tired to argue anymore.

"Can you move your arms again?"

"Yes," I said tentatively, lifting them to see for myself.

"Well, why are you sitting here then? You have sprints to do," he barked.

I jumped to my feet and crossed the gym, pretending that nothing was wrong—that I hadn't just learned something that bothered me a hell of a lot more than any boy with green eyes. My body *did* have physical limits, as much as I denied it. That meant I wasn't invincible, and I hated that, because it told me one thing. I wasn't unbeatable, and now everyone in the gym knew it too.

CHAPTER 17

School had never been my strong point. I didn't care, and my grades reflected it. I'd always made straight Cs across the board, apart from gym, but I was okay with that. Lily and Alexandra were my focus, not some mundane school for humans. Now, I was facing a small dilemma in that department. I was failing three classes and school was getting harder by the day. Without Lily's help, I wasn't driven to study and it showed. I thought about my sisters often, but they didn't need me anymore, and I was still pissed with them.

Early Saturday afternoon in late September, there was a knock on my door.

"Who is it?" I yelled, not even bothering to get off the floor.

Lily walked in.

"What do you want?" I said coldly. My jaw strained, and I nearly broke my pencil.

"To talk."

I looked back down at the textbook, pretending to be ambivalent. "Well, then; talk."

"I'm sorry, and I miss you," she said.

I stayed silent.

"Selena, talk to me," she pleaded.

"What do you want me to say?" I said, not looking up.

"That it's okay. That I made a mistake. That you're still my sister."

I chuckled. "I'll always be your sister. You can't change that."

"Are we okay again?" she asked. I looked up at her. She seemed sincere, and her brown eyes looked hopeful. I wanted to say yes, but . . .

"On one condition."

She stayed silent, waiting.

"I don't ever want you to bring up my ability, or how it affects me, again. Got it?"

She sighed, but nodded anyway.

"Okay." My shoulders released the tension I'd been holding in sudden relief.

She took a seat on the floor next to me. "What are you working on?"

"History. I have to write a paper on the difference between the American Civil War and the Revolutionary War," I said. I was bored just talking about it.

"You don't sound very enthusiastic."

"Could you tell?" I said, my voice dripping with sarcasm.

"I've got an idea. Let's make a deal," she said.

I examined her, slightly guarded now. She was trying

too hard. When she tried to be, she was too innocent, and it always gave her away.

"What kind of deal?" I questioned.

"I'll tutor you in your classes if you teach me how to fight." She tried to seem indifferent, but didn't quite pull it off.

"Why do you want to learn how to fight?" It didn't really matter why—I wouldn't teach her—but I still wanted to know.

"Because . . . everyone here knows how to," she said meekly.

"Bad answer. Why'd you come to me?" It dawned on me that this was the real reason she'd come here today. I didn't know whether to be angry or hurt. She'd just lied to me so that I would teach her how to fight.

"Because you're better than anyone I know?" It came out like a question. Lily was a terrible liar, but that didn't make this any better.

"Okay, Lily, why don't you stop lying to me?" I refused to look at her. The pencil snapped. "There's no way I will *ever* teach you how to fight. So just get it out of your head."

"Why not? You fight. Alexandra fights. Why can't I? I just want to be good enough to impress everyone in Battle Simulation." Whatever grand notions I'd had that she would be ashamed were gone. She was pissed because she wasn't getting her way. Like a child.

"Because that's who *we* are, Lily, not you. Besides, what would our parents say if they knew you were trying this just for a stupid class?"

Her eyes flashed in a way I hadn't seen before. "I don't care what they would say. Our parents are dead, and they're never coming back. When are you going to get that? You always hold them over me like I'm still ten. I'm not a little girl anymore, and they're gone!" she yelled.

I was stunned.

"Get out," was all I was able to say.

She was already gone, slamming the door behind her.

~.~.~

"We need to talk." I was at Alexandra's door less than a minute after Lily left.

She was busy painting her nails, gossiping with Hannah, and didn't want to leave. Only after I threatened to drag her out by her hair did she actually come into the hallway.

"What do you want?"

"Lily. What's her new kick with wanting to learn to fight?"

"Well, if you were being her sister instead of ignoring her, maybe you would know," she said.

"The sooner you tell me, the sooner I leave."

"Okay, I don't know . . . she, like . . . she came to me yesterday and asked me to teach her. Something about fitting in—I don't know." She flipped her hair and made an annoyed sound.

"Wait. Why did you tell her no?" I asked her.

"Probably the same reason as you. Besides, teaching Lily how to fight is like teaching a cat how to be a dog. Okay? It just wouldn't work." She tapped her nails impatiently on the door as she waited for me to move.

"And why do you think I said no?"

Her eyes flashed. "Because her fighting takes her down a path that could go one of two ways, and you have no guarantees what it will do to her. Will she be like me . . . or you?" She looked away.

It was the only secret we kept from her. The real reason I fought, the reason I would train with Alexandra but not her. Alexandra didn't have the "killing gene," as I called it. My father tested that before he died. I did.

"Keep an eye on her," I said by way of goodbye as I walked away.

On my way back to the gym, I bumped into Elizabeth. We hadn't seen much of each other since starting school, and I suspected it had to do with boxing becoming my entire life. She was dressed in her usual black skinny jeans and graphic tee. Today, however, she had on knee-high black Converse and a studded choker. Um . . .

"Going somewhere?" I asked, eyeing the choker.

"They're taking all the middle schoolers who've manifested to Vegas," she said with a smirk.

"What for?" I asked.

"To see the market," she said, like it was obvious.

"What market?"

"The black market? You've never been to one, have you?"

"I didn't even know it existed," I said, and she laughed, but it didn't reach her eyes.

"Well, they have one in all the major cities. New Orleans, Vegas, New York, San Francisco, even Detroit."

"Mm hmm . . . So, what's at this 'black market?'" It sounded too witchy, like something out of a book.

"They sell *everything* there. For some reason, the school

thinks it would be good if we saw this." She shrugged, finding her hands fascinating.

"Well, enjoy your trip," I said.

"I will, and when I get back, we have to catch up. I haven't seen you in over a month."

"Yeah, that'd be fun . . ."

"I've got to get going. Don't want to miss the plane," she said awkwardly.

We went our separate ways. As I got back to my room, I couldn't help feeling that there was something she wasn't telling me.

CHAPTER 18

It was a week after our brief meeting when I saw her again. She was sitting in the library reading a book and sipping a cappuccino. No surprise; the girl mainlined caffeine. I walked up to her and took a seat to her left.

"How was the black market?" I smirked. It really sounded kind of stupid.

"Interesting," she said, without taking her eyes off the book.

"So what are you reading?" I asked.

Without talking, she tilted the cover so I could see it. *Mystical Creatures of the Supernatural.* What was she doing with that? I started to ask her when something caught my eye.

"I've got to go. We can catch up later," I said over my shoulder as I walked away.

She didn't reply. What was her problem? I shrugged. Maybe she was just having a bad day.

I walked over to the corner where a flash of red hair had caught my attention. Either my eyes were fooling me, or

Alexandra was in here. I rounded the corner and my eyebrows rose.

Alexandra was studying, actually studying, with Michael. Her head was lowered, and she was reading something out of a book, taking notes every now and then.

"What are you doing here?" I asked her, even though it was pretty obvious.

"I was just helping Michael— hey—"

I snatched a few papers out of her folder. They were tests, and she was failing. I flipped back and forth between them. The highest grade was a forty-nine.

"What are these?" I asked, holding them up.

"Michael, could you give us a second?" she asked him, but it was an implied command.

He stood and disappeared behind the shelves in the library.

"What are these?" I repeated.

"Who do you think you are, my mother?" She snatched the papers away, stashing them in her bag.

"Why didn't you tell me?" I didn't have the energy to go another round with her, but I refused to walk away and let it go.

"Because, newsflash, you haven't exactly been around," she snapped spitefully.

I winced, but tried to downplay it. "I would have put our problems aside for this." I took a seat. She'd failed tests before, but never like this. She always managed to pull a mostly passing grade, and when the end of quarter came, she passed. Barely, but she did.

"Look, I don't need your help," she said.

"Bullshit," I spat.

"I'm doing perfectly fine without you."

"You're failing, and I know you don't like studying with your boyfriend."

She considered this. "Okay, what am I supposed to do? He's the only person doing well in these classes, and while I'd rather do other things—I need to pass."

I silently thanked my lucky stars she didn't know I was failing. I would need to start actually trying to do better if I was going to be able to help her.

"You're supposed to come to me, that's what you're supposed to do." I had taken care of her for years. Both of them. It was what I knew. It was what they knew. This whole new world of independence wasn't something we'd prepared for.

"Well, you're here now, and you're not helping. So either find a way for me to start passing or get lost, because I only have another half hour with my boyfriend to try to learn about the Declaration of Independence." She crossed her arms.

"Pick three days a week. We'll study, and no one will know. You'll start passing again, and you won't have to spend all your time with your boyfriend studying." I sighed.

"What's in it for you?" she asked, expecting a catch.

"I don't have to deal with you when you fail at the end of the semester," I said bitterly.

She looked me up and down like she didn't believe me.

"Okay, here's a better one. If I don't help you, who will? Because whatever your boyfriend has you doing, it's not working. Otherwise you'd be passing."

She sighed in frustration. "Fine, but I'm not doing it on the weekends. We can do it on, like, Monday, Tuesday, and

Thursday." She crinkled her nose like a snob. "Now, if you'll excuse me, I would like to spend a little time with my boyfriend." She practically pushed me out of my chair when Michael came around the corner.

"Nine o'clock?" I asked her.

Her response was a single nod and a fire-filled gaze.

I disappeared behind the bookshelf and found myself facing where Elizabeth had been sitting moments before. Her book was lying open on the table.

I stared down at a man with jet-black hair and fire in his eyes. Literally. You could see the flames through the deep and endless black pits. He was handsome in an unearthly, unsettling way. The title on the page next to it read *Demons*.

Now why would she want to know about demons?

CHAPTER 19

It was almost October, and rain and thunder rolled in across the mountains from the west coast. The warm summer breeze passed and became gray and drowsy as the days went on. Today, however, was the best day we'd had in a while.

As I looked out of my bedroom window, I couldn't help noticing how pretty the sun looked with the clouds. It would rain tomorrow, but today it was beautiful.

I sighed and turned away from the window, heading outside to the gym. I strode back to the third room, and immediately walked to the mat.

Before I could even drop into a split, Coach Avery called me over. "I want to start you on a new routine."

"Why?"

"Your first match is less than two months from now. I need you to build up your endurance in the ring." He glanced away, almost nervously.

"So what do you want me to do?" I prodded.

"You're going to train with a partner from now on, and

we'll see how it goes. He's the only one I think could compete with you, and he's already agreed to it."

My heart sped up a little. I had a suspicion about where this was going. "Who?"

A figure appeared at my side, and I felt a gentle shift in myself.

"Selena, meet Lucas. Lucas, Selena." I swore I could see a slight twinkle in his eye.

I turned my gaze toward Lucas, who put his hand out tentatively. I placed mine in his for a second, careful to keep my grip gentle.

He wore black gym shorts and a white t-shirt with the sleeves rolled up. His muscles flexed with the slightest movement of his arms. His hands were rough and callused. I didn't want to feel them. I snatched my hand away and threw my shields up.

His face was careful and guarded as he examined me for a moment, but his eyes . . . they gave away his surprise. I smiled slightly, meeting his gaze, and gave a slight nod before turning back to Coach Avery.

"Selena, Lucas is my best boxer. I've been training him since he was yay high," he motioned to a point on his chest, several inches shorter than me. "He's the only one at your level. Your footwork is impeccable, you have the fastest sprints in gym, and your punches are precise. You're going to need more than that if you want to win. I think you both have a lot you can learn from each other," he said. "Will you train with him?" He pushed the question at me after a short silence.

You made a promise. You train, no matter what.

"Sure," I said.

"You guys can work out the exact schedule, but I want you to start running, both of you. Selena, you need the endurance. Lucas, you need the speed. You both need to get in the ring more too. Like I said, the first match is approaching, and it's only going to get harder from there. I have the rest of the gym to prepare, so don't be expecting as much one-on-one time." It was a nice way of saying he's leaving me alone with Green Eyes for extended periods of time in extremely close proximity.

Lovely.

"When do you want us to start running?" I hid my smirk at his stupidity. Endurance? Apparently, he needed reminding of who I was.

"Today," he said, giving us a serious look before leaving.

It was silent for a moment before Lucas spoke.

"Are you ready? There's an eighteen-mile run around the school wall—"

"Give me five minutes. I'll meet you out front." I walked off.

I went into my split and raised myself, careful to take deep breaths and maintain tranquility. Once I was upside down, I closed my legs into a handstand and kicked backward, landing in a bridge. I flexed my stomach muscles and heaved as I pulled myself up to standing. My warmup was a type of meditation for me, only it required considerably more strength.

Lucas was standing next to the ring, watching me, completely ignoring what I'd told him to do. I sighed and walked out the doors. This was going to be a long day.

"We can start at the front gate—"

I was already running. Coach had told me I had to train

with him, not be with him every minute. Besides, they might not have known it, but running wouldn't challenge me.

I bounded toward the front gate and turned sharply right when I reached it. Within minutes, I was speeding down the wall. Faces blurred by as I passed buildings and trees. After a while I was starting to get bored, when I heard footsteps and steady breathing behind me. I kicked it up a notch, but he was still there. He came up on my side and fell into step with me.

When I glanced at him out the corner of my eye, he was smirking. I shook my head slightly and kept going. There was a curve coming up, and I was going to lose him on it. My heart pounded as I increased my speed until I felt like I was flying. I lost my sense of . . . well, everything. I raced along the wall like a cheetah hunting its prey. My mind blurred, and all I knew was running; all I felt were my feet racing over the ground below.

I ran for what seemed like forever, but before I knew it, the gates were in sight. I pushed harder, harder than I had to get here, harder than I had with weights, harder than anything. I ran past the gate and slowed to a gradual stop about a hundred yards or so from it.

My heart was pounding. Sweat was slick across my skin. I breathed slow and deep to cool off as I took in my surroundings. The sun started to set, and I wondered how long we'd been out here.

I turned around and jogged back to the gate, where Lucas was lounging against the wall.

"You're fast," he commented as I came to a stop in front of him. Was that a slight southern accent I heard? Great, not only was I stuck with this guy, but he was also one of those good ol' fashioned southerners.

"The fastest," I corrected. To him, it may have seemed like bragging, but to me, it was just a statement.

"You're observant," he noted.

I gave him a questioning look, and he tapped his head with his index finger.

"Stay out of my head," I spat at him. Narrowing my eyes, I threw my shields up as well as I could, given my lack of practice.

"I wasn't prying. You're actually very good at blocking me, for the most part. Let me guess, you're a psychic shield or something?" He sounded intrigued by me, perhaps even a little admiring. There was no lust in his eyes. In fact, he seemed more guarded than most—although, I would've been too if I'd had my ass handed to me in two minutes flat.

"No, I just know how to keep my thoughts from cheaters like you," I said snidely and started to walk back.

He dropped into step next to me. "A cheater? That's what I am?" he asked, amused.

"Yes, a cheater." I tried to ignore him, but it wasn't working. There was no humor or invitation in my voice, yet he kept coming back.

"How did you know?"

"Know what?" I said, too lost in thought to pay attention.

"You didn't know my name or anything about me. You just appeared . . . and yet you still knew. You knew what I could do almost immediately after stepping into the ring. How?"

We were back at the gym, standing in front of the third

door. I turned to him and a small, knowing smile found its way to my lips as I looked up to him.

I shook my head slightly. "Like you said, I'm observant." I walked into the gym, but not before spotting the confusion on his face.

Despite what he could do, he was nothing like my father. But we were still young, and . . . perhaps he would grow. I was born to be what I am, but I was different. Not all are born to be great. I shook my head. I needed to get back in the game. This boy was making me a sentimental fool.

I worked for another three hours before leaving the gym. We didn't talk again, but I had a feeling I'd given him something to think about.

After boxing, I went back to my room and took a very long shower. Letting down my shields, I practically purred in pleasure as the tension of keeping them up released. The hot water beat at my back, and I groaned. Boxing might've been doing what it needed to do, but it could be hell on the body. Lucas had gotten me hard in the ribs today; even though I'd moved to dodge it, the bruise was still there. I'd punched him harder in the gut in return. I bet he'd have a bruise a hell of a lot longer. I smiled to myself.

I changed into sweats and a t-shirt for dinner. After grabbing a salad and water, I headed back to my room to eat. I didn't feel like seeing anyone tonight.

I met Alexandra in the library after my quiet dinner and meditation. She grinned up at me from the hard wood table, her nails freshly painted, and face less tense than it had been in weeks. She looked good.

"You passed," I praised when I looked down at the eighty-three she'd made on her test.

"Thank you." The words came out in a rush. She was looking at her hands because even if she hated to admit it, she still needed me, and that made her uncomfortable. I was the only one she'd let help her all these years, and she still didn't trust anyone else to do it, even Michael.

"You're welcome." No point making it harder on her than it needed to be.

We studied for hours. Eventually, the librarian, Ms. Rivas, had to come and tell us to leave. I listened to Alexandra's speech for Health as we walked back to our dorm, and when I was finally satisfied, we said goodnight.

That night I lay in bed, listening to Amber snore and Tori watch YouTube videos about cats. It was so normal for them; for Alexandra, for everyone else to find their place in the world. They had a future, all of them, and everyone wanted something. Yet when I thought about my future, I saw nothing. There was a time I had dreams, but they were long dead, and I had changed. My sisters were growing up, and I was losing my purpose. They still needed me . . . for now. But what would happen when they didn't anymore? What would happen when they'd grown up, and I'd "won the war"? *What happens to me?*

I didn't know, but I wondered . . . what would it be like to want something for myself? To want *someone*?

I snorted at the thought, and rolled over—falling into a restless sleep where I dreamed of a cabin far away, and a man with eyes that made me feel something, deep in my lonely heart.

CHAPTER 20

Today, I found out why they called it Battle Simulation. For the last two months, all our class had been doing was studying Supernaturals: why we had our abilities, manifesting, classification, etc. Today, we were fighting.

Vonlowsky picked two kids to go into the simulation room, and the rest of us would watch them battle it out. Afterward, he would critique it, tell them what they needed to improve, and what they'd gotten right. Sounded simple enough, right? Wrong. The first two people he picked were Alexandra and the youngest girl to manifest in our grade.

His attention was all on them, which gave me a chance to talk to Lily. I yanked a piece of paper out of my binder and wrote: *How long do you plan on staying mad at me for not teaching you how to fight? Do you know how stupid that sounds?*

I probably shouldn't have said what I meant if I wanted to get a response out of her, but I couldn't help it. She *was* being stupid—even if she didn't realize it. I folded the paper up and threw it three rows to my left. I heard a slight *swish* before it landed neatly in front of her on her desk.

She looked over at me and glared, but opened it, none-theless.

As I waited for a response, I focused on Alexandra. She was locked in hand-to-hand combat with the girl. She swung, the other one ducked. The other girl aimed a kick at her knee, and she jumped. They continued like this for several minutes before someone tapped my shoulder.

I turned to see Tori sitting next to me, holding out a note. I took it from her and unfolded it.

I don't care how stupid it sounds. Just like I don't care that you won't teach me. That doesn't make it okay between me and you, so just forget it.

I sighed and put the note in my pocket. I was just going to have to deal with her another day. The sight of flames caught my eye.

Alexandra's hands were on fire. My sister had her oppo-nent by the throat, dangling her a foot off the ground. My eyes widened. What kind of teacher would let this go on? Our people were brutal, sure, but these were kids. This was wrong.

Before I could say anything, the overhead bell rang.

"That will be all," he said into a microphone on his desk, and Alexandra dropped her.

She landed on the ground with a thud, and Alexandra turned to leave.

"We'll review tomorrow—"

The girl was on her feet with a pissed look in her eye,

and she was holding one hand out as if she were gripping something.

Alexandra hovered several feet off the ground, her face turning redder by the second as she struggled.

I didn't think. Within seconds, I'd silently slipped into the now-open room, and advanced on her. She didn't notice me until it was too late. In the back of my mind, I heard someone scream—a warning, maybe?—but I wouldn't listen.

I grabbed her hair, forcing her to break eye contact. She looked at me, and I knew she would try to hold both of us at the same time. It didn't work. I punched her. I only did it once, and I didn't hit her hard—just enough to knock her unconscious for a while. I was vaguely aware of the group forming around us when she fell.

I started to step away when I felt a hand on my shoulder. Professor Vonlowsky opened his mouth—

"I don't know what the hell you were thinking," I yelled. I would've gone on, but I needed to get to Alexandra.

I wove through the thinning group of children to reach my sister. She was passed out on the floor, but the color was steadily returning to her face.

When she regained consciousness, it took her a moment to realize where she was, and what had happened.

"I'll kill her," she spat, and fire danced in her eyes. She tried to stand, but I had her by the shoulder.

"You'll do no such thing," I said, forcing her to turn and look at me. "No such thing."

She looked away but made no further move after the girl. She knew better.

"Can you take her back to her room? I think she just

needs some fresh air," I said to Lily. Michael appeared at her side, and they started coaxing her back to the dorm.

I waited until the girl started to stir before I went back to my dorm. Shit. Was it too much to hope that no one would mention this in the gym? I already had a reputation for being slightly dangerous.

I was the first back to the room—my roommates must've still been in Battle Simulation. Hurrying, I grabbed my things and shoved them in a duffel bag. As I made my way out of the dorm, the whispers started. I ignored them and kept walking.

When I got to the gym, I made a beeline for the third door and went straight to Coach. When I walked up to him, he appraised me, and I knew what he was seeing: school uniform, hair down, no workout clothes.

Before he could even ask, I spoke. "I had a slight mishap today," I blurted before I could think of something clever. "Is there a bathroom or somewhere I can change?"

"Girls' locker room. It's always open."

As I walked to the door, Lucas caught my attention. He was talking to one of the guys, but stopped when he saw me. I felt him watching me as I walked into the locker room. I changed quickly into shorts and a tank top. I hastily pulled my hair back and washed my face with cold water before leaving.

I threw my bag in the back and started my warm-up. In the middle of lifting myself out of a split, Lucas appeared in my line of sight.

"Coach wants a word with you before we run," he said.

I continued until I was standing again. Silently, I walked over to Coach Avery who was already watching me.

Does everyone feel the need to stare at me today? I mean, goddamn, don't they have anything better to do?

Lucas stood next to him, saying something too low for me to hear. I did a quick check to make sure my shields were up as I approached them.

"Coach?" I asked with hesitation. I knew I was in trouble.

"Some boxers have approached me with concerns about you." He looked away. I didn't think he wanted to be having this conversation any more than I did.

I had to resist the urge to roll my eyes. "Like?"

"Selena, it's not okay to interfere with a fight in Battle Simulation. Especially not when you knock them unconscious. Just because you have the power doesn't make it okay." He didn't understand.

I had to look away from them to keep myself from screaming. *No one gets it.*

"You don't understand," I managed to say.

"Then explain it to me, because I can't train you if this happens again." He sounded frustrated.

Join the club.

"I can't," I mumbled. I had to say something. I was here for them, just like I'd intervened today for them. *They come first.* Even though it made me selfish, sometimes I wished things were different. *And if wishes were fishes, we'd all eat sushi.*

I hated sushi.

"If you can't be open with me, I can't do anything."

I stayed silent for a few moments, trying to work out how much I should say. "It was wrong." I paused. "I didn't step in until I felt it was necessary. The fight was over. He'd told them to stop, and Alexandra did. I knew if I didn't do anything, Alexandra would. I couldn't let her," I said quietly. It wasn't intentional, but emotion seeped into my voice. "I was careful. I didn't break anything. I just couldn't chance it. Alexandra's my sister." I looked away and fought the strain in my jaw to grit my teeth. I hated talking about myself, my sisters, any of it.

"I understand that, but you can't hit someone for no reason," he reasoned.

Even though I heard sympathy in his voice, I instantly recoiled. I'd just explained to him why I'd done it, and he still thought I was wrong? No, I refused to believe that. I would do it a thousand times over before I let Alexandra get hurt.

"It wasn't for no reason," I said with my face completely void of expression. I wiped all emotion from my voice, and looked on with indifference.

"That's not the point, Selena. I understand that you were worried about your sister, but I've seen what you can do. That hit could've been a lot worse if you'd slipped up. My point is, that next time you need to find a different approach, or let your sister take care of herself."

"I can't do that," I said.

"So you're telling me no?" An edge slipped into his voice, as if I were questioning his judgment.

"She comes first." I stood my ground.

We stood in silence for a minute before Lucas turned and whispered something to him. Damn him for being quiet enough to get past me.

Coach nodded then turned his gaze back to me. "Okay, that's all for now. Go start on your run."

I walked away. Lucas followed close behind, but I needed out. Out of this skin, and these responsibilities. I broke into a run across the gym, bracing myself for when I hit the door to the outside.

I heard his footsteps behind me and knew he was trying to keep up, but I wanted to be alone. I burst through the gym door and took off at a sprint, leaving him in the dust.

As I ran, my thoughts came pouring down on me. I was suffocating. Drowning.

I knew we should stay. I knew this was best for us. That didn't mean I had to like it. My father once told me that there was a perfectly easy, straightforward solution to anything. He was wrong. Sometimes what was best for you was also difficult. Growing pains came to mind.

While I wasn't happy, I was happier here than I'd been in years. I was more distant from my sisters, but I had my own life now. I had boxing, school . . . I even trusted a few people—not that I'd admit it.

There was a movement to my left, and Lucas came into view. I ran faster, but I couldn't outrun him.

Still, it was obviously a struggle. His breath was coming short and heavy, and sweat glistened on his tanned skin. His eyes; they'd never looked so alive, so green. In them, I saw determination, but he was distracted. His gaze flashed toward mine, and I immediately looked away.

For the rest of the run, I faced forward, not even daring to glance toward him. I was too unsure of where we stood. We were partners—equals, according to Coach Avery. Anything more felt like asking too much. I trusted him, but only to a degree. A very small degree.

As we approached the gate, I steadily decreased my

speed, coming to a gradual stop in front of it. I turned on my heel and started toward the gym.

"So what year are you?" he asked, suddenly appearing at my side again.

"Sophomore," I said in a clipped voice.

"And Alexandra?" he asked.

"Sophomore."

"Twins?"

"Triplets," I replied.

"Is she weak?" He was testing the waters on the day a hurricane had blown through.

"No," I snapped. I knew he was trying to find out more about the Battle Simulation incident. That didn't mean I wanted to tell him.

"Then why did you get involved in her fight?"

"Because she's too powerful and I'm the only one who can stop her." I didn't know why I was telling him this. It wasn't the whole truth, but then again, it never was. It was close enough to make me question myself, however.

Before I could get lost in thought, he spoke again. "Your parents can't control her?" he asked, turning the conversation to even darker topics.

"My parents aren't around," I mumbled.

"What do you mean?"

Without breaking stride, I told the truth for the first time in a very long time. "They're dead," I said in a hollow voice. There was no point avoiding it or covering it up. He would find out eventually, even if I didn't tell him.

He opened his mouth to say something, but I cut him off with my hand. "I don't want sympathy. It is what it is.

Just don't go snooping in my head, and we won't have a problem."

I took a deep breath. *Remember, they come first.*

The mantra that had once brought me peace now felt like the bars in a cage of my own making.

CHAPTER 21

ALMOST INSTANTLY AFTER I TOOK MY SEAT, CLASS STARTED, AND I just *knew*. I didn't know how or what, but I knew that, somehow, he was going to make my day hell.

"Yesterday's fight got a little out of hand when students cheated and *interfered*. I'm here to tell you, too bad. In real life, if you were to fight someone, tell me they wouldn't play dirty?"

No one answered.

"Exactly. That's why I've already decided who I think would benefit most from this lesson." My stomach plummeted when he looked at me. "Ms. Foster, I think today we'll see you and . . . " He looked around the room until his eyes rested on someone. I followed his gaze. I was going to throw up. "Ms. Foster." He pointed at Lily, and motioned for her to come up.

At first, she looked shocked, but then, slowly, she made her way up.

If I could've figured out how to make my mouth move, I

would've gaped at her. No, I would not fight her. He could stick me in there and lock the door, and I still wouldn't do it.

"The rules are the same as yesterday. Until one of you wins, I'm not letting you out."

Was that even legal? Was any of this even legal? Maybe not in the human world, but we belonged to a world of our own.

He walked over and opened the door, motioning for us to go through. I walked stiffly, not saying a word, with Lily following behind me.

"Well, don't just stand there," he said.

I turned toward the door. Out of nowhere, she hit me in the face. The punch was so weak I didn't turn toward her or even flinch. I walked to the door.

I reached for a handle, but there was nothing but smooth metal. I pushed against it, but it didn't budge. I took a step back and kicked the door as hard as I could. It shuddered and moved slightly, but didn't give.

"Oh fuck it," I muttered and turned away from the door just in time to see another punch flying toward my face. I grabbed her fist mid-air before it was even close. She threw another one at me, but it was so slow I intercepted it long before I was in any danger of being hit.

I looked her in the face. "What's wrong with you?"

"What, do you think you're too good to fight me?" she spat.

"It has nothing to do with being too good. I wouldn't fight you even if you were better," I said.

She tried to break free; I didn't move an inch. "Then

what is it? That I'm your sister?" I could hear the struggle in her voice—she was wearing herself out.

"That's part of it," I admitted and backed her gently against the wall.

"Why? You fight Alexandra, you box, and you even knocked that girl out yesterday." Her voice dripped with venom.

"That's not fair," I whispered to her. She didn't understand. It wasn't her fault.

"Why not?"

"Alexandra and I get in fights because she's actually dangerous. You're not. I box because I have to. You don't. And I dealt with that girl yesterday because she was a threat. You aren't. So. Get. Over. Yourself." I dropped her hands and walked away.

I felt a flash of pain when she yanked me back by my hair. I went into a backbend to keep myself from falling.

"Stop this," I told her.

"Not until you fight back," she said low in my ear.

I saw her boots in front of my face before she kicked me. My vision turned hazy, even as I reminded myself she didn't know any better. She went to kick me in the face again, and I tried to grab her boot. I tried to stop her. She slammed her heel down on my wrist. There was a *snap*, and pain flooded me. I collapsed to the side, bringing my wrist to my chest as I sat up.

It was already purple and blue, and the bone was sticking out at an odd angle. Blood streamed down my arm as I held it up to assess the damage.

Lily had done this. Lily hurt me.

I stared at my wrist with bizarre fascination. Lily. Innocent, golden-haired Lily had done this. She lost her inno-cence the second I realized that. She wasn't good, or sweet, or kind. Yet my mantra played in the background, like a sarcastic funeral march.

They come first.

What a load of bullshit.

Lily gaped, covering her mouth. A door opened, and Vonlowsky strode in. The bell rang overhead, and I couldn't help but think that it always rang when something bad happened in this class.

Lily's healing power washed over me, but I tore my arm away. I didn't want her healing.

I rocked back then pushed all my weight forward so I could stand. I was a little unsteady, but Professor Vonlowsky put a hand on my shoulder to keep me from fall-ing. I jerked away from him.

Lily was saying something, but I didn't hear her, or Vonlowsky, or even Alexandra, who was trying to get my attention. He'd put us in here, said fight, and Lily had will-ingly gone along with it. She'd kicked me in the face and broken my wrist. She hadn't just gone along with it. She'd reveled in it.

I looked at her, and it felt like I was really seeing her for the first time. Was this what she saw when she looked at me? I didn't know. I didn't care. Everything I'd done had been for her. For them.

She reached for my wrist again, but I jumped back and bared my teeth. The animal inside sharpened its claws on the tattered thing I called a heart.

"Selena, please, I'm sorry—"

Alexandra cut her off. "Just let her heal you, Selena. You can't box with that wrist."

That was true, but right now I wanted nothing to do with her. I might've been a monster, but even I had boundaries. I'd never truly hurt them. Either of them. Not once in the six years that Alexandra had been fighting with me had I ever knocked her unconscious. I'd never even laid a hand on Lily; she was innocent then. Untouchable.

I was too busy processing to realize that Lily had taken my wrist again. When I pulled away, she was already done, and all that was left was a massive migraine.

"You've done your job. Now can you please leave?" Vonlowsky said impatiently to my sisters.

"Excuse me?" Alexandra said, but Lily tugged on her arm, and Alexandra went with her, but only after giving him one last glare and flipping him off as she walked out the door.

He didn't appear to care.

"What?" I spat at him. I assumed my usual position with my arms crossed and face blank.

"Why did you refuse to fight?"

I didn't answer; I simply stood there staring at the wall behind him.

"So you refuse to fight *and* refuse to answer. Is there anything else I should know about you?" he demanded.

"What do you want?" I said, anger heating my voice. I could've decked him right now. I could've hit him so hard he would never look the same again, even with his Supernatural blood. I wouldn't, though; not yet. I had to be on my best behavior for Coach Avery or he would pull me from the lineup.

"I want you to fight back. I saw you hit that girl yesterday when you thought your sister was in trouble. There was no hesitation; it was perfect. Precise. Today, I put you in here and you refuse to do anything. She kicked you in the face, and you still refused. Why?"

"Why does it matter? I don't have to fight if I don't want to. You can't make me do a damn thing! You locked us in here and told her to fight me. You put my sister against me. Do you just hate me? Are you naïve? Ignorant?" My head pounded to the beat of the song my blood was singing. It called for murder. It wanted me to paint this room red. "No, I don't believe any of that. I think you do it because you're twisted, and you think it's funny." I got right up in his face.

The brown eyes narrowed as his jaw clenched.

Try me. I dare you.

"You're cruel."

"You think I'm cruel? Let me tell you something about life: it's not easy. Our world is full of cruel people who do things simply for power. When you leave here and learn something about it, then you can come back and tell me I'm cruel." He advanced on me, but I wouldn't step back. Step down.

"I did that because you need to learn. You need to get past whatever childlike illusions you have of protecting your sisters. You interfering yesterday didn't help Alexandra. It made her rely on you. It made you in control. That's what your issue is—you don't know how not to be in control."

I didn't answer.

"You need to let it go, and let them take care of themselves. Don't interfere again, or your next lesson won't be so kind."

His emphasis on *kind* made me snarl.

"Leave me alone," I growled.

I walked away, and I realized I didn't have anywhere to turn.

Not anymore.

CHAPTER 22

I was already running late when I walked into my dorm, but when I stepped inside my room, I knew there was no avoiding it. Tori was curled in a ball on her bed, crying. Amber was already long gone. How could she have left her like this?

I walked over and took a seat at the edge of her bed. "What's wrong?" I said softly.

She looked up at me, and moved into a sitting position. "My grandma just died," she whispered between sobs.

All my anger and frustration faded as I held my arms out to catch her. She fell into them, and her cold hands wrapped around me, holding me tight.

I knew a thing or two about loss. When my parents died, I was in mourning for weeks, crying silently. I never let anyone comfort me. No, I'd thought it was my job to comfort my sisters. I had to be strong.

She didn't have to be strong because, right now, she had me.

I was still holding her, stroking her hair, when there was a knock at the door.

"Come in," I called without turning or releasing her. I heard the door open, and soft footsteps.

I was staring out the window when a person I hadn't expected stepped into view.

His face was sad, and his eyes, normally so green, were reddened and bruised. He didn't look weak or frail; just guarded. Always guarded.

"What do you want?" Today wasn't a good day to bother me.

I looked away from him, and rested my cheek on her hair. Maybe we'd never really been friends—mostly because of me—but right now it didn't matter.

"Victoria." He said her name softly.

She moved to look at him, and I lifted my cheek. Realization dawned on me as I stared into his eyes—which were fixed on her.

Their eyes. They both had the same bright, emerald-green eyes.

They were brother and sister.

She released me, and I let her go. She looked back, and I smoothed her hair, giving her a small smile before retreating.

When I was at the door, I turned and looked at them. She was sobbing on his shoulder as he whispered words of reassurance. His eyes met mine and with a single nod, I left.

CHAPTER 23

After that, everything changed. My sisters were no longer my concern. I took Vonlowsky's advice and left them to their own devices, especially Lily. For so long, I'd drifted through life with no purpose but them. I was my own purpose now.

I started skipping classes, working out to greater extremes, and even going without sleep for days. At first, I was confused about where it had all gone wrong, and then I didn't care. Lucas met me at the gym every day, and we practiced for hours, but he never mentioned that day in my room. Meanwhile, Tori now waited up for me at night. I would come back around midnight to popcorn and YouTube videos. It was so unlike anything I'd ever done, and yet it felt normal now. Tori had somehow filled up part of the hole that had been ripped out of my chest when Lily kicked me in the face. She wasn't my sister, but for once, I was glad of it. She was something entirely new to me. A friend.

I was getting both better and worse as the weeks wore

on. I had my own life, but one day, out of nowhere, I reached the day I couldn't go without pills. At first, it was Tylenol here and there. Then I found Hydrocodone in the bathroom. It only went downhill from that point on. The bottles were prescribed to Amber, and after the first week of me getting into them, she started giving me sly looks. She never said anything, so neither did I. Tori was either the most oblivious person I'd ever met, or she'd turned a blind eye to us.

On the first day of November, Professor Vonlowsky told me to stay after class. After that afternoon, he'd never called on me, and I'd never volunteered. I didn't know why he would want to talk to me now. When I saw my sisters staying as well, I had a feeling.

I picked up my notebook and walked to the front of the classroom.

"What?" I demanded. I had places to go and people to hit. The gym was both a haven and a prison. The clarity I felt nowadays, the way I could breathe freely. I wouldn't let that go. I enjoyed being there—it gave me purpose.

But it was always a question of just how hard I could hit —how much I could hurt—before Avery pulled me. Sometimes I wondered if he saw the darkness inside me, or if he chose to turn a blind eye like Tori.

"We're worried about you," Lily whined.

I turned to her. It was the first time since that day that I'd really looked at her. I laughed humorlessly. It wasn't me talking to them, but the monster inside me.

"Isn't this what you guys wanted?" I gestured to myself and laughed again.

"No, this isn't what we wanted. Selena, you need help," Lily persisted.

"I don't need anyone's help, especially *yours*," I said. Somewhere inside, something whispered that this was wrong; that it shouldn't be this way. I was worse today than usual. Amber had run out with us both raiding her stash, and she wouldn't have more for another day or so. I clenched my fists to keep my hands from shaking. They couldn't know. No one could.

She covered her mouth and started to cry, turning toward Alexandra, who just stared at me.

"Ms. Foster, your sisters have a valid point. I've noticed it over the last few weeks. You're emotionally cut off. You need help. Maybe with the guidance of a close friend or—"

"No one asked for your input. In fact, I never asked for any of yours, so just fuck off, why don't you?" I stormed out of the building.

CHAPTER 24

The next day Coach Avery approached me. I was done
warming up, and Lucas was waiting out front for me.

"Has something been bothering you, Foster?" he asked.

I just shook my head.

He watched me for a moment before sighing. "If something's bothering you, you know you can tell me, right?" he said uncomfortably.

I nodded.

"Okay, well get going." He sighed again.

As I walked away, part of me wished I'd told him, or that I could tell someone. The monster raged inside me. I was a prisoner.

Outside, the cold air whipped at me, and I shivered. My usual tank top and shorts were definitely not November clothes.

"You're confused," a voice said from behind me.

Seriously? I yelled, "What did I say about reading my—"

"I didn't," he said.

"Oh," was all I could manage. Strangely, after everything that had happened, he was the person I had the most respect for. I preferred training with him over *anything,* and the silence between us was welcoming. He understood me better than most.

"It was your expression—the way you hold yourself." He shrugged.

"Mm hmm . . . really? Since you know me so well, how do I hold myself?" I glared.

"Well, if you insist, you're very . . . guarded. Generally, whenever you're around people, you appear hostile. I don't think you are, though."

"What do you think I am, then?"

"I think you close people out because you're scared of getting hurt."

"I don't know what you're talking about," I snapped and broke into a run. Unfortunately, he caught up. I guess we weren't done talking.

"See? You run away from confrontation." He gave a half-hearted laugh.

I turned and glared at him, but he only raised his eyebrows and smirked.

"How do you know this anyway?"

Stalker.

"Hardly," he growled with a somewhat annoyed expression.

"How many times do I have to tell you to stay out of my head? I don't think you realize this, but the longer I have to block you, the less energy I have." Increasing my speed, I closed my eyes and imagined building a brick wall around my mind, using my main emotions to keep him out—a technique I'd learned long ago.

"It's hard not to hear when we're the only two people out here. It goes from silence to quick thoughts that are just thrown at me. You don't exactly make this easy on me," he grumbled.

I vaguely remembered something my dad had told me about that, but before the thought could fully form, he spoke again.

"I know this about you because we're partners. It's my job to know." He paused. "Whether you like it or not, you're stuck with me."

"Yay me," I said sarcastically as we rounded another corner.

"You agreed to train with me," he reminded me.

"It's not you . . . it's just . . . I work alone usually," I admitted.

"That's because you're scared to get close to anyone," he repeated.

"Is that such a bad thing?" I found myself saying.

"When it keeps you from the people you love most."

I stopped dead in my tracks. The knowing look in his eyes told me everything. He saw a lot more than he let on.

"What if those people have changed, and you don't really know them anymore?" I asked him.

"Think about it. Is it really them who have changed? Or is it you?"

The problem wasn't that I didn't know the answer; it was that I didn't want to admit it.

CHAPTER 25

After that day with Lucas, I cleared things up with my sisters. The things I'd said to them when I was dealing with withdrawal bothered me, and I needed to make it right. This past month had taught me several things. They were no longer my purpose for living, but they were the most important people in my life. There was blame to share on both sides, but if we could find it in ourselves to forgive each other, maybe we could get past this. First, we had to come to several agreements.

I had to stop shutting people out. My symptoms may have been getting better, but I still needed someone to be there for me like I was for them. I needed them, but not like before. Then they were all I had, and I wouldn't go back to that. I had friends now. I had Lucas.

If our relationship was going to work, they had to stop questioning me. I was sick of hearing that I needed help. All that did was piss me off, and then they thought I was getting even worse, when really my temper was just short-ening. It was an endless circle, and the only way to stop it was for us to compromise. This didn't fix everything, and I still had a chip on my shoulder with Lily, but it was getting better.

After that, Alexandra and I started studying again. For me to help her, I had to start going to school every day again. At first it was difficult—I didn't feel like going, and I preferred being in the gym—but after I made myself go, it got easier.

I couldn't give up the pills, and my only saving grace was that I was pretty sure only Amber knew. It wasn't until the day of my match when Lucas said something that I knew that wasn't the case.

We were sitting in the boxing gym while they moved the ring into the real gym. Outside, the walls lined with bleachers were filled with a few hundred or so students and faculty.

I was sitting cross-legged on the floor, stretching with Lucas. Over the last few weeks, we'd developed a close friendship, and talked a lot. He wasn't like other guys. There was something different about him, something that kept me coming back for more.

"Don't hook yourself up on painkillers before the match," he said in a hushed tone.

I glanced at him out of the corner of my eye. "What are you talking about?"

"Don't play stupid." He glared.

I turned away so that he couldn't see my face. "Fine. Why?"

"It'll numb your senses. You don't know what ability the guy you're fighting will have, and you need to be prepared." He was more hostile than usual; far too blunt.

I got up and crossed the room. There was a chest filled with ice and water bottles; but I wasn't getting water. Sitting on my knees, I took a deep breath and plunged my hands into the cold water. By the time my match came, they would be numb, and any pain would be delayed.

"All right, I won't take anything before a match," I agreed, a little ashamed that he knew.

"You should stop taking it, period." I expected him to go on, to tell me why, to threaten to tell people, and even go as far as to say I needed help. But he didn't.

"I tried; I really did. It's not that easy," I snapped. My excuses were weak, even to me. My hands clenched in the ice water.

"Tell me something." He took a seat next to me, and I couldn't help looking at him as he spoke. "If your sisters were doing what you're doing right now, would you sit by and watch them kill themselves? Because that's what I have to do." He looked angry and sad at the same time.

I looked away, unsure of what to say, what to do.

"It's not going to be easy. Nothing's easy. Nothing that's worth it."

His words echoed my father's from years past.

I released the pressure of my fists and sighed. He was right. I had to quit, for good. I couldn't just try, I had to. Not just for myself—for Alexandra, Lily, Lucas, Tori . . . my parents.

"Okay," I agreed. I would probably have my slips in the beginning, but I had to try. I had to do it.

The silence stretched between us while I let my hands freeze. They were starting to ache, but until fifteen minutes before my match, I didn't even dare to look at them. They were blue and purple and even starting to wrinkle a little. I was scared they would warm up too quickly if I took them out now. I waited another five minutes.

Just as my coach walked in, I was pulling my hands out. I quickly wiped them on my shirt and met him next to my partner.

"I just met with the other coach, and we ran into a little problem. They only have two level five boxers, and we have three. One of you can't compete today." He looked back and forth between Lucas, me, and Aaron, who was lounging against the wall.

"Which one of us isn't competing?" I demanded.

"I haven't decided yet." He sighed.

"But the tournament begins in ten minutes." I raised my voice.

"Aaron and Lucas have been here longer, but putting you in the ring will definitely throw them off . . . so who to choose?" he muttered to himself.

I glanced at Aaron, and he didn't seem concerned. That irritated me even more. There was no way he was walking out there instead of me. Even if that meant I had to make sure he couldn't walk.

"Coach, you've watched me fight. You know I'm better than Aaron," I insisted under my breath.

"The hell she is. Besides, you even said it. I've been here longer."

Now he wants to pay attention.

"I'm the best," I retorted. "I'm faster, more experienced, and I don't get distracted. You may look more dangerous, but we all know when push comes to shove, I can pack a punch better than most. I am better than you, I was when I walked into this gym the first time, and I deserve to fight."

I didn't argue over many things. I thought of myself as above that. When it came to standing up for myself, I had no problem saying something. I deserved this, whether I'd started out wanting it or not.

"It doesn't matter what you think. I was here first," he responded coldly.

"You're only saying that because that's literally the only way you have a chance. Just face it. If we fought, I would win." I turned to glare at him. He glared back. His black eyes homed in on me, but I wasn't the prey here. I was the hunter.

"Then fight me for it." He took a step toward me.

"When and where?" I stepped up to meet his challenge, staring straight into his bottomless eyes.

"We don't have time for this," Avery barked. "The match starts in less than five minutes, and Aldric Fortescue is here." Aaron backed away; his jaw strained as he turned to our coach.

We went silent.

"I think you all would do great," he said slowly, "but when it comes to odds and skill alone . . . Selena and Lucas are above you, Aaron."

All I heard next was a long stream of curse words that was quickly drowned out by a whistle.

"I've made my decision. You don't have to like it, but, as a boxer, you have to respect it," Coach Avery scolded.

Aaron's eyes bored into mine. First, I'd ratted him out with his girlfriend, then I'd rejected him, and now he couldn't even compete because of me. Yet . . . his gaze wasn't hostile. I couldn't tell what he was thinking, but the intensity was scalding. I looked away.

"All boxers report to the ring. I repeat, all boxers report to the ring." An overhead speaker boomed through the gym.

Show time.

CHAPTER 26

When I entered the gym, I was met by the dull roar of the crowd, which had increased since I saw it last. Now there were probably just under a thousand people, a third of which were faculty. Coach Avery called me up to the judges' table. I walked forward, blanking myself of all my emotions in an attempt to appear even more confident. Part of me felt bad about what I was going to do today, the rest of me smiled on. I didn't know which part to be ashamed of—the sociopath . . . or the compassion?

"Coach?" I asked hesitantly.

Three judges presided over the match. The first was a young man who appeared to be in his early twenties with brown hair and closed eyes. From what I knew, he was here simply to make sure no other Supernaturals' powers were interfering with the match. The second was Professor Vonlowsky, who was currently smirking at me, as usual. The final judge was an older man with a very composed appearance and delighted smile. His hair was white, and the wrinkles clearly showed, but he was strong.

I could feel him and the others watching—for what, I had no idea.

He stood and offered me his hand. "I'm Aldric Fortescue, Member of Court. Dimitri here has told me so much about you, Ms. Foster," he said with perfect formality.

"Pleasure's all mine," I responded, shaking his hand.

"Well, I wouldn't want to keep you from your match any longer. Good luck."

Coach Avery steered me away from the judges and toward the ring.

"What did he mean by *Member of Court*?" I asked.

"Now's not the time. Ask me another day," he said, staring into the ring.

"When's my match?" There was already another boxer in the ring. He was at least six-feet-tall and bulky, with a mean scowl and ugly face.

"Now," he said, holding the ropes for me.

I was startled, but climbed in, nonetheless.

"Remember, Foster, he's stronger than you. Speed and endurance are the key," he whispered in my ear then pushed me to the center of the ring.

Overhead, a loudspeaker came on, introducing us, but I blocked it out. The crowd gasped when they learned I was boxing.

Out of nowhere, Lucas's voice came from the crowd. "End this quickly, Selena."

I nodded once and took my place.

"What's a little girl like you doing here?" The hulk-like boxer teased, clearly amused that I was his opponent.

I brushed off his comment and waited for some kind of indication that the match had begun. When a bell rang, we began circling. Lucas's words repeated in my head, and I knew what I had to do. I already relished the clarity that was soon to come.

"Do you really think you're going to fight me?" He outright laughed at me.

A spark of anger ignited in me, and I swung, aiming for his mouth. He was too busy laughing to see it coming. My fist connected with his teeth. There was a slight pain in my hand, but it was too numb to register—just as I'd hoped. Blood splattered the floor, and he spat out teeth. Almost all his front teeth were missing, and the impact had cracked his jaw. I guess he shouldn't have insulted me.

I didn't even wince at the gruesome sight; instead, I smiled knowingly. The crowd went quiet, and I was feeling almost sadistic about what I was going to do to him. The killing gene, as I called it, was active.

He tried to say something, to threaten me, but all that came out was red. It was less than thirty seconds in, and I'd already covered the ring in blood.

He came at me, stumbling in his rage. I sidestepped just before he reached me and turned to him. His distorted face looked like something out of a horror movie. I flashed him a smile, and he roared. He swung at my face, but I caught his fist mid-swing. I closed my fingers around his fist, digging into the skin. This was the biggest fix I'd get for a while, so I needed to make it hurt.

I bent it backward and snapped it with a flick of my wrist. Pain filled his already broken face, and I twisted his arm. He hunched over, and I drove my elbow into his sternum. Several sharp snaps filled the ring as I destroyed his ribcage. Using all my weight and strength, I drove him backward and sent us both falling through the air. He landed flat on his back, with me on top of him. One foot landed flat on the ground with my knee on his stomach, and my elbow still lodged in his chest. His head banged against the floor, and he started to black out from blood loss.

I looked down at him, both sickened by what I'd done and relieved that the darkness was gone. For now. I wanted to say something to him. To explain myself.

The words never came.

I looked around the ring for a moment, examining the blood, teeth, and unconscious body left in my wake. Out in the crowd, students, teachers, even the judges were gaping. The timer read 1:16.

I lifted a bloodstained hand and pushed a stray hair back. The medical staff on hand rushed into the ring, hauled him onto a gurney, and carried him away. When I stepped out of the ring, I was instantly surrounded. Most faces I didn't recognize, and I started to feel flustered. My heart pounded as frustration rose in me. My eyes glazed over, but I wasn't in danger right now. My gory victory had assured that. The killing gene was sated.

"Get back to the stands. Now." Coach Avery's voice boomed over the others.

I walked over to an empty chair and took a seat while I let my mind return to normal. The urge to pop some pills was overwhelming, though the conversation with Lucas was still fresh in my mind. In the end, I decided against it.

"You never cease to surprise me." Lucas appeared from behind me.

"It's when I don't surprise you anymore, that means

you've known me for too long." I examined my knuckles. The ice had been a good call. I would be bruised tomorrow.

"So, you've been holding out on me," he accused. He didn't sound upset, but I knew he would take note of what had happened here. I was a living weapon, honed to be lethal. I thanked my lucky stars I'd been able to stop myself this time.

"Don't you have a match to get to?"

"Well, actually, I don't because I believe someone decided to turn the ring into a bloodbath. Which brings me back to my original statement—you've been holding out on me."

I shrugged.

"Why?" he asked.

Again, I shrugged.

It was quiet for a moment or two. Then, "Can I ask you something?"

"You just did," I retorted, recalling the day I'd said the same thing to Aaron. This time, however, it was followed by silence. He wasn't chasing me, and I was again reminded of just how different he was.

"You can ask me anything, Lucas. You know that. Whether I'll answer it or not is a completely different question." I sighed.

"Will you answer it? Truthfully?"

For a moment, I considered just telling him yes, allowing him one question, any question, and giving him the answer. Truthfully. But I couldn't . . .

"That depends. What's the question?" I asked.

"How do you do it?"

"Do what?" I frowned at him.

"Everything. It just doesn't make sense. You're abnormally strong, even for a Supernatural. I've never seen anyone run like you can, not unless their speed is their ability. When you fight, you know exactly what's going to happen. Somehow, you can keep me out of your head, but I know you're not a shield. How?"

My mouth dropped open slightly. He'd completely caught me off guard. "Lucas, you really don't want to get into this—"

"Stop avoiding the question, Selena. Do you trust me or not?"

It wasn't a matter of trust. It was a matter of safety. If people knew what I could do, just how powerful I was . . . I didn't know how they would respond. I was *dangerous*—that was what I feared most. If he knew, would he even accept me? Doubtful.

I couldn't lie to him either. Lucas was my closest friend. I could be myself with him—or, at least, almost myself, apart from the secrets. I had to tell him the truth, just not the whole truth.

"I do," I finally said when I got my head together.

"Then how is it possible that you can do all these things?"

"My ability," I said, not entirely lying.

"What?"

"I can do all these things because of my ability." I laughed lightly, trying desperately to lead him off this path.

"Why didn't you just say that?" He laughed too.

"I don't know. I think I'm paranoid." I smiled.

We talked for a few more minutes before he left for his match. I wished him luck and watched as he destroyed his opponent, minus the teeth and broken bones. It didn't get by me that he'd been holding out on me too. His opponent was unconscious with a busted lip, black eye, and probably broken jaw. We were both effective, but he had the blessing of not being forced into brutality. I sighed and let it go. I knew the consequences that came with my survival.

Soon afterward, Alexandra caught up with me; Lily had to go somewhere. We went to lunch and talked about my match, school, even boys . . . and our birthday—which I'd managed to completely forget about, somehow, even though it was tomorrow.

CHAPTER 27

I groaned. "Are you almost done?"

"Almost," Alexandra chortled.

Birthdays. They're supposed to be fun, right? All the friends, presents, and food—if you're Lily. Wrong. I hated birthdays. Well, I hated *my* birthday. Not because I was turning another year older, but because twelve years ago I was forever changed. Nothing had been the same since that day. I want to say that before my fifth birthday I was happy. Normal. But I can't remember that far back, and the struggle is all I've ever known.

With our parents gone, I actually had to participate on our birthdays, for the sake of my sisters. That was why every year I allowed Alexandra and Lily to dress me up like a Barbie doll and take me to a party or something.

"Blink," she ordered, holding the mascara wand under my eyelashes.

I resisted the urge to roll my eyes and did as I was told.

Heels clicked against the tile floor as Lily entered the bathroom. "Oh my gosh!" she gasped.

"What?" I said, instantly tensing up but fully aware that Alexandra was holding a stick of mascara less than an inch from my eye.

"She looks hot," Lily said in awe.

Alexandra and I both started laughing.

"Well, I guess my job's done. Open your eyes," she commanded, spinning my chair around.

Well, damn. There was no denying it. I was hot. Alexandra had shoved me into a bright, blood-red dress. It only had one long sleeve down to my wrist, and it was *tight*. It was so short it made it past my butt by about two inches, at most. I wore Alexandra's shiny black stilettos and a pair of simple silver hoops. My eyes looked like liquid silver with all the black eye makeup, and my lipstick matched the red of my dress.

I stood up and admired myself for a moment before turning to Alexandra. "I look good," I said, offering a half-hearted compliment. This was still her thing, not mine.

"You're welcome," she said sourly, but I knew she was pleased.

"Well, they're waiting. You guys ready?" Lily nearly squealed.

Alexandra looked past me at herself in the mirror, as if for reassurance. The sequins on her silver dress sparkled as she turned on her heel. Unlike mine, hers was loose, but just as flashy. Her black metal pumps clicked as she led the way out.

The sun was setting as night approached, a quiet hush had taken over the campus, and my sisters' silent anticipation was all but tangible. A wind blew lightly as I walked outside, stirring my hair. Music was coming from Building Eight, the recreation center, and Lily's smile widened as she hurried to the open doors, which were decorated with black streamers that hid everything behind them.

Lily saw my slight grimace and flashed me a smile, squeezing my shoulder lightly. "Loosen up some." She disappeared into the black mass, leaving me with Alexandra.

My other sister turned to me. "She's right, you can take a break once a year and have a little fun. It's never killed anyone," she offered jokingly, but it had a very different effect on me.

"It almost did," I whispered.

Her smile faltered then dropped, and her eyes met mine. "We're not little kids anymore. And you're dormant now. You deserve tonight. Don't waste it." She squeezed my hand, and with a single step, she was gone.

The wind blew harder, turning my hair into a swirling mass of black. She was right. I'd worked hard to get past that day for twelve years, and my insanity was finally under control thanks to boxing. I did deserve it. Tonight was my night, and I *could* do this. I took a deep breath and plastered a smile onto my face.

The room was alive. Lights danced across the moving bodies while the stage lit up to welcome my sisters. Off to the side, a few classmates of mine were playing beer pong, and— Was that a keg? Holy shit, Aaron's ex was holding herself in a handstand as she guzzled god knew what out of it. I turned to see a massive three-tier cake covered in chocolate frosting. Sparklers sat next to it. Were they actually going to use those as candles? Alexandra would burn the building down. I groaned.

I joined Alexandra on the outer edge of the party. As I neared her, she turned and smiled, handing me a fruity-looking iced drink with salt around the rim. Alcoholic, probably. I took a sip and turned to the group. My roommates gaped at me.

"Selena?" Amber asked, a subtle rudeness to her tone.

I dropped my smile into a slight grin. "Hello to you too."

"You're absolutely stunnin'," Tori said in her country twang.

"Thanks," I said lamely. I didn't take compliments well. Not that I was insecure—quite the opposite. I knew I was hot. I just didn't care. Looks fade. People grow old. There are more important things in life.

"So, uh . . . Amber and I are havin' a movie night tomorrow night. You in?" Tori asked. For a while now, we'd been staying up late to eat snacks and watch comedians on YouTube. We never really did anything as roommates. Maybe it was time to change that.

"Sure." I nodded. "I'll make the popcorn."

Tori smiled brightly, and her eyes slid to something, or more like someone, behind me.

"Happy birthday," Lucas's deep voice rumbled next to me.

"Thanks," I said, turning from the stage to him.

"I'll let you enjoy your party. See you later," Tori said, dragging Amber with her to the keg.

I cut my eyes at Lucas to see what he thought of his baby sister joining in that, but his eyes were all for me.

"Does that have alcohol in it?" He motioned to my drink.

"Probably," I said, gulping the last bit down.

"I'm surprised you drink," he said.

I snorted. "I have a lot of self-control. I'm not a prude."

"Fair enough. So how old are you turning?" He flagged down one of the servers. I snatched a mimosa from the tray, and he took a beer. Vile stuff. Such a waste of good alcohol.

"Seventeen." I coughed. Some of my drink had gone down the wrong way.

"You okay?" He laughed, and tried to take it from me.

I maneuvered it away from him. "Nice try." I coughed again, but brought it back to my lips. "So, is that a problem?"

"What?"

"Me being seventeen. Is that a problem?" Why was he acting so funny?

"No." He smiled genuinely, shaking his head.

"Good." I laughed, drained my second cup then sang along to the song playing overhead.

"Is there anything you aren't good at?" He motioned to me.

I laughed lightly and reached for another red drink. "Nope," I replied, giddy. Colors flashed by, and my life kicked into fast forward. I stumbled, just a little, and a strong arm looped around my waist.

"I beg to differ," his deep voice rumbled in my ear.

"I'm on my third drink. Give me a break." I wasn't even bothering to go easy. It wasn't like it would make me sick. I would likely have to be at it again in the next half hour if I wanted to keep the buzz going.

"You want to have some real fun?" He smiled devilishly.

"What did you have in mind?" I grinned.

"I don't know yet, but I'm sure we can think of something if we put our heads together." His eyes were brighter than I'd ever seen them.

I would've gone anywhere with him.

CHAPTER 28

The train station was cold tonight. Filled with people from my life. A whistle blew, and I knew what was coming. This couldn't be happening.

Smiling faces passed me, but no one stayed. First, it was people I used to know, and then others came. My cousins and roommates boarded before the whistle called again. I saw my family boarding. I panicked when I saw Lucas.

I tried to talk to them, to get their attention, to stop them from leaving me, but they slipped past. I screamed and yelled, throwing my hands in the air for the most dramatic temper-tantrum I could come up with. No one stopped.

I tried to run, but my legs were like Jell-O. I needed to move faster. They couldn't leave me. I had to stop them. But how?

My sisters and parents stood there with Lucas, waiting. They were waving and motioning for me to follow, to not get left behind, but it was a wasted effort. Soon Lily and Alexandra walked away, then my mother, and, finally, my father. Lucas stayed; he stayed right there on the platform, looking at me expectantly. Motioning for me to get up—to keep moving.

I slowly made my legs work. Forcing my body along in a crawl. The train doors slammed, and it started to roll away. But Lucas . . . he stayed.

He stayed.

I ran to him, taking his outstretched hand.

My dream shattered.

I bolted straight up as my eyes flew open. Cold sweat trickled down my back, and my heart raced.

Tori was leaning over me, and her hands were clamped around my shoulders as she shook me. Her sharp green eyes were wide and scared. "Are you okay?"

I nodded, and she slumped back onto my bed.

"Bad dream?"

"Yeah." I nodded. "Can you do me a favor?"

"What?"

"Don't tell anybody about tonight. It'll be our little secret." My sisters had freaked last time this happened.

"Okay, I promise," she agreed, and we sat there in silence. "Do you wanna talk about it?"

"No." It came out harsh, but that wasn't my intention. "It's just something I have to deal with on my own. Thanks, though," I added.

"Okay." She shrugged as she got off the bed. Tori was still dressed in her clothes from the party, so she must've just gotten back.

Lucas and I had practically drunk the night away, and talked until three in the morning. How I'd ended up in here was a blank. I'd have to ask him about it later. I was still wearing the dress from the night before, but the shoes were missing. I kicked my legs out of bed to stand up.

"Ow! What the—"

"Your shoes?" Tori said, reaching down and picking them up.

"Oh," I muttered, a little baffled.

"You look confused," she commented as she stripped out of her clothes.

"I am."

"About?"

"How exactly did I get back to our room last night?"

"Oh. Uh, you fell asleep, and Lucas carried you back. I'm surprised you're up . . ."

I cursed under my breath. I had been pushing it toward the end of the night. I couldn't have told you how many drinks I consumed. My Supernatural heart beat steadily, and any effects were long gone. I was sober.

"What time is it?" I sighed.

"Almost seven," she said, falling back on her bed.

If I'd stayed up all night, I would want to sleep all day too.

"Selena, I was wonderin' . . . uh . . . you and Lucas—"

"No, we're just good friends," I interrupted. "Why do you ask?"

"When you were screamin', you said his name and— I was just wonderin'." She clearly wasn't saying everything, but I did *not* want to be having this conversation right now.

"No, it was . . . just a bad dream." I turned away and got up to shower.

"And, Selena—"

"What?" This topic wasn't up for discussion. All I wanted was to take a shower in peace.

"I'll keep quiet, and if you ever need anythin', I'm here for you."

I wasn't sure how to respond. We'd been friends for a while now, but we never talked about deep things, and I never asked for favors. It was . . . strange. My only real friend here was a guy. That kind of put me at a loss. "I . . . I appreciate it." The words felt too formal.

She laughed at my lack of conversational skills. "You're not used to hearin' that, are you?"

"I've never had friends."

She climbed out of bed and walked to me. I froze when she hugged me. Since the day her grandma died, we hadn't had any physical contact. I put my arms around her, and tried to relax.

"Where I come from, thank you works just fine," she joked, pulling away, but still holding me at arm's length.

"Thank you." I squeezed her arms, grateful she'd at least tried to understand how bizarre this was for me.

We laughed together, and for the first time in a long time, I felt normal.

CHAPTER 29

"Hurry up, Selena! We're already late," Amber yelled from the other side of the bathroom door.

Movie night had gone great: we'd laughed and talked, and I'd actually had a good time. We'd watched the X-Men movies, which had kept us up until four in the morning. It wouldn't have mattered, except it was a Sunday night, and Tori had forgotten to set the alarm.

"Tori forgot the alarm, not me!" I yelled back through the door. I'd woken up at 6:23, and ever since then, we'd been in a rush.

There were another few bangs as Amber pounded on the door. I didn't say anything, just kept blow-drying my hair.

Next thing I knew, there was something in the shower, and hair crap was falling all over the place. Tori walked out of the shower, and I almost screamed.

"What the hell was that?" I yelled at her over my blow-dryer. The door was locked, and two seconds ago, she'd been outside the bathroom with Amber, trying to get in.

"I'm a teleporter," she said, giving me a look that said, *what the hell did you think it was?*

"I'm still not done," I said.

"Well, we need to use the bathroom!" Amber yelled through the door.

Tori reached around me and unlocked it.

Amber instantly pushed me out of the way and claimed the bathroom.

"Excuse you," I said, grabbing the hair dryer.

"We're gonna be late to first period," Tori said.

"Oh shit." I scrambled out of the bathroom to grab my things.

Tori and Amber bounded after a few seconds later.

"First bell just rang," Amber swore, and we bolted from the room. We had about two minutes to get to Building One, and it was all the way across campus.

I sped up once we hit the pavement and didn't stop until I was in the classroom. As we walked in, everyone stared—probably because Tori was gasping for air like she smoked a pack a day. The last bell rang on cue, and we took our seats just as Brighton strolled into class.

"Foster, Headmaster Daizlei wants you immediately," he said, taking a sip of his coffee.

"Which one?" Alexandra asked.

"Selena," he responded without looking up.

I got up and headed over to the main building. What could he need me for? Had they learned my secret? Had Alexandra or Lily said something? I highly doubted it was for drinking. It could've been for skipping class, but they would've said something already. It had to be that they'd found out . . . but how? Alexandra wouldn't have said anything, would she? No, but neither would Lily. How else—

"Something on your mind?" Lucas said next to me.

"I got called to the Headmaster's office, but I'm not sure what for," I mumbled, which was when it hit me. What if he'd found out when I was drunk? He could've read my mind; what if he'd told? I looked over at him suspiciously. No, he wouldn't have told even if he knew. But . . . did he know?

"Me too," he responded.

It couldn't be that, then. My secret had nothing to do with him—but boxing did.

"Can I talk to you about something?" I had to know if the alcohol had lowered my senses enough that he'd found out what I was.

"Sure," he said, a little guarded. He glanced sideways at me with a confused look. Whenever I asked things like that, it usually didn't go well.

"When you read someone's mind, have you ever come across . . . a barrier like mine?" I asked.

"No, unless they were a shield. But if I really wanted to know something, I could break them." His response was immediate; didn't even require thinking.

"Could you do that with me?" I asked.

"Is this your way of asking if I tried to invade your privacy, Selena? I thought we were past that." His voice turned dangerous.

"Just answer me," I snapped.

He'd avoided my question. I had to know.

He stopped walking and turned to face me completely.

My eyes were hard, and my heart was closed. I waited.

"No, I haven't gotten around your barriers. You're different. Most of the time it's silence, but every now and then, out of nowhere, I hear you screaming. I wish I did know what you were thinking, but I haven't tried to read your mind in months." His eyes never left my face, and I looked away out of embarrassment, even though it wasn't my confession.

I ignored what I thought he was hinting at. Of course he would want to read my mind, any Supernatural would. I was an enigma to him. A challenge. We were friends; and more importantly, partners—and he'd kept any curiosity at bay, respecting my boundaries.

"What do you mean, I'm 'screaming?'" I would address the necessary and leave the rest for another time.

"You're silent. I can feel your presence, so to speak, but nothing more. But if you're distracted, and not using any of your Jedi mind tricks, I can only assume I'm actually hearing what it's like to be inside the mind of Selena Foster. You sound like you're screaming." He looked away. There was more he wasn't saying, but I'd heard enough.

This conversation had taken a way too personal turn, and I needed to backtrack quickly. "Does alcohol change that?" I asked, getting straight to the point. We didn't have much more time for idle chitchat when we were expected to be there any moment now.

"You're very . . . different." His voice sounded a little off, too short. Different? What the hell did that mean? Good or bad? *Oh, screw these stupid mind games.*

"Define different," I pushed, ignoring how uncomfortable this had become for both of us. I knew Lucas saw more than he usually let on, and he chose not to double-cross me and keep what he'd learned to himself. It worked for us. Some secrets can't be kept quiet. They have to be buried.

"You're just different. It's like going from silence to overload with you. There were so many thoughts running through your mind, I couldn't keep up. It was like listening to a hundred people at once. Except it was all you," he said softly. It was like the calm after the storm with him. We were either in it or not, never in between.

"Did anything . . . stand out?" I asked, trying not to be completely obvious. He knew I still had secrets; he just didn't know how big they were.

"No, Selena, nothing stood out. I had to drink enough to numb my ability throughout the night, so I couldn't hear you." Shit. He was pissed. I'd crossed some sort of invisible line; one I hadn't even known was there.

Instead of apologizing, or telling him the truth, I let us walk in silence until we reached Headmaster Daizlei's office. I'd never been here before, and if it weren't for Lucas, I probably would've gotten lost. Not that I was going to tell him that, or thank him.

Inside, everything was made of wood: the floors, the long desk, the bookcases, the couches, even the two chairs. Along the walls, bookcases were piled high with books of every age, color, and size. The long desk sat in front of a huge window overlooking campus, and sitting behind it was the headmaster himself. We weren't the only ones in the room. Coach Avery was leaning against the desk, while several others from the gym were seated at various spots.

"Take a seat, guys." Coach motioned to the only remaining couch open.

I sat next to Lucas and waited patiently for the lecture.

"First off, you all did great at the tournament this Friday. We had strong start this season, and Belleview was completely blown away. Especially by you, Selena, but I think we were all surprised by the gore in that match." He looked away, and I could practically feel the weight of the room shift. The tension between Lucas and me didn't fade.

"We've just received an invitation to Vermont's School for the Supernaturally Gifted. I'm taking twelve of you, no more, no less. Lucas and Selena, your places are already secured. That means there are ten slots open, and eighteen of you. Aaron, you'd best get your act together or you won't be on that flight, understood?"

I couldn't help smirking when he shot me a look. He didn't turn away; he kept his eyes on me, and they seemed so sad. I turned back to Avery, ignoring Aaron and his burning gaze. His intensity was staggering.

"The tournament is three weeks from now, and a week before Winter Break. I'm leaving and will be out of town for a few days, but I'll let you know who's going within the next two weeks. This trip is a week-long deal, and it is a privilege. One that can be taken away from those of you who choose not to show appropriate behavior in and out of my gym. Is that understood?"

"Yes." One word echoed through the room as every boxer responded.

"You're dismissed. Head back to class immediately."

I was shuffling toward the door with the others when Coach spoke again. "Except Hunter and Foster. I need to have a chat with you two."

I turned back, not even bothering to take a seat again. When the door was shut behind us, he spoke. "Your places are secured as of this moment. I have, however, been informed by Headmaster Daizlei that we have some things we need to talk about. First, Miss Foster, we need to deal with the fact that you've missed so much school that you're now failing three classes. Again. You have to bring your classes up to at least a C before we leave on this trip, especially Battle Simulation. Because there's so little time, I'm going to ask Lucas if he'll tutor you until we leave."

My heart sank. I had no clue I was failing all those classes. I also didn't want to deal with this while we were pissed at each other.

"I'll tutor her," he said, far too somberly. Normally, he would've given me crap for failing Battle Simulation, and I would've made a joke about how BS stood for Bull Shit.

"Selena, I need your help to teach him this season," Avery continued, ignoring the obvious tension.

"Teach him what, exactly?" I asked, a little skeptical.

"To fight without relying solely on his ability, to predict the competition, and to be a step ahead. I need your help to make him better. As his partner, can you do this?"

"I can," I assured him with a nod.

"I would appreciate it if you refrained from any long-term injuries, please?"

I rolled my eyes. "I'll try."

I saw Lucas smirk out of my peripheral vision.

"You're dismissed. Get back to class."

We let ourselves out and walked in silence.

"Lucas, I don't know what you're pissed about, but you need to get over it. If we're going to be partners, you need to accept that I have secrets, and that's not going to change.

What you see is what you get. I've always been honest with you about that."

He sighed, and I was expecting another argument. "So, how do you manage to fail Battle Simulation?" he asked, letting it go.

I fought back a smile as he grinned, and settled for elbowing him instead. "Shut up."

CHAPTER 30

We started studying after boxing practices, during lunch, and all day on the weekends. I felt like I was being grilled on school every second of the day. He was a good tutor. I could at least understand it when he explained things, as opposed to Professor Anderson, who was definitely more boring than listening to Alexandra every time she got a new boyfriend.

Teaching him to be a better boxer was much trickier than memorizing types of rocks or dates. I had to come up with ways to stop him from automatically reading everyone's minds. Sometimes, I blindfolded him and made him listen to commands while I threw things at him. Sometimes he listened, sometimes not, but after getting hit with a few baseballs, he got the hang of it. Other times, we would just spar, and I would remind him to watch with his eyes, not his mind.

Progress was slow on both fronts, and we were spending nearly every second of the day together when I wasn't in class. By the time the tournament came around,

I'd brought all my grades up to passing, even in Battle Simulation, where I was very careful to tread the line between doing just enough to get by and failing. Fighting in Vonlowsky's class wasn't enjoyable. And, unlike like boxing, it wasn't to keep the darkness at bay. I kept myself on a tight leash whenever he tried to sic me on some under-prepared sophomore. The fights were quick, and most of my classmates were thankful that I held back in class. Word had spread since my first match, and even those who weren't there were hesitant to fight me. What they didn't know was that I was holding off for Vermont, not wanting to dismember the boys who'd grown on me in the gym. Lucas might've had something to do with that.

As the weeks ticked by, Aaron pushed my buttons less and less, though he never stopped staring. It bothered me, but I tried not to let it show. I didn't know what his problem was, and I didn't think he did either. He was always in trouble in class nowadays, and was spending nearly as much time at the gym as Lucas and me. Coach noticed the change, and applauded him for getting his act together—finally securing that coveted spot on the plane. I didn't think he was really straightening out. I thought he was teetering on a cliff and didn't know what to do with himself. In a way, I felt bad for him. I didn't know what was going on, but I knew I was finally seeing what it was like for Lucas to watch me fall. To watch me lose myself.

For once, I knew the compassion that Lily had always had. The very feeling that always seemed to elude me.

I hoped he figured it out. I hoped he found peace—even if I could never bring myself to tell him that.

CHAPTER 31

I was standing outside in jeans and a sweatshirt with my duffel bag and eleven guys, who were also waiting for the plane that would take us to Vermont. It was five in the morning on a Saturday, and bitterly cold. That didn't stop Jack from throwing a giant snowball at Aaron's face, or him getting pissed and responding in kind. I thought it was funny until they all joined in. Next thing I knew, powdery white ice exploded on the back of my head. I turned. Lucas was standing there, snowball in hand.

"Don't you dare."

"Oh come on, Selena, have a little fun," he taunted, hurling it at me.

I sidestepped the throw. "No."

When the plane finally pulled in, I was the first one inside and took my seat as far away from the baboons that called themselves boxers as I could. Did that stop them from irritating me? Not a chance.

I threw my duffel bag into the chair next to me and

pulled out my iPhone, relaxing into a semi-comfortable position. I didn't even get thirty seconds into the song when there was a tap on my shoulder.

"What?" I snapped. My irritation levels were through the roof at the moment. Probably from lack of sleep since I'd had another all-night movie marathon with my roommates and then had to pack.

"Is this seat taken?" Lucas asked me, motioning to my duffel bag.

I shook my head and stashed it under my seat.

"Everyone take your stuff up to the front. If we win, you can sit wherever you want on the way back," Coach Avery boomed through the cabin.

I sighed. Great. My only chance at peace had just dissolved into thin air.

"I'm going to listen to my music so that I can maybe make it through this flight without killing somebody."

Once the jet was up in the air, it didn't take long before I passed out.

The forest seemed much darker this time. Lonelier. Desolate. It was dead silent as I walked through the fog. I knew it was here.

Ever since I'd started school, it was always here, watching me. I frowned as a chill went through me. Tonight, it was closer than usual. I started to walk a little faster as the dream took on the realness of life. I was getting caught up in it again, and again.

A twig snapped, and something moved to my side. I ran. Sprinting through the woods, I looked behind me and in every direction as I headed to nowhere. I knew better; these woods were never ending, and it was only a dream . . . but it was so real.

Something brushed my arm. I whipped around, but nothing was there. A wicked laugh rang through the air, and I stopped running. It had found me.

"Show yourself," I called to it.

I started to take a step back when I bumped into something. I turned to see myself, grinning maliciously with glowing violet eyes and a monstrous laugh. I put my hand over my mouth to keep from screaming.

I jumped two feet out of my seat, shocked back into reality. My eyes snapped open, only to see the back of the seat in front of me. My heart raced as I closed my eyes and leaned back. My skin was clammy, covered in a cold sweat, and fear still gripped my heart. What the hell *was* that?

"What's wrong?"

My eyes fluttered open to meet Lucas's intense green gaze. There was worry in his voice, and I felt his mind reaching out. Testing me, or checking on me, I didn't want to think about which. I kept my barriers up.

"I'm fine," I stuttered. I was not fine, nowhere near it. The monster stalking me in my dreams was . . . *me.* At least, some form of me.

"Why are you afraid?"

"What?" His question threw me off guard, and his eyes searched mine.

"I can't read your mind clearly, but I can feel your fear. What are you so scared of?"

"Nothing, it was just a nightmare," I said, and turned away. Effectively ending the conversation.

Outside the window, the jet was descending into fields of white, and a single pop of color stood apart from the snow. The forests around it were dense and filled with ice. Not a soul could be seen, and the wall that protected it had spikes, so very like the one at Daizlei.

We were here—Vermont's School for the Supernaturally Gifted.

CHAPTER 32

"FASTER, HUNTER!" COACH YELLED FROM THE SIDE OF THE RING.

We'd been sparring for the last three hours, and Lucas was still struggling. We'd arrived two nights ago and were only three days away from the tournament.

"Watch my hands. Watch my eyes. Watch my feet. Nothing should get past you," I instructed, while ducking his next blow. "I will slap you if I see that glazed look on your face again." I kept on his case. He wouldn't get better if I didn't, even though it irritated him.

"I'd like to see you try," he taunted.

Faster than he could see, I lunged out and hit him on the back of the head just to prove that I could do it.

"I would like to see *you* try," I retorted.

He did.

I knew I didn't have time to block it. I braced myself as the pain came at me in a full-blown punch to my stomach. I fell to my knees. Holy shit, that hurt. Damn his temper.

I lay there for a minute while Lucas crouched to his knees. "You okay?"

It wasn't like me to show pain, ever.

"Fine," I wheezed. My whole stomach felt like it was exploding. I rolled onto my side as a wave of nausea hit. It took everything in me not to throw up right then and there. I knew I shouldn't have eaten breakfast.

"Foster, is there an issue?" Coach called.

"No, Coach," I called back.

"Then get up, and this time, block yourself better."

I felt it coming up and fled the ring. I jumped over the ropes and onto the floor, sprinting to the trashcan. I heaved as my breakfast came up, and tried not to fall in.

When it stopped, I wiped my mouth, took a swig of water, and spat it in the trash. Stomach acid was some foul stuff.

When I turned away from the trashcan, Coach was watching me with concern. "Please tell me you're not sick."

"No, Coach. I shouldn't have eaten." After climbing back into the ring, I rubbed my stomach once before preparing to fight again.

"If you can block yourself better, you can go after this, and take Hunter with you," Coach said, and we began circling again.

I aimed for his gut, which he'd expected, but when he caught my arm and pulled me in, he didn't expect me to go for his shoulder. I dislocated it with one hit and aimed my rebound for the center of his chest. I struck with deadly accuracy, and the air left his lungs in a *whoosh* as he fell back. He landed on his butt and couldn't get up again with his arm hanging uselessly at his side.

"Hold still," I instructed as I crouched next to him. I

popped his shoulder back into place, and he groaned. Good thing Supernaturals heal quickly.

I climbed out of the ring and landed next to Coach Avery. A few seconds later, Lucas stood to my left as we waited for whatever work he was giving us.

"Vonlowsky was very specific about your Battle Simulation work. He wants three essays on his desk Friday afternoon. These are the topics you can choose from." He handed me the manila folder with my name on it.

"From you, Anderson wants a detailed ten-page essay on the Court and how the system works. She said to remind you that this is twenty percent of your grade, so take your time." He handed Lucas a single sheet with requirements on it, and turned away, dismissing us.

"What is this Court? That guy from the last match brought it up too. 'Member of Court,' I think."

They both just stared like I'd grown another head.

"You've never heard of *The* Court?" Lucas asked, and I shook my head.

"How exactly did you get accepted into Daizlei?" Coach Avery asked me.

"I'd just moved in with my aunt, and she had everything worked out." I shrugged, annoyed with this conversation already. They didn't need to make me feel stupid for not knowing this.

"No one bothered to explain this to you?" Coach pushed. Did he think the answer was going to change?

"No. Explain what?" I crossed my arms and cocked my head impatiently, waiting for an explanation.

"Go get started on your paper, Hunter. I'll deal with her," Avery said, taking a deep breath.

Over his shoulder, Lucas mouthed, "Meet me later."

Go. I motioned back with a quick nod before Avery saw.

"The Court is our form of government, I guess you could say. There's a Council that consists of the oldest and most powerful ruling families. This Council takes care of everything that has to do with Supernaturals, and also gives advice to the Head of Council. The Head of Council is also a Member of Court, the highest-ranking form of government in the world. Are you with me so far?" He was trying to be patient in breaking this down for me.

My irritation lessened; at least he was trying. "So there's a Council that controls everything with Supernaturals and the head of it is called the Head of Council, who also belongs to the Court?"

He nodded and continued. "The Court consists of the four Heads of Councils, one from each of the ruling species. Each of these Heads of Council is from one of the current ruling families of each species. They also have two representatives from the Council, usually family, giving the Court a total of twelve members. The Court controls *everything*, do you understand?"

"I think so," I said. "So how do these ruling families take control?"

"Usually, the Heads of Council pass on their title to the oldest, or in our case, most powerful child, when they get too old or die, but it *depends...*" The Court sounded familiar in a way that was almost eerie.

"What if another family wants to rule? Or the Council doesn't want certain people to rule? What if the kids are little when the title's passed on?"

"It all depends on the case. It's sad to say, but not too

many people stand up to the ruling families—they rule for a reason. If the Council didn't want someone to rule, they could fight for the title. That hasn't happened in a long time."

"Do other families ever join the Council?" A weird prickling sensation was making its way up my spine.

He laughed once, as if that were absurd. "No, it's strictly the oldest and most powerful."

"What are the ruling species?" The question earned me another incredulous look.

"Supernaturals, Vampires, Shapeshifters, and Witches."

"How many species are there?" I asked.

"Many. Much more than four." He was watching the other boxers now. I was clearly cutting into his training time.

"That doesn't seem fair," I said.

"It's been that way for over a thousand years. Now, you have three essays due when we get back, and they're not going to write themselves." He dismissed me.

I felt numb walking down the hallway. A whole other world existed—one with multiple species and ancient oligarchies. What bothered me the most was that the words seemed so familiar. Not just the Court, but the Council and all of it. I felt like I've heard it before. I just couldn't remember where.

CHAPTER 33

"Focus, Selena. Your match is up first, and you need another strong win," Lucas urged.

I grabbed the tube of Icy Hot and applied it to my black and purple stomach.

"I shouldn't have hit you." He sighed, glancing at my stomach.

"Don't even go there. I should've done better." I pulled my shirt down.

We were inside their gym, waiting to start the tournament, and the crowd was growing larger by the second.

"Boxers to the ring. I repeat, first match boxers to the ring," the intercom announced.

"Knock 'em dead! Not literally, Selena," Lucas backtracked when he saw my malicious grin.

I entered the ring and faced a wicked-looking guy, who was tall and muscular with dark brown hair and eyes that had a tinted reddish glow.

"Is this a joke? Come on, sweetie, who put you in here?" He hooted with laughter, looking around the ring.

"Well, I can see they didn't tell you." I glared, cracking my knuckles. This was humiliating; I didn't like being made to look foolish.

"Tell me what?" He looked at me suspiciously as if the idea had just crossed his mind.

The intercom came on again to introduce us.

"I'm your opponent, *sweetie*."

"Hey, yo, I ain't fightin' no chick!" he yelled to his coach outside the ring, completely turning his back on me.

My mouth dropped. "Oh, hell no." I saw red.

"Calm down," Lucas called from the side of the ring.

The bell rang.

I let the monster loose.

When I tapped the guy's shoulder, he turned toward me, and I slammed my fist into his jaw and felt it unhinge as Lucas's had—the exact same hit. The cheekbone was shattered, jaw broken, and there were several fractures in his mouth. I smiled . . . and his eyes turned a glowing red as fire consumed his fists.

Several people gasped, but I laughed—like, actual open-mouthed, hysterical laughter. I suppose I looked a little mad. My sister's ability? That was what I was up against? Why didn't they just hand me the win because I could guarantee that she was more powerful than this troglodyte.

I took a step back as he lunged, then ducked when he swung for my face. Why were they always so predictable? I sighed when he was too busy swinging blindly to notice my hand go under his and hit his shoulder, likely doing more than dislocating it. He fell back for a second, giving me time to aim for the place right below his ribs.

"Ugh!" he cried out. His entire body shifted forward.

More. I needed more if I was going to hold out over Christmas.

Placing my fingers lightly around his boiling hot throat, I pressed my lips close to his ear. "I shouldn't feel bad in the slightest for what I'm about to do, but it isn't really your fault. Even if you don't remember this, I'm sorry." I gave him the words I couldn't give my last opponent. I didn't believe in apologies. Somehow I could never bring myself to give one—to feel sorry for something. I'd chosen myself over him, and I could be sorry for that. I could be sorry that I was going to do this to countless other men for the rest of my life.

I snapped his wrist and twisted his arm behind his back, moving with it. After a final shove, he crumpled to the floor with me on top of him.

My heart slowed. I felt the pull, the killing gene.

It needed more.

I grabbed his hair, drawing his head back.

Silently, I cursed myself to hell for my cruelty, for what I was about to do.

I slammed his head to the ground with a vicious *crack*. He was unconscious. I stood and stepped out of the ring without another word.

"I thought I said don't kill him," Lucas groaned, giving me a disapproving look.

"I didn't," I retorted. He could never know. No one could. It was easier to think I reveled in brutality than to realize that every body left in my wake was a sacrifice to my demons.

"You smashed his head into the ring so hard that it

cracked. He could have brain damage or be a vegetable for the rest of his life." He sounded almost disgusted by me. He should've been.

"That's not dead," I said, taking a bottle of water from the cooler. I acted indifferent, but all I really wanted was to scrub the blood from my hands and burn my clothes.

"How can you be so . . . " He couldn't find the word.

"Heartless?" I offered.

"Yeah." He sighed.

Was that disappointment?

He took a seat next to me, and we watched while they carried the guy out of the ring.

"Years of practice," I concluded, looking into the distance. *Keep the barrier*, I reminded myself.

"You're not like that with me." Ah, yes, the inevitable statement that had hung between us since the very beginning. I was different with him.

"You're my partner." I shrugged.

"What about that first match? You didn't pound my head into the floor or knock out half my teeth." He leaned forward an inch. He was right, but my demons wanted more now. The killing gene wanted more. I loved that I could have friends and feel normal sometimes. So I gave it more.

Again, I shrugged. "You didn't insult me, I guess . . . I don't know."

"You got Lily to help me. Why?" he persisted, unable to accept my answer.

"I felt bad. You didn't ask to fight me. I picked you." I was grasping at straws because that wasn't completely true. I'd told my sisters the same thing that night, but it wasn't true. I didn't know what was.

"They didn't ask either," he pointed out.

"But they insulted me—. Just listen, Lucas, you're not going to win this one. I have my reasons for things. Just let it go." I was getting more and more uncomfortable with where this conversation was heading. He didn't know the real reason behind every body carried out on a gurney. He didn't know the monster with violet eyes. Yet, he stayed by me. I couldn't fathom why.

"Lucas, you're up!" Coach Avery shouted from the ring.

"Good luck." I smiled as he got up to leave.

"Thanks," he said, giving me a half-smile before leaving.

Tori's voice filled my head, asking if we'd ever be more than friends.

No . . .

I didn't need that. There was no point even thinking about it.

CHAPTER 34

"Congratulations, boys . . . and Selena. That's another win for Daizlei. At this rate, we'll make it to the championship this year!"

True to his word, everyone got to sit in the back on the couches and play poker. I set my things in the seat by the window and joined the table with Lucas.

He gave me a questioning look.

"Did you think I had to be wasted to have fun?" I asked him, taking my cards.

"You make me wonder sometimes . . ." I had a feeling it had to do with me being 'heartless.'

Three hours and four hundred dollars later . . .

"Okay, boys, I'm feeling charitable. Take your money." I dropped the wad of cash, and everyone immediately scrambled for the pile on the table.

"Why?" Lucas asked.

"Because I have a heart," I joked, and he shot me a glare.

"Why?" he repeated.

"I don't need it, so there's no point taking it." I shrugged.

The plane landed, and I grabbed my things and shuffled out the door.

"Selena," he called me back. The snow fell on his rumpled hair and tanned skin. His green eyes watched me, and I half-smiled.

"What?" I called.

"Have a good Christmas and Happy New Year. I'll see you when we get back." He was going back to Tennessee to see his family; Tori hadn't shut up about it since I last saw her.

"You too." I waved before turning and heading for the dorm.

The snow crunched under my boots, and I hummed happily to myself. I'd been looking forward to this break ever since I'd learned we could stay at the school instead of going home. I'd signed up right away.

Outside, our dorm had been redecorated with lights, ribbons, and music. Somehow, one of the technopaths had gotten the doormat to sing Christmas tunes and never stop. I walked in to find that the inside had been changed once again. Mistletoe hung from every door, and the walls had been repainted green and red. When I reached my room, the door was already open, but the room was empty. The beds were made, the bathroom cleaned, dirty laundry missing, and no girls. I guessed they'd already left for break, leaving me the room to myself for two whole weeks.

I threw my bag on the bed and grabbed my manila folder with all my work from the last week. As I was leaving to drop it off, my sisters came bursting in with duffel bags.

"What are you doing here?"

"Nice to see you too," Alexandra said sarcastically, throwing her stuff down.

"Did you win your match?" Lily chimed in.

"Of course, but seriously, what are you guys doing here?" I asked again, nicer this time.

"Well, we decided to stay with you over break while your roommates are gone," Lily said happily.

"Oh. Okay, well, I, uh . . . " I paused, not letting any disappointment show. "I've got some stuff to drop off, so I'll see you guys at dinner. Oh, and don't screw up Amber's bed, or I'll never hear the end of it." I motioned to the bright red twin-sized bed.

"Whatever." Alexandra plopped down on my bed.

I left the room without another word and headed to drop off my work. Most of my teachers were already gone, so I slipped it into their mailboxes, and the ones that were here just hurried me out so they could leave. The real reason I was even doing this was so I could get to the library before it closed. The Court sounded absolutely fascinating, and I was dying to find out more.

When I finally made it to my last drop off, my hearing perked up when I saw Elizabeth standing with Vonlowsky. I'd assumed she had gone home for break.

"Professor Vonlowsky, where do you want these?" I interrupted.

"Desk," he said, giving me *the glare*. Of course, with our current relationship, I didn't really blame him. I mean, I had said 'fuck off,' hadn't I? Just because I was coming to class now and giving the bare minimum didn't mean that all was forgiven.

"If you expect to be on the trip this spring break, you have to be perfect for the rest of the year. No screw-ups. Understood?" he told her in a hushed tone.

"Yes, sir," she begrudgingly agreed.

I tried to mask my laughter with a cough; the look I got from him said I hadn't done it very well. I walked out the door before he could say anything and hurried down the path to the library.

"Selena, wait up!" Elizabeth called, and I stopped. I turned to see her jogging to catch up with me. Her shoe slipped on the snow, and she fell to a crashing stop at my feet.

"What was all that about?" I asked while helping her up.

"Oh, I've just gotten into a little trouble as of late, that's all," she said nonchalantly, brushing the ice off her jeans.

"How much is a little?"

"Skipped a few classes, disappeared on some trips, nothing major . . . " Her tone made me skeptical, but I let it go. We all had our secrets.

"So why'd you stay here for the holidays?"

"Going on a ski trip with my mother and sister is not my idea of fun, if you know what I mean," she scoffed with a look of distaste.

"Well, if you don't have plans, you can stay with us on Christmas," I offered halfheartedly as I tried to bring this conversation to a close.

"Thanks, I might do that," she said, looking over my shoulder. "Well, this has been fun and all, but I've kind of got somewhere to be. Don't be a stranger." She hurried away as I continued to the library.

CHAPTER 35

"Do you have any books on the Court?" I asked.

Ms. Rivas peered at me from behind her glasses, dark eyes taking in who I was. "Follow me," she said, leading me down another aisle. "What exactly are you looking for?"

"Anything. I just want to learn about it—how it works. What would you recommend?" I knew from experience that being polite went a long way with this librarian.

She reached up to the top shelf and pulled out a book labeled *Court: The Innerworkings of the System.*

I took the book from her and flipped through it quickly. It was a few hundred pages long, complete with pictures and quotes. It looked easy enough to read. "I also need one on species."

"You need to be more specific. What exactly do you want to know?" She made a *tsk* noise.

"Um, I guess something with facts about the different species, and their relationships with each other?" I wasn't entirely sure what I was looking for.

"I know exactly what you're looking for." Without

moving, she stretched her arm around the aisle and out of view, only to come back with a book that looked oddly familiar. She handed it to me.

As I read the title, I knew for certain I'd seen it before. *Mystical Creatures of the Supernatural* was printed on the cover in gold. I flipped through the pages . . . and then I remembered. As the word *Demons* caught my eye, I turned the page to see the fiery man with black hair and eyes like the pits of hell. This was the book Elizabeth had been reading when I'd stumbled upon her.

"Will that be all?" she prompted.

"Yes, thank you. You've been very helpful. When exactly do I need to return these?" I asked as she walked me to the counter to check out.

"In two weeks, when school comes back in session." She handed me the clipboard for my signature.

I thanked her again as I left the library and went on my way.

The sun was setting, casting shadows across the snow. I ran by my room to drop the books off before I went to dinner but stopped in the doorway and cursed when I saw the nail polish stain on my bed. We were going to have a talk about that. As I turned to leave, the air rushed from my lungs.

"What happened?" I tried to calm myself as I looked at Lily.

Her arm was black and blue, clothes tattered. Bruises darkened her face, and her lip was bleeding. She walked toward me with a slight limp.

"I fell down the steps on the way up and hit my head a

lot. Do you have any Tylenol I can take?" she asked meekly, sitting on the edge of my bed.

I turned and grabbed the bottle out of my dresser then handed her two and a bottle of water. "Hold still, and follow my finger," I ordered, watching her eyes. I let out a sigh of relief; no concussion.

"Thanks." She handed me the bottle.

"Don't mention it." I frowned, putting it on my dresser. "So what exactly did you do again?"

"I was coming back because I forgot something, and the ice on my boots made me slip on the stairs."

"What did you forget?" This sounded sketchy.

"Ugh . . . my phone." I watched her suspiciously, but she retrieved it from her duffel bag. I guess it really wasn't all that surprising that she'd fallen and hurt herself—she did it all the time.

"Are you okay to walk to dinner?" I asked.

She nodded.

"There's no need to keep Alexandra waiting, then." I started to leave the room.

"Wait up. Let me change real quick and then we can go." She ripped her bag open faster than I would've thought possible for her.

"You should be more careful," I chided and tapped my foot. The second she was done, I held the door open for her, waiting.

"I try."

A thought occurred to me as I glanced at the books on my dresser. "Have you heard of the Court?"

"Yeah, why?"

"Does Alexandra know?"

"Probably." She shrugged.

"Why am I just hearing about this?" I demanded, a little disgruntled by this news.

"Well, my roommates told me. Alexandra's probably told her, so . . . I don't know." She shrugged. What she really meant was it was my own damn fault for being an antisocial bitch when I got here.

"Oh," was all I could say.

"So how was Vermont?" she asked.

"Cold," I grumbled.

"What I meant was, what did you do there with your week off?"

"Boxed, made up work, and then boxed some more." I yawned.

"Really? You have to have done more than that."

"No, really, that's all we did. You can ask anyone who was there. Coach Avery had us in the gym at least ten hours a day." That was not an exaggeration.

"Well, it wasn't much better here this week. I had essays and tests in every class except Brighton, and that's only because he got sick and the sub was lazy." Her nose turned up on the word lazy, like that was the worst thing someone could be. It was a wonder her and Alexandra ever got along.

"Personally, I'm ready for a break from all this schoolwork. I've never had to work this hard at a public school, and I've never actually failed classes." We walked through the doors to find over half the student population missing.

"You failed?" Lily gasped in horror.

"No, but almost," I corrected, giving her an annoyed look.

"I made straight As. This semester was so easy for me." I knew she wasn't trying to brag, but it still got on my nerves.

"Applause goes to you for being smarter than the rest of us," I said.

"Not really. Alexandra didn't make lower than a B minus."

"I highly doubt that," I said lightly.

"Doubt what?" Alexandra asked.

"What was your lowest grade this semester?" I turned on her.

"I didn't tell you? B minus in history. It's so boring, but with tutoring, I pulled it off," she boasted with complete satisfaction.

"Congratulations," I said, disappointed in myself. How did I make worse grades than Alexandra? I was the one who'd tutored her.

"What was your lowest?" she asked, picking at her pizza.

"A C in Battle Simulation," I grumbled.

"Okay, that's not bad. Lily's a genius, and I cheat off the smartest kid sitting next to me. It's not a big deal," she tried to console me, but I waved her off.

"Let's get dinner," Lily said quickly and yanked me out of my chair, clearly feeling better.

"The food's not going to disappear," I muttered as she dragged me to the counter.

"Look, your grades aren't the best, but we both know you've missed quite a bit of school. Just do better next semester," she said while grabbing the fattiest food she could find.

"How do you stay so skinny?" I asked her, changing the subject.

"What do you mean? You're skinny." She pinched my side, but it was solid muscle. Skinny wasn't the word I would use. Athletic, maybe, but not skinny.

"Yeah, but with the way you eat, you should be an Oompa Loompa . . . " I muttered, grabbing a salad and water.

"I'm only going to be young once, and I don't want to spend it eating like a guinea pig. Besides, I got mom's metabolism, and it doesn't look like I'm going to get any bigger." She laughed, getting a root beer and taking her seat.

I took the only empty seat across from her and started picking at my salad.

"So has she told you about William?" Alexandra asked me with a not-so-subtle grin.

"Who's William?" I asked Lily.

"Just a guy . . . " Lily said as heat rushed to her cheeks.

"A guy that she's, like, *talking* to," Alexandra said.

"What is he?" Not so long ago, I would've been appalled by this question. *Funny how Daizlei changes you.*

"Super strong, so not that impressive, but he is kinda cute. So not my type. He's insanely smart . . . Can you believe he's the Andersons' kid? The worst teachers in the school are married and have a kid?" she gossiped with the most enthusiasm I'd seen in a while. "So how are you and Michael?" Lily asked, desperately trying to change the subject and cover up her blushing.

"Not good. I think I'm gonna break up with him," Alexandra said while pretending to examine her pizza.

"Why?" Lily asked in exasperation. Alexandra always did this.

"Do tell," I said with slight sarcasm. I didn't really care, but I was used to this being part of our conversations over the years.

"Well . . . okay. I know this sounds bad, but I'm bored with him," Alexandra confessed.

"That's just mean," Lily scolded.

"It's the truth," Alexandra declared with her usual attitude.

"That doesn't make it right," Lily said.

"I can't change that I'm bored with him, and I'm ready to move on." She tossed her hair and made a face.

"I'm not surprised," I said. They both turned and looked at me. "She's a heartbreaker, and you're a heartbreakee, that's why you don't get it."

Alexandra laughed and semi-choked on her pizza.

A look of shock crossed Lily's face. "How would you know? You've never had a boyfriend," she snapped.

"Because, according to Lucas, I'm heartless, so I think that puts me in a whole other category." I sighed.

"Wait. Are you guys *talking*?" Alexandra shouted with excitement.

"Spill," Lily commanded, completely forgetting about my comment.

"No, of course not. Who do you think you're talking to? Lucas and I are friends and partners—that's it," I said firmly.

"It sounds like more than that to me," Alexandra said in a singsong voice.

"That's because all you think about is boys and who to gossip about next," I said.

"True," she admitted.

"Well, if you ask me, I think he likes you," Lily said, very matter-of-fact.

"And that's why I didn't ask you," I said.

"Oh come on. You've never considered it?" she asked dreamily. She was such a romantic.

"No." I glared.

"I think you're lying. You just don't want to admit it," Alexandra said, sharing a gloating smile with Lily.

"Bite me," I snapped bitterly and got up to throw my food away.

CHAPTER 36

"Merry Christmas!" Lily yelled, waking me from my extremely unpleasant dream where the *other me* had just shown up. She came every night now.

"Good morning to you too," I grumbled.

"She's awake. I'm opening my presents now," Lily said.

After the first squeal, I knew I had to get up. I kicked my legs out of bed and walked to the bathroom to brush my teeth.

"Oh, thank you, thank you, thank you!" Lily called and ran to give me hug. She had opened the brand-new copy of *The Notebook* I'd gotten her for Christmas. The last one was lost in the move, and she'd been dying to see her favorite movie again.

"You're welcome," I groaned, stifling the urge to push her off me. It was too early in the morning for this.

"Come open yours," she yelled as she ran back to the presents.

"Shhh," I whispered. Why was she so loud?

"Shut up," Alexandra said, reinforcing my point. She

was still in bed with the pillow over her head, while Lily sat on the floor unwrapping gifts.

"Thank you!" Lily ran and jumped on top of Alexandra to hug her.

"Get her off me."

"Maybe after a shower." I ducked into the bathroom and closed the door.

"Well, hurry up then," Alexandra complained.

Damn, she could be pushy. I stripped off my pajamas and turned the shower on. Outside the bathroom, there was another squeal. I sighed. She was the only person I knew who still acted like a kid when it came to holidays and gifts.

I took my time in the shower, allowing the sleepiness to wear off. I think the break had gotten to me—it usually didn't take so long for me to wake up. When I was done, I dried myself and wrapped my hair. Christmas. How could the year already be halfway over? I guess it's true what they say—time flies when you don't have to find ways to fill it.

I dressed in jeans and a royal blue turtleneck before I turned my attention to my hair. I combed through the knots and blow-dried it before it drenched my clothes. I looked in the mirror and thought of the other me. She looked like me, but she didn't. Did that make sense? The way she held herself, the look in her eyes, her laugh, it was . . . chaos.

"Selena, I know you're done," Lily yelled.

I jumped, and opened the door.

Alexandra was still curled in a ball sleeping with her head under the pillow, and Lily's pile of gifts had gone down to zero.

"Get up," she commanded, taking Alexandra's pillow and whacking her on the head with it.

"That's it," Alexandra screeched and sprang for her. Lily screamed and ran to the door. Alexandra followed, chasing her out into the snow, where Lily had the advantage. Alexandra hated the cold.

"Not so bad now, are you?" she taunted her.

"Think again!" Alexandra called, wailing her in the side of the face with a snowball the size of my fist.

"Hey!" Lily shouted and started after her again.

I stood at the door, laughing at them. Fools.

Thump.

A snowball smacked into my chest.

"Oh, hell no," I bellowed and tackled Lily to the ground.

Alexandra burst out laughing as the snowball fight took a turn for the worse. *Wham.* A snowball hit her square in the face, wiping the smile right off it.

"Oh, it's game on," she called and started after me.

Thirty minutes later, we trudged back into the room, cold and shaking, but laughing, and Alexandra and I opened our gifts. Tori had sent a box of homemade brownies with a card that read: *Merry Christmas from the Hunters.* It showed a picture of her, Lucas, and an older, blonder version of Lucas. Their parents stood next to them, arm-in-arm and smiling. I pinned it to the wall next to my bed where a few other photos showed the slow bonds I'd been creating this year.

I spent the rest of the day reading up on the Court and the different species while we watched *The Notebook.* Coach Avery was right. There were a lot more than the four main species. Werewolves, pixies, trolls, mermaids, nymphs, faeries, elves, even dragons. They all existed—well, dragons had existed a thousand years ago, but they were extinct today. Apparently, all those tales of knights in shining armor saving the damsel in distress from a dragon were based on true stories. The Middle Ages were the last time that almost all humans still believed in the paranormal, more often than not mistaking my kind for gods.

I also learned that not only are there demons, but angels too. They weren't on earth to battle for heaven and hell or higher beings, but to protect people and do good things. Demons, on the other hand, were only here to collect souls and wreak havoc.

The worst problems came from politics; not good versus evil. There were so many political problems with all these species that I doubted half of them even knew why they hated each other anymore. The whole werewolf/vampire dichotomy was based on the story *Helen of Troy*, which turned out to essentially be true. A vampire named Helen was married to a member of the Court. At the time, the werewolf population was under consideration for representation in the Court, and Paris was the werewolf sent to secure their spot. Helen ran off with him and risked a hybrid species being created. Neither species wanted to deal with that, but Paris wouldn't listen. The werewolves of Troy burned Helen alive at noon, angering the Vampire Council, which led to an all-out war that lasted three thousand years.

Numerous accounts followed. *Tristan and Isolde* were the sole cause of families in the Supernatural Council splitting. *Sir Lancelot and Guinevere* started the original witch burnings that lasted well into the eighteen hundreds.

Cleopatra and Mark Antony created the bond between Supernaturals and Shapeshifters—they're generally considered allies in Court now, and our history hasn't been nearly as bloody.

When Elizabeth knocked on the door, I put the books up, and we headed out for dinner.

"What happened to your arm?" Elizabeth asked Lily.

"I fell down the stairs," she said stiffly.

"You should be more careful," Elizabeth said.

"That's what I told her when she showed up looking like she'd just gotten mugged, and then a week later, she's running down the stairs again." I threw a hand up in exasperation.

"I wouldn't have run if Alexandra hadn't chased me."

"I wouldn't have chased you if you hadn't hit me with my pillow when I was sleeping," Alexandra grumbled.

"I'm hungry. Why are we even talking about this?" Lily babbled, trying to change the subject.

"You're always hungry," Alexandra snapped.

"Do you really want me to get dirty snow all over that brand-new cashmere sweater of yours?" Lily threatened.

"You wouldn't," she said, eyeing her.

"Try me," Lily dared.

"What would William say if he saw you right now?" Alexandra taunted.

"Oh, don't even go there," Lily lashed out and kicked snow at her.

"Do they ever stop arguing?" Elizabeth asked me.

"No," I said, shaking my head. A flaming fireball materialized in Alexandra's hand. "Hey! What are you thinking?" I yelled at her.

"She got shit on my sweater," Alexandra said.

"So wash it!" I bellowed in exasperation.

"You can't just 'wash' cashmere," she said, glaring at Lily, but the fireball extinguished.

"You know, I just realized, you never told me what your ability is," Elizabeth cut in.

"Enhanced senses," I said curtly, trying to shut her down.

"Really? That's weird. I mean, Alexandra's a fire user, and Lily heals, so I'd assumed you were even more powerful . . ."

"Ow!" Lily yelled. She was down on all fours, but Alexandra was helping her up. Her knee was scraped, leaving behind bloody snow.

"How did you manage to trip on snow?" I asked her.

"I don't know, it's like I ran into a ro—"

Alexandra said hurriedly, "Selena, you should take her to the nurse. I think she should have it cleaned. Elizabeth and I can get a table." Her smile was far too big, and she gave a slight nod, so I knew she'd tripped Lily on purpose, making Elizabeth forget the entire thing.

"Good idea," I said as thanks, towing Lily along with me.

"That was close," Lily whispered when we were far enough away that Elizabeth wouldn't hear us.

"Tell me about it," I muttered. My "enhanced senses" were a shitty excuse at best. How many more people were going to start asking about me—and, more importantly, how long could I hold them off?

CHAPTER 37

"Selena!" Tori shrieked and ran to give me a hug. "Where's Amber?" Her lively gaze looked over the unpacked clothes lying on our roommate's bed.

"She left a while ago." I shrugged.

"Oh, okay. How was your break?" she asked, throwing her bag down.

"Good. Yours?" I was getting better at small talk.

"Great!" she said. "We went ridin', I got to bake, and see Alec!"

"Who's Alec?"

"My brother—the blond one on the Christmas card." She pointed across the room at my wall.

"Oh. Why don't you get to see him usually?" I asked while digging for gym clothes.

"He graduated last year and now he works at the Court." She sounded disappointed.

"Really?" Now that piqued my curiosity. "What does he do there?" It wasn't uncommon for stronger or more influential Supernaturals to work with the Council, but at Court you had to have some serious magic tricks.

"He has a certain ability they find . . . favorable." She hesitated. "He can make others see what he wants them to."

"Cheater," I muttered.

"What?"

"Nothing." I glanced at the clock. Bright red numbers read 4:59. Crap, I was late. I pulled my hair back into a ponytail and tied my running shoes. "I have a meeting to go to, but we can talk more when I get back," I called over my shoulder as I walked out the door.

The hall was crowded with girls coming back from holiday. It must've been nice to have a family. *Don't even go there*, I scolded myself.

The second I was outside, I raced for the gym, dodging people and their luggage. I burst through the gym doors and continued to the last door on the right. Twenty pairs of eyes turned to me as I took my seat on the edge of the ring.

"You're late," Coach Avery said.

"You're observant," I retorted.

"Don't let it happen again," he said before turning back to the group. "We have one more match coming up in the middle of March, and if we win, we'll be invited to the Council for championships. I don't know how many I can take, but if you don't win in March, you're not going. End of story.

"Now, if you're failing or on probation, I've been informed that you won't be allowed to participate in March, so if you need to, you can come see me during prac- tice today and we'll figure something out. Selena and Lucas,

I want you in the ring." He turned away before I could talk to him alone.

"Actually, can I have a word with you?" I interrupted, getting up from my seat.

"What, Foster?" I could almost hear the eye-roll, but he returned to hear me out.

"Can you please inform this school that I am female? I'm tired of my opponents laughing at me." I crossed my arms and raised an eyebrow.

"You've actually earned a nickname after the last match. I think their coach gave it to you." There was amusement in his voice.

"What?"

"Heartbreaker."

"You have got to be kidding me," I groaned and turned away. "Forget I asked," I called over my shoulder as I stepped into the ring.

He was still laughing at me.

"Heartbreaker, hmmm . . . I think it fits," Lucas commented with great amusement.

I elbowed him in the ribs as I walked across the ring. "What did I say about readi—"

"Not yours. His." He motioned to coach as the whistle rang shrilly in my ears.

"Stalker," I muttered under my breath so he couldn't hear me.

"How was your break?" he grunted, aiming for my stomach.

"Okay." I paused to step sideways. "I read up a lot on the Court."

"Sounds boring," he said, but he stiffened at my words.

Hmmm . . . .

"Oh, and I heard about your cheater brother," I said with nonchalance. I aimed for his abs, taking advantage of his surprise.

"What about him?" he growled as my hand slammed into his rock-hard body.

Interesting . . .

"Oh, nothing in particular . . ." I cringed as he took my hand and pinned it behind my back. His foot swept mine out from under me. I dropped to the floor.

"So you heard about his . . . talent." It wasn't a question.

"Why do you hesitate when I mention him?" I brought myself into a crouch, and he moved closer to keep his hold on me.

"He's dangerous," he whispered in my ear.

"So am I," I said and brought my free arm up to flip him. He hit the ground with a thud as I stood.

"I know," he groaned, but I had a feeling he meant it in more ways than one.

"So why does he bother you so much?" I said.

"It's different. He's not you." His face had taken on a sharper, much older look. He was completely serious, but why?

"You should keep in mind that there's still a lot you don't know about me." I cut myself off before I could say more, and turned away to get some water.

I could feel his eyes following me. Lucas knew I had secrets. He just didn't know how many, or how deep the lies ran. If he had, he never would've accepted me. I didn't think I could handle him walking away now—even if I had to lie to keep him.

CHAPTER 38

"It's the first official day back, which means your break is over." Vonlowsky was beginning his class much like the rest of our teachers, by trying to calm everyone down. I sat back and relaxed as I waited for whatever speech he was going to deliver today.

"To start off the new semester, I'd like to give some people second chances to prove themselves and raise their grade." He sounded downright gleeful. Fuck me.

"Hunter and Foster, go inside the simulator." Fuck him.

"Which one?" Lily asked, but I already knew.

"Selena."

I got to my feet and walked to the front, where Tori was waiting.

The bare minimum, that's all you have to do. Take her down and walk away.

"Professor, I really don't—"

"Ms. Foster, I really don't care," he said coldly.

"And what if I refuse to fight?" I came across as bold and

insubordinate, but inside I was scrambling for a foothold on a wall made of glass.

"Let me be clear, Ms. Foster. If you do not fight, I will fail you. If I'm correct, that would mean your chances of going to the championships would be zero." He held the door open while I stood there, debating.

This is Tori, your friend, and Lucas's sister. You must only do the bare minimum. I walked through the door and turned to face her.

"I can't fight you," I said under my breath.

"We don't have a choice," she said.

The door shut behind me, locking us in.

"If one or both of you chooses not to fight, I will fail you both," Vonlowsky said over the intercom.

I had no choice.

End this quickly.

I swept my foot under her in a flash. She fell back and vanished into thin air. Shit, I'd forgotten she was a teleporter. The next second, I felt myself being pulled back by my hair.

I grunted. "Do not grab my hair."

"I'm sorry, but I can't fail this class," she whispered as she brought me into a headlock.

"Neither can I." I reached up to grab the back of her neck then squeezed tightly, putting pressure on it until she let go.

I was moving to flip her over my shoulder when a void enveloped me, sucking me through a vortex. I found myself lying flat on my back with Tori pinning me.

"How—" Then realization dawned.

"I just teleported with you."

I don't know why I did it. Maybe I just got caught up in the moment, but I actually punched her. I didn't really get that I'd hit her until she fell back, clutching her stomach. She rolled off me and onto her side as she vomited.

"I-I didn't mean to," I stuttered. What could I say?

"It's fine," she gasped but started vomiting again.

Blood.

Shit.

I knelt over and held her hair back as she finished throwing up.

"Take her to Love. Try to get the vomiting to stop," Vonlowsky said, and Aaron appeared in my line of sight.

He reached down and picked her up like she weighed next to nothing. The door closed, and yet Vonlowsky was still there, and I was still staring at my hands, wondering why the hell I was even born.

"I've dismissed class early. I think we need to have a talk," he said from behind me.

"I have nothing to say to you." I got up from the ground and walked toward the door.

"Don't even think about walking out of that door. I'm not one of your silly little peers who you can ignore. I'm your professor, and you will treat me like it."

"Maybe you should act like it," I turned and shouted at him.

"You're angry. That's good." He nodded, watching me with cold calculation.

"No, it's not." I gritted my teeth.

"Anger is power. That's one reason you're so good at boxing." He motioned to the blood and vomit.

"Don't you dare talk to me about boxing," I spat. I put

my hands on my hips to try to control how badly they were shaking.

"It's true."

"Anger does not equate to power. It's terrible. Anger causes death and destruction. Nothing good comes from it." I knew from experience. I turned away from him, fighting the flashbacks threatening to make their way to the surface.

"That's where you're wrong. It all depends on how you use that power." He made a *tsk* sound, and I realized that I wanted to kill him. For what he'd made me do. For feeding my demons. I wanted to destroy him because he was *right.*

"Get to the point—I have somewhere to be," I snapped.

"You're powerful yet weak. Why do you refuse to use your ability? They say you have enhanced senses, but I know better. I see through you, Foster."

My blood ran cold, and I knew I needed to shut this down now. "Why do you care? In fact, why does anyone care? It's my ability, my choice, and my life, why can't you butt out—"

"Because you're making a mistake. You could be great."

I couldn't believe I was actually listening to this. "But it's my choice! You might be my teacher, but you don't have that right. It's one thing that you make me fight, but this is none of your business!"

"Why are you so scared of yourself?"

His analysis was too close. This needed to end. "What?" I asked, both exasperated and desperate. I hoped he couldn't tell.

"You're scared. I have no idea why, but it's the reason

you won't fight—not really. The reason you refuse to use your ability."

"Let's just get this straight. You know nothing about me. Stay the hell away if you know what's good for you." He thought he saw potential in me. A prodigy in the making. What he didn't realize was that if he wasn't careful, he would find out just how powerful I was.

"You'll regret this," he called after me.

I stopped dead and turned my head to the side. "I've had regrets in my life, but I can promise you this won't be one of them."

Lock it up and throw away the key. The anger. The resentment. He can never know the truth. No one can. If they knew ... they would come for us. They would fear us. Then they would kill us.

With a look as cold as the weather, I left to seek the blessed heat of blood and sweat on a gym mat.

CHAPTER 39

"UGH!" I GRUNTED AS I LASHED OUT.

The air left his lungs as he grasped his throat.

I turned and swung again, this time breaking his nose.

Aaron groaned. "Can you not control yourself?" he snapped, clutching his bleeding nose.

"Can you not fight better?" I retorted angrily as I stormed out of the ring.

I grabbed a bottle of water from the cooler and downed it in two gulps. I was burning, and my heart felt like it was going to beat out of my chest. I still hadn't cooled off from my confrontation with Vonlowsky.

I dropped the bottle in the trash and pressed my palms to my temples; the headache wasn't going away.

"Selena, what's the deal today? You just broke Aaron's nose, and that's only fifteen minutes after you fractured Michael's shoulder," Coach Avery said from behind me.

"Nothing. I'm fine," I lied.

"Foster, something happened. Is there anything I can

do?" He was offering to help me, but I was well aware that he was also trying to push me to talk to him.

"No, there's nothing you can do, so I don't see the point in talking about it." I started to walk to the bench.

"What happened?" He put a hand on my shoulder to stop me.

I took a deep breath and turned to him. "Vonlowsky won't stay out of my business, and to make me fight, he's threatening to fail me," I said quietly, trying to keep Aaron from hearing.

"Why won't you fight without him having to threaten you?" Avery asked.

"I am, but he doesn't think it's enough unless I destroy them like I do in here. It's not like boxing, and honestly, I don't think he has a right to ask me to do that to a bunch of inexperienced teenagers." My voice was rising again, and Aaron had most definitely heard me—along with half the gym. I closed my eyes, massaging my temples in a vain attempt to calm down.

"I'll make sure it doesn't happen again," he said.

My eyes snapped open. "You can do that?" I asked in disbelief. I didn't think he had that kind of sway with other teachers.

"Selena, you have a real reason for being pissed with him, and he knows better . . . hell yes, I can do that," he said and left me.

I sighed and positioned myself on the bench.

"What was all that about?" Lucas asked, coming up to the side and doing pushups.

"Just some stuff I needed to sort out," I said, pressing the one hundred- and forty-five-pound bar.

"Did it have to do with you breaking Aaron's nose?" I could hear the grin in his voice. Nosy bastard.

"Maybe." I smirked despite myself. I still didn't like Aaron, even if I felt sorry for him.

"And did it have to do with you fracturing Michael's shoulder?" he continued.

"Maybe," I repeated, less enthused.

"So he was asking you about your aggression issues?"

I outright laughed at that. "If you already know what happened, why ask?"

"I actually wasn't paying attention. It's your constant anger that's sending off flares in my mind." His voice was deeper and more gruff than usual; must've been the pushups.

"Oh . . ."

"We need to go running," he said suddenly, getting up from the floor.

"I just started bench pressing," I argued.

He took the bar out of my hands and put it on the rack. "Too bad." He started for the door. I bounded after him. "What has you in such a bad mood today?" His tone was husky as he led the way out.

"You mean you can tell the difference between my usual heartlessness and bad days?" I mocked.

He glared at me as he held the gym door open. "Usually."

We walked in silence for a few minutes while I decided what exactly to tell him. "I got into an argument with Vonlowsky today," I finally conceded.

"About?"

"I refuse to dismember my classmates, but he insists on

threatening me so that I will. Which is ridiculous, because it's not like I'm not fighting at all, I just want them to be able to walk when class is over. Is that really so bad?" I threw my hands up in frustration as I paced. I needed to run—to burn this energy off. I turned and took off down the wall.

"No, I don't think it is," Lucas said quietly, matching pace with me.

"I hurt Tori today." I told him, not able to let it weigh on me any longer. "I didn't mean to, but it was instinct. She teleported, and I flipped. I punched her in the stomach, and she started vomiting blood."

Lucas was quiet for a minute. A whisper of panic moved through me. I couldn't lose him. Not over this. She would be okay. She had to be, because not only had I punched one of my only friends, she also happened to be my best friend's sister. Ouch. Karma's a bitch.

"Is she okay?" His voice was concerned but not angry.

"Aaron took her to Love's right away," I assured him.

"You shouldn't be fighting sophomores. You're too far above them. Maybe if they move you up to a more advanced class, it wouldn't be as hard to hold back?"

"Maybe," I said. I didn't want to fight in class at all; there was no reason for it. Boxing had a reason—suppress the insanity, feed the demons, control the killing gene.

Battle Simulation was to prepare lesser Supernaturals for the killing that comes with being one of my kind.

"I know it sucks right now, but as you get older, it changes from one-on-one. They do teams or use the Simulator." He was sweating despite the cold, and his ragged breathing made him sound gruffer.

"I'm more upset because he thinks being my teacher means that anything's up for discussion and that's definitely not the case. I don't even like seeing him on a daily basis." I think I was talking more to myself than Lucas.

"Did he say anything else to you?" He panted.

"No," I lied.

Lucas thought my ability was my enhanced senses and strength, but Vonlowsky knew better. I couldn't mention the part about me never using my ability. It would invite too many questions, which meant even more lies to keep up with, and I just couldn't afford that right now. Not if I wanted to stay dormant.

CHAPTER 40

"Selena, it's time to open presents," Daddy called.

I dropped my baby doll and ran to the door where my father was waiting. He scooped me up in his massive arms and kissed me on the forehead.

"How old are you turning today, my big girl?"

"Five!" I shouted in glee, smiling from ear to ear.

"So how many presents are you getting?" he prompted.

"Five," I repeated, holding up my hand to show all five fingers.

He set me down inside the dining room where our presents were scattered on the table.

"Honey, can I see you in the kitchen real quick?" Mommy said from the door.

"Be good, girls," he said as he left with her.

"I'm gonna open this one," Alexandra announced, holding up a big box wrapped in pink.

"And I'm going to open this one," I declared, holding up a box just as big in purple.

"Wait for Mommy and Daddy," Lily commanded.

Alexandra and I giggled. Why wait? We ripped open our presents to find two almost identical dresses in different colors.

"Ooooh, I'm telling Mommy," Lily yelled as she ran out of the room.

"I like yours better." Alexandra pouted. She was looking at my pretty purple dress; hers was black.

"So do I," I gloated.

"I wanna trade," she whined.

"No."

"Yes!" she yelled and tried to take it from me.

"Mommy said you're both in big trouble," Lily yelled but stopped walking toward the table.

"I said no!" I shouted and stamped my foot as I pushed her. She went flying straight through the wall, and my anger evaporated.

"Alexandra?" I asked in a small voice.

She didn't answer.

"Alexandra?" I screamed.

I turned back to the door to see my Mother's face white as the cake that now lay at her feet. I trembled. The room was moving.

"Daddy?" I fainted.

I woke up with the picture of my father's face imprinted in my mind. The moment it had happened, the moment he knew what I was. The first time I ever saw fear.

I tried to calm my breathing as I looked over at the clock. 3:07. I sighed and closed my eyes, trying to forget.

CHAPTER 41

I wanted to cry and that was saying something for me. As I hit the bag, all I could think of was *them*. The two people whose lives I'd stolen.

I swallowed my pain and continued with my training. That was what he would've wanted. I hit it over and over again as bruises slowly formed then turned red and bloody. My knuckles hurt. My hands hurt. I couldn't stop. It was the only thing getting me through today.

"Selena, stop," Lucas commanded. It was eight o'clock already, and the gym was empty apart from us.

"I can't," I breathed and smashed my fist into it again.

"Stop." He grabbed my hand as I swung.

"I can't."

"What's wrong?"

I stopped fighting and turned to him. "My parents died on February twenty-third, six years ago." I hung my head in despair. I was anything but rational today.

"Come with me." He took my hand and led me out of the gym.

"Where?" I asked, but it really didn't matter. Nothing would for a few more days when, hopefully, I'd start to feel like me again.

"Just on a walk." We veered off the path and toward the wall where we ran.

I didn't say anything; I didn't feel like saying anything. It was cold outside, and the tank top and shorts didn't help much. Even when I started shivering, I said nothing.

"Are you cold?"

I nodded.

He took off his sweatshirt and handed it to me. I slipped it on without protest.

"What happened to your parents?"

There it was. The question had been between us for so long now; never the first thought, but always close behind. Just one of the many secrets I kept.

Why not today?

"Six years ago, my parents left us with a babysitter while they went out. It wasn't until the next morning when I woke and answered the door that I found out what had happened. They'd died in a car crash on the way back from their date. Somehow, the car swerved, and they went off a two hundred-foot cliff. After that, we were shipped off to the first of the relatives."

I didn't remember much of my parents' deaths. I was young. My aunt took care of the funeral arrangements. We buried them right outside our yellow walls, inside my mother's beloved white picket fence. I hadn't been back to that house since the funeral, even though I technically owned it. Well, my sisters and I owned it.

"I'm . . . sorry."

"Why? It's not like you killed them. I did that on my own." And there was the crux of the matter.

"You just said they died in a car crash." I could see his confusion in the way his eyebrows knit together, the slight frown, earnest eyes. He didn't understand, and I couldn't blame him. It was only ever half-truths with me.

"They did." I sighed. I couldn't completely tell him how it was my fault; he would never understand that I could've saved them.

"Then how did you kill them?" Our voices we barely above a whisper, and the wind howled in our ears.

I stared down at the glistening snow in silence. "Before my parents left that night, I'd been getting headaches because I just had this feeling. I knew something was going to happen, I just didn't know what, and when they asked me about it . . . I said nothing." My hands clenched into fists as I remembered. "I said nothing . . ." I whispered.

"Selena, you didn't kill your parents. They died in a car crash. It wasn't your fault."

He didn't understand. No one did.

"It's not just the feeling, Lucas. I don't know how, and I know it doesn't make sense, but in my heart—I know I killed them." It was like I was forgetting something; I just didn't know what. I was the greatest murderer in history— even I didn't know how I'd done it.

I stiffened when he hugged me. The smell of the outdoors and him overwhelmed my senses. Easing the pain I'd felt on this day for six years. It felt . . . right. I wasn't alone, and for once, I needed that. I closed my eyes and leaned against him, wrapping my arms around his firm waist.

"You're not alone. Never again."

CHAPTER 42

"It all comes down to today. Everything we've worked for this year depends on today. This is the hardest school we've faced yet, but if we win, we'll be invited to the championships." Coach Avery was finishing up his usual pep talk before the big match.

"First match boxers to the ring. I repeat, first match boxers to the ring."

I started to get up when Avery stopped me. "We switched up the order. You'll be going last today instead of first."

He hadn't thought to tell me this before now? "Why?"

"Because I requested it. I'm the coach. End of story."

Asshole.

As the next couple of hours passed, I paced back and forth, waiting anxiously. The room emptied one by one, and when it was finally Lucas's turn, I went out with him, turning the light off as I left. I wished him luck as he entered the ring and wasn't surprised when, ten minutes later, he'd won.

"Selena, it's all on you. This match will decide if we go to the championships. Don't let me down," Coach Avery said, clapping me on the back.

"No pressure," I muttered, but it really didn't bother me.

As I stood inside the ring, I waited for the other boxer to get in, rubbing the calluses on my knuckles out of boredom. I glanced over at the corner to see a boy around six feet tall talking to an older man, who I assumed was their coach.

"So, this is the Heartbreaker you were talking about?" he said to his coach, not even trying to pretend he wasn't outright staring at me.

Oh god, that fucking name. I wanted to kill him already.

"That's her."

"Consider it done," he said with misplaced confidence, and he climbed into the ring.

The intercom came on, and I stepped up to fight. Pulling my fists up into fighting position, I took one single deep breath, and the bell rang.

"Look, I don't want to hurt you. Why don't you just withdraw, and I'll take you out for ice cream?"

Same old bullshit. My eyes narrowed. I threw a punch at his side, but he jumped out of reach.

"Feisty. I like it." His blue eyes roamed over me with interest.

I sent one straight for his head, and he caught my hand.

"You really don't want to fight," he said in a deeply seductive voice. His eye twitched, and something weird came over me.

"Selena! Selena!" Tori yelled from the side of the ring.

I blinked and snapped out of it. "What?" I yelled, not taking my eyes off him.

"It's Lily. She's going to kill her!"

Without a word or glance, I turned away from him. He grabbed my arm, and I turned back.

"Withdraw," he persisted, and I decked him—one single punch, thrown at him with everything I had, straight into his face.

I didn't even stick around long enough to see him fall. I ran and jumped clear over the ropes and out of the ring, sprinting behind Tori. I didn't have to go far. I found her right outside the gym.

The crowd parted to let me through. It was completely the opposite of what I'd expected. Lily had April pinned against the brick wall, holding her by her neck.

April's face was already blue and purple from lack of oxygen, and she looked like she was losing consciousness. Her skin was ashen, unnaturally pale, and she scrabbled weakly at Lily's hand.

The most shocking part was Lily; she looked radiant. Her normally kind brown eyes were almost black. Power came off her in waves. She was draining the life from April and into herself. That was when I knew. She had the killing gene.

I strode forward and grabbed Lily's arm, trying to pull it off the girl's throat. She held tight, and April gave a strangled cry.

"Lily, let go of her. Now," I commanded.

She didn't listen to me; it was almost like she couldn't. There wasn't even the slightest recognition in her eyes.

April didn't look like she had much time left. I had to stop this.

I tried to pry her fingers from the dying girl's throat, but the effort was wasted. She gave me no choice. Grabbing her wrist and locking her arm before she could push me away, I struck down hard on her elbow and felt it give as I snapped it in two.

She instantly released April as she stepped back, rage clouding her lovely features. April drooped to the ground, unconscious. I reached down and pressed two fingers to her neck, sighing in short-lived relief when I found a pulse— faint, but there.

"What the hell was that?" My voice was razor sharp, and my sister flinched ever-so-slightly. She knew to be afraid. She knew what I was. The real question here: what was she?

"Just a fight. What does it matter to you?" Her eyes were watering, not unreasonable considering the bones in her arm were sticking out awkwardly and her blood ran free.

"What's it matter to me? *Who do you think you are, talking to me like that*? I just had to leave my match to pry you off some chick, so when I ask you a question, *you answer it.*" I let my voice rise and advanced on her. "So, let's try this again. What the hell was that?" I saw a look in her eye, one I hadn't seen in months. Unease crept up my spine.

"A fight. What do you want me to tell you? She was talking crap about you, and I had your back. You should be grateful," she spat at me.

"My back? You think that's having my back? Well, you are sorely mistaken, then. I'm a grown woman. I can take care of myself—something you obviously still don't know how to do. And since when can you fight? Because if I remember correctly, I told you no." I wished now that I'd told her why. I wished she knew. I wished I'd done a lot of things differently with her.

By this point, she looked like she was going to cry. Out of pain or anger, I couldn't tell.

"You're not my parent, Selena. When are you going to get that through your thick skull? I don't have to listen to you, and I'm not going to, because I'm stronger now."

I watched in sick fascination as the tendrils that had been leaching April of life reknit her bones and healed her like she'd done for so many others. I was torn between the part of me that saw this as a way for her to finally protect herself, and what it truly meant—whatever monster lived inside me had a twin inside her.

"You call that strength? You know nothing. Lily, you almost killed her, do you understand that? Can you actually grasp the idea that you almost ended someone's life? Because I don't think you can. I don't think you understand the guilt that would haunt you until the day you died. It would consume you."

"No, I don't think *you* understand. This is my power now. I've evolved. So why deny it? I'm stronger than the rest of them, and now they know it." She motioned to the crowd gathered around us, sweeping her arms wide as she cackled. "One person. That's all it takes to make a point. Why don't you just accept that I can take care of myself? I don't need you anymore."

My heart sank. I was sorry for her—for what she was going through. I knew how it worked, and pushing her would do no good. Until she could see the difference between her and the monster, she would be controlled by it. I only had one choice; one chance to bring her back to me.

"You know what? You're right. I'm done with you."

"What do you mean you're done with me?" She sneered, but underneath her anger, she flinched. She was on her own now. I hoped I was making the right decision.

"I mean exactly what I said."

Even though it killed me, I turned and walked away, leaving her to suffer in her own dark glory.

CHAPTER 43

"Hey . . . I saw what happened," Lucas said from the door.

I stood in the middle of the ring, pacing back and forth. Thinking. I felt him come closer. "Of course you did." The words were mostly to myself; I knew he didn't expect an answer. He didn't make me bother with the normal social conventions that frustrated me.

"I know you're upset, but I think you did the right thing."

Did he see the monster when he looked at her? Did he see the way it snarled? The way it smiled? Did he see that in me?

"I don't know." I sighed. I was so confused right now. Nothing made sense.

"What are you talking about? You saved a girl's life, and you saved your sister from the guilt of killing someone."

"But where did I go wrong? I always taught her to be herself. I taught her morals, and I was there with her when she manifested. I've gotten her through everything up until now. Where did it all go wrong?" The truth was: I knew where it had gone wrong, and it wasn't Lily's or my fault. Not really. Much like me, she was born this way. Inheriting our mother's sickness.

"I don't know what to tell you, but I think you should focus on the championships right now and not your sister. I get that you love her, but you have your own life to worry about, and she'll be here when you get back. It's only two weeks."

I didn't have a choice. Today wasn't enough to suppress me through the summer, and if I was going to have any chance of helping her, I needed to have my insanity on a leash. Even if it meant leaving her for a short while. The only thing worse than one monster was two.

"You're right. I need to worry about me." He didn't know the half of it.

CHAPTER 44

"Are you ready?" Tori asked me.

"Almost," I said, pulling a Daizlei sweatshirt on over my head. I reached down and grabbed my duffel bag while Tori opened the door.

"Good luck. I'll keep an eye on Lily for you." She hugged me.

"Thanks. Have fun in California." I walked out the door.

The dorm was silent; no one was up this early on a Sunday.

When I got outside, I was disappointed to see the snow had melted, leaving damp green grass in places. The fountain had also defrosted, and water was running smoothly from the arrow mounted on the angel's bow. As I neared the landing area, I didn't expect to see flaming red hair and a pair of brown eyes searching for me.

"What are you doing here?" I asked her.

"I decided to see you off," she said, yawning.

"Oh, well, thank you," I said awkwardly, taking in her pink fuzzy slippers, pajama pants, and hot pink tank top.

"So are you ready?"

"Always. I never lose," I said, remembering how my last match had ended. I should've been disqualified, but extenuating circumstances and all that . . .

"Okay, what's wrong?"

"Nothing." I twirled a strand of my hair.

"It's Lily, isn't it?"

"I just worry." I sighed, when suddenly *the feeling* came over me. Something was going to happen. I just didn't know what.

Breathe, I reminded myself. *She'll be all right. You have people watching her. Tori, Alexandra, even Amber . . . There's no way she'll get past them.*

"Don't. I'll watch her, and Elizabeth's helping me. She won't leave our sight," Alexandra assured me.

"I know." I looked away.

See? my subconscious chided me, *even Elizabeth is helping. She'll be fine.*

"It's the feeling again, isn't it?" she said.

I nodded. "I would just feel better if it were me watching her." I finally bolted to the trashcan about five yards away and hurled.

"Are you okay?" Alexandra yelled, running over to me.

"Fine," I gasped, wiping my mouth and hoping the jet would get here soon so I could brush my teeth again.

"Selena, she'll be fine. I promise. We both know why you need to go on this trip." She gave me a knowing look.

I nodded again and sagged against the trashcan.

"You missed some." She pointed to the corner of her mouth.

I grimaced and reached up to wipe it away. "Thanks."

"Did I tell you I broke up with Michael?" Well, that was a change of subject. She was watching something over my shoulder.

"No."

"I got a new boyfriend." She smiled.

"Who?" I was only half-interested.

"Aaron White."

That got my attention. "You're joking." Word around the gym was he hadn't dated since his ex had dumped him back in August. I wondered what had changed.

"No, and he's, like, really *fine*." She wiggled her eyebrows, and rolled the last word on her tongue.

I wanted to gag again. "Alexandra, he's a terrible boyfriend."

"Why? How would you know? You haven't dated him," she said.

I sighed. "Whatever. Do what you want, just keep an eye on Lily, please?" I didn't need to deal with this right now, not on top of everything else.

"I will." She rolled her eyes just as the jet came into view.

"It's about damn time," I muttered, looking at the time on my phone.

"Okay, have a good trip. I'll text you," she called as she went to give her new boyfriend a hug.

I didn't even bother trying to respond.

Aaron only kissed her on the cheek before boarding. She looked sour, and I was pretty sure she'd also noticed.

Good, I thought, climbing onto the jet after him. *Keep your hands off my sister if you know what's good for you.* I took a seat and sat back, closing my eyes while the feeling washed over me for what I hoped was the final time.

"You okay?" Lucas's deep voice rumbled next to me.

"Fine," I lied as the plane doors closed and we took off.

The only thing worse than one monster is two, I reminded myself.

I looked out the window one last time and tried to push all thoughts of Lily from my mind.

CHAPTER 45

"We're almost there," Lucas said, waking me from my dreamless sleep.

The trip was about ten hours from Montana all the way to the Alps in northern Italy. I glanced at my watch. It was a little past eight in the evening, local time.

"How far away are we?" I asked groggily, leaning back in my chair again.

"You can see it if you look out the window."

Spires of onyx jutted out against the lush green landscape of Italy. Perhaps even more elaborate than Versailles, these were the homes of the Council, and they had been for centuries. They were bigger and older than Daizlei, but I could see where my school's architecture came from. There was no gate for protection, but from what I'd heard about the members of the Council and their servants, I doubted they really needed one.

"It's beautiful," I whispered, feeling a strange sense of déjà vu.

"I've seen better." He shrugged. The tone in his voice

made me want to ask, but something told me to leave it—that I might not want to know the answer.

"Have you been here before?"

"Twice. I've gone to championships the last two years, but never won."

"I really feel like I've been here before." The words popped out suddenly as we got closer.

"That's unlikely. Unless—" He stopped mid-phrase, looking at me with concern.

"What?"

"Unless your parents took you here," he said.

I stayed silent for a moment, and he looked away.

"You do realize I'm not going to break down and cry every time someone mentions them?" He was trying to be considerate, but I couldn't help being annoyed by the implication that I wasn't strong enough to talk about them.

"I know that, but I also know you don't like to talk about them." The ice in my voice hadn't even phased him.

"Not always," I murmured as the plane came closer to the Council.

"Are you nervous?"

I followed his eyes to where my fingers where tapping impatiently. "More of a mix between tired and excited." The jet touched down.

"About?"

"I'm going to the Council, a place I've only read about in books. I'm going to meet and see the most powerful beings that walk the earth. It's . . . gratifying, even if I am walking into a lion's den. I'm tired of being on this plane, and I really need a shower." Meanwhile, my brain was replaying two words over and over: *we're here*. I felt like I was on the precipice of something.

"I understand completely," he said as we stood to leave.

As I stepped off the plane, I immediately felt out of place. Tall buildings towered over me, stuck in their ancient beauty. The cool breeze lifted my hair, and the setting sun heated my pale skin. Directly ahead of me stood a garden— the smell of roses overwhelmed me, bringing me back to my childhood home and mother's garden. I was going to have to take a walk very soon.

"I see that you find my home resplendent, Ms. Foster. I'm happy to say that *your* beauty alone can compare." Aldric Fortescue came striding up, and I was struck by the assuredness that radiated from him. Such confidence—so like my own. He came from the ruling family; a Head of Council, and Member of Court—I was just a wolf in sheep's clothing.

I glanced down at my thinning tank top and baggy sweatpants. "Thank you, but on the contrary, your home is much more magnificent than any beauty I possess," I purred, allowing myself to take on a very formal tone. I hated having to bother with pleasantries, but I knew it would go a long way here.

"You are quite refined for someone so young. I commend you." Such lovely words in such a dangerous place. The Supernatural Council was known for being even more brutal than I was when it came to our enemies, or those who displeased them.

"I do not believe my attire is exactly what you would call refined." I laughed a sophisticated laugh, such a lilting sound. I hated it.

Fortescue smiled as Coach Avery came walking off the plane with Aaron.

"Mr. Fortescue, it is an honor. To what do I owe the pleasure?" Avery's tone had also changed, and that never happened. The Fortescues were the equivalent of royalty. They'd been the ruling family for as long as anyone can remember.

"Ah, Christian Avery, I simply came to welcome you and your students to my home. My servants can escort you to your rooms. Before I leave, however, I would like to make it known to you three that wandering the buildings is not advised. I'm sure you all understand what I mean." His smile was too cunning, too kind. It wasn't real, and all I heard was the threat in his words.

"Thank you for reminding them. I'm positive they'll heed your warning," Coach Avery assured him, casting a sideways glance at the three of us.

"I have business to attend to, and I am sure you would all like to put your things down. Marcus, please show our guests where they will be staying," he ordered the younger man next to him. With a final nod goodbye to Avery, he strode away, leaving a beautiful, tall, dark-skinned man in his place.

"Follow me," he rumbled and began walking.

I fell into step next to Lucas as we came into the court-yard just outside the garden. I studied the servant with his lithe body and glowing golden eyes. Was he of my species, or another? Many of the Council members had servants that were acquired for their ability. The way I had read it, slave felt like a more accurate term.

"You're quite charming when you want to be," Lucas said.

"Charm is easier to fake than sincerity," I countered.

"Always the realist." He seemed satisfied by my answer in some way.

"Of course. What else would I be?"

A half-smile formed on his lips as he contemplated his answer. "Haven't you ever had dreams or imagined you could do the impossible?"

"I did once, a very long time ago. Then life happened, and I had no choice but to see the reality of things. Besides, there's no point in imagining things when I can already do the impossible," I said with my own sad half-smile.

Marcus had led us around the outskirts of the garden and onto a pathway. The legendary Fortescue mansion loomed in front of us, and, oh, what a mansion it was. Spires so tall I had trouble seeing their tops looked dark and foreboding in their onyx encasement. It was the dark castle, plucked straight from a Grimm fairytale.

"The Fortescues have graciously put aside three rooms for your stay," Marcus announced as we walked through the double doors. He had such a thick, smooth foreign accent. Lovely. His voice was too lovely. I kept my distance.

Inside, I found a place of luxury with famous paintings, Persian rugs, and antiques. Despite all the riches, this place felt *cold*. How many of these beautiful priceless things were stolen from those they'd conquered?

"This is your room, Ms. Foster," Marcus said, holding open a door to reveal a bedroom fit for a king.

"Thank you." I dismissed them with a nod.

As I looked around the room, I thought about Aldric's

words. *Wandering the buildings is not advised. I'm sure you all understand what I mean* . . . An almost eerie feeling came over me as I thought about what kind of secrets this place must be harboring. I was the master deceiver; the murderer who couldn't remember. As far as I was concerned, it was a toss-up on who would come crashing down first.

CHAPTER 46

I stepped out of the shower and wrapped a silk robe around myself. I grabbed a brush and ran it through my hair as I entered the room.

On my bed was a dress bag with shoes and jewelry, along with a note that read:

You have an hour to get ready for a dinner party. Lucas will pick you up at 7.
P.S. You're being watched.

I groaned internally, but gathered everything and dropped it on the bathroom counter. I began transforming myself into the respectable socialite I needed to be. I started by blow-drying my hair, then bumped up the back half and used a silver headband to keep it in place. I kept the makeup light—I'd never liked it anyway—and put on the matching black diamond jewelry. The undergarments were the perfect size, and I didn't want to think about how any of them knew. Turning from the mirror, I eyed the Louboutin pumps. That heel was steep, but I'd worn worse. I slipped my feet into them, and found they were surprisingly easy to walk in, and the height difference was staggering. I had to be near six feet now.

There was a knock at the bedroom door.

"Come in," I called.

The door opened and closed. "Selena, you ready?" Lucas asked. He was in the bedroom, but I heard him like he was right beside me.

"One minute," I murmured and turned to the dress.

It was strapless, short, and black. I slipped it off the hanger and shimmied into it. When it was all the way up and positioned perfectly, it was still too loose. I felt for the back zipper to see if I'd forgotten to zip it, but all I found were lacings. I turned around and looked at my back in the mirror. The entire waist had to be laced-up.

"Lucas, can you do me a—"

He opened the bathroom door. I turned to see him standing there in a black tux with the corners of his mouth turned up in an amused smile.

"Turn around," he said, walking toward me.

I placed a hand on the counter to steady myself and used the other to keep my dress in place while he pulled and tightened my dress.

After a few moments of silence, I decided to speak. "Thank you," I whispered, thinking back on this last year. So much had changed.

"For what?" he asked.

"Being there for me . . . putting up with me. I know I'm usually not the best company," I said. I saw his half-smile over my head in the mirror as he pulled the back tighter.

"You should give yourself more credit."

"No, I know who I am."

He sighed as he gave a final tug on my laces and tied them in a bow. I pulled my shoulders back, standing straight with my head held high. The dress did fit me perfectly.

"How do I look?" I asked, turning to face him.

"Beautiful," he murmured, looking me up and down. He sounded like he was talking more to himself than me. He held the door open, motioning for me to go through.

"What a gentleman," I teased, walking into my room. I went over to the nightstand and picked my phone up. I only had two messages—one from Alexandra and the other from Tori wishing me luck. I clicked my phone on silent and put it in my bra as we were walking out.

He took my arm as he escorted me. "Such a lady," he countered, amused smile still in place.

I smiled a little uneasily as a vision from my past came to me. I was only four or five and dancing in a hallway that looked oddly familiar. I was dressed in a gown, laughing and playing with my sisters. My parents were following behind, and when I saw them, I stopped. I heard the words "such a lady" come from my father's lips, and the vision faded.

"But aren't I?" I whispered. He gave me a curious look, and I laughed once. "I forget, there's still so much you don't know about me," I said bitterly, wishing things could be different. No need to go into that tonight.

"All the more fun when I unravel you," he murmured, and we laughed as he opened a door.

"Such a gentleman," I repeated, walking into the dining room.

There was only one table, and while it was sprawling, we very clearly had a private audience with the ruling family for the night. An archaic chandelier similar to my aunt's hung low, probably to showcase its fine details. I didn't recoil as I'd done so many months ago. I kept my gaze roaming.

I only got two feet before I stopped in my tracks. The easy smile I wore faded, and my eyes narrowed slightly. She was sitting at the table with a knowing smile, but rose and came to me as we got closer.

She had creamy skin, high cheekbones, and almost every feature, angle, and color on her was *mine*. Except for her curly hair and stormy blue eyes, I was practically looking in a mirror.

"So it is true," she murmured, taking as much interest in me as I was in her. "I am Anastasia Fortescue, Member of the Council," she announced, offering her hand.

"Selena Foster, Daizlei boxer," I challenged, taking it.

"And you are?" She turned to my escort.

"Lucas Hunter," he said, his voice stiff as they shook hands. His posture was closed, and he eyed her aggressively. She was not welcome, which pleased me. I frowned.

Not good, Selena. Not good.

"Why don't we all take our seats." She phrased it as a suggestion, but I was well aware it was an order.

I started to follow Lucas when she touched my arm and motioned for me to sit next to her. I had to restrain myself from physically removing her hand. After following her around the table, I took the seat on her right. We weren't the only ones here. Coach Avery, Aaron, Professor Vonlowsky, and several others I didn't recognize filled the seats closest to us. The words from Coach Avery's note replayed in my mind:

You're being watched.

I took a deep breath. My gaze caught Lucas's, and he gave me a questioning look, asking if I was okay. I nodded once.

"Yes, quite interesting, isn't it?" Anastasia mused beside me.

"Hmm?" I asked politely.

"How much you and I look alike." She was goading me. Watching. Waiting.

"And why do you think that is?" I returned the subtle prod.

"Oh, I have no idea. Must be a trick of nature." She watched me intently, looking for a reaction. Something about her statement bothered me, and I realized she was lying.

"So, I hear you're the only girl boxer in the tournament."

"That's right," I agreed, pushing my salad around the plate.

"Why are you good at it?" she asked.

Pushy, much?

"I started when I was young and took a liking to it," I

said casually. I had to play this cool. Get the attention off me and my past.

"Oh, come now. There must be a reason you're the only girl in the championships. What makes you so good?" The way she licked her lips made me uneasy.

I needed to respond. I thought for a second about the many reasons I was good, but it really came down to one thing.

"I'm merciless," I declared with an edge to my voice.

She smiled, obviously hearing the warning in my words. My doppelgänger was treading too closely. Like the lioness I was, I showed my claws.

"That's good. So many Supernaturals have gone soft, and that's why we're dying." Her voice was sad, but her eyes were hard; cruel. She was talking about the building tension between Supernaturals and Vampires in the Court, but our supposed softness wasn't the reason for the tension at all. Her family had a very interesting history with the Court from what I'd read, and some of its methods weren't exactly . . . humane. I supposed you didn't stay in power by being humane.

Merciless. The word rang through the air as clearly as if she'd spoken it.

Telepathy. I slammed the door shut on my mind, and her eyes narrowed ever so slightly. Judging by Lucas's blatant stare, he must've heard it as well.

"That's one theory," I said in response to her original comment, working hard to keep my voice neutral.

She studied me for a second. "So, tell me about your family, since you seem to know so much about mine."

I ignored her comment, and tried not to let the tension

show. Across the table, Lucas's eyes widened, and the rest of the table had gone quiet. "There's not much to tell. I have two sisters," I said.

She saw what I didn't say, and things took a turn for the worse. "And your parents?"

"Gone." My tone made it clear this topic wasn't preferred discussion. There was no hesitation, emotion, or room for weakness in my voice.

"How'd they die?" she continued, taking a bite of salad. She spoke to me so casually, you would've thought we were old friends.

"Car crash." I hated playing along, but I had no choice.

"Really? That's strange, unless they were . . . weak."

My jaw locked. "My parents were not weak."

"Selena," Lucas warned from across the table. I could feel him monitoring my mind, and I shut him out immediately. He flinched, and even she did a double take. Every telepath at the table probably felt my mind slam shut this time. I was struggling to keep the shield with her prying. This was not good. I was not good.

"You're protective of your family, I like that. So if your parents weren't weak, what could they do?" She'd stopped the nonchalant act, setting her fork down and turning to face me head on.

"My mother was a necromancer, and my father . . . my father was a telepath." I immediately averted my eyes from the table. Lucas and I had talked about my parents before, but never this deeply. I was keeping secrets—secrets that affected him.

"Interesting . . . " she murmured, lost in thought.

"Ms. Fortescue, may I have this dance?" Aaron interjected, cutting into our conversation.

"You may." She smiled and rose from the table.

They strode out to the dance floor and danced leisurely to the music playing.

Professor Vonlowsky followed, leading a woman I didn't know, and I found myself wondering why he was even here. Aldric Fortescue danced with an older-looking woman I assumed was Mrs. Fortescue, and another couple I didn't recognize followed. Most of the dancers seemed clumsy compared to Anastasia and Aldric.

I used to dance. Only a year ago, I was still taking classes—pop, ballet, jazz, ballroom, modern, even a little Latin. Then I came to Daizlei and everything changed, but I still loved to dance.

"Would you like to dance?" Lucas asked me.

"How many times have I told you not to read my mind?"

"I wasn't," he countered, but he still sounded pleased.

I turned to him. "Can you dance?"

You're playing with fire. I welcomed the flames.

"A little." He smirked.

I sighed and rose from my chair.

He held out his arm, and I took it as he led us to the dance floor. The music changed just as he pulled me by the waist, close to his body, and a tango began. He slid his hand down to my lower back as we started to dance. I glided through the steps, moving swiftly across the floor.

"I never took you for a dancer." His eyes twinkled in the candlelight cast by the damned antique chandelier.

"There's a lot you don't know about me," I repeated my

mantra as he moved me backward. My heels clicked. This was the perfect dress for this. Short enough to let me move, and modest enough to keep it from looking scandalous. What better to tango in?

"Oh really? I think I know you better than you assume." He let go, and I went spinning across the floor. My legs moved swiftly, carrying me as I fell into the heat of the moment. I stopped before there was too much distance, my arms at my sides and head high. I smiled to myself as we crossed the floor, meeting again. He wrapped his arms around my waist as he held me close. I tried to ignore the smell of his skin, the way his hand felt on my back, and how he was ever so slowly caressing my skin with his thumb. We'd been close to each other all year, but this felt different.

"Oh, is that so?" I dipped.

"Yes." He grinned and whirled me around.

"What's my favorite food?" I asked, amused by this little game. I was well aware I was flirting with him now, but it felt so good. I didn't stop.

"Double cheeseburger."

"Color?" I asked.

"Black—"

"Hah!" I cut him off as he backed me up again.

"—looks best on you, but purple's your favorite."

When I didn't say anything, he gave me a smug look.

"What's my middle name?" I smiled. I so had him.

"Analysa," he murmured, looking at me in a way that would've made a lesser woman blush. He should've known better.

"How do you know that?" I knew for a fact that only two people at that school knew my middle name. I'd never told anyone. It was my mother's name, but—as good as he was—I highly doubted he knew that.

"I have my secrets," he replied, a ghost of a smirk on his lips. That bastard. Quoting me? Fuck him.

"There's a lot more to me than a silly color and some food," I said haughtily and let go of him on the twirl, causing me to go spiraling across the floor. His mouth popped open as he watched me.

"Oh, I know." He laughed taking me back into our tango, which was coming to a close. "We'll have to do this again sometime." His voice held a promise as he pulled me in for the end.

"Maybe." I drew my leg up, wrapping it around his waist as he picked me up.

The music stopped, and he looked down at me for a second before putting me down.

Bad Selena, I reprimanded myself. Oh, I was in so much trouble. I should not have done that because now I would dream about the smell of him for weeks.

The room broke into applause, and I turned to see that everyone had stopped dancing to watch us. I smiled as I walked around to take my seat back at the table.

"Thank you," I mouthed to Lucas.

Smirking, he nodded once.

"You're quite light on your feet, Ms. Foster. I've rarely seen such grace," Aldric Fortescue complimented me.

"Thank you, but I'm a boxer. I have to be light on my feet. If I'm not, well . . . I shouldn't be boxing." I faked joviality as I sipped my wine, and the waiters set plates of food in front of us.

"That's very true. A girl your size could be killed in the ring if not careful," Aldric agreed.

"I suppose, but I don't think I'll have to worry about that anytime soon," I said vaguely, taking another bite of my salad. I was completely aware of Anastasia watching me with peculiar interest.

"Why is that?" His dark brown eyes locked on mine.

"I've never lost, and I don't plan on starting now," I declared with the confidence I'd always had. Fighting came naturally to me. It was second nature. I could tell he didn't quite understand this.

"You've never lost. That's quite a feat. Let us toast to victory and the many more to come," he announced, raising his glass.

"To victory," I murmured, touching my glass to Lucas's and Anastasia's. A smile found its way to my lips as I sipped the wine. I could still feel the heat of the tango, the feel of his hands, and I knew deep down that I'd crossed a line I couldn't come back from.

CHAPTER 47

"You made quite an impression on the Council tonight," Lucas noted. We were strolling through the garden and I felt strangely at ease.

"Yes, I did, didn't I? I think part of that's because of Anastasia." My mind was still reeling from dinner. My heels clicked lightly as I walked, and I occasionally smelled a flower here and there.

"She looks a lot like you. If you curled your hair and wore contacts, you could almost be twins."

I turned and looked at him, my eyes narrowed. "Almost is the key word there, because we are *not* twins." My voice was indifferent, but my gaze told him everything.

"Only in looks. Past that, you're very different." His green eyes glowed in the moonlight, and his black hair was as dark as the tux he wore.

"Can you read her mind?" I inquired.

"No. They had several shields there blocking all the Members of Council. It's customary. They know too much." He didn't need to say that she'd communicated with me through them. I was aware of how powerful these beings were. I'd never had so much trouble maintaining my mental barrier as I did tonight. She was the strongest telepath I'd ever encountered.

"Interesting . . ." I murmured and turned away. I knew what was coming; what he'd been waiting to talk to me about.

"You never told me your father was a telepath."

"I have my reasons." It was all I could bring myself to say.

"You always have your reasons, Selena, so please enlighten me. What were they this time?" His voice was cold, almost heartless.

I didn't flinch, but I knew then that I'd made a mistake in not telling him. But I'd done it for him. "When I learned you were a telepath, I immediately thought of my father, and I was always comparing you to him. But I soon learned that you fell short of the man he was. You haven't quite figured out all the tricks of the trade. If I told you about him, you'd want to know more. You'd start to rely on me to explain things, and you would never grow. He got to where he was because of the struggle. I wanted you to get there too. So, no, Lucas, I didn't tell you. In time, maybe I would have, but more than likely not."

He paced back and forth, and I started to leave. This was a mistake.

"You did it because you care," he concluded.

I stopped walking and turned back to him. His green eyes were alive and fiery. "Some things you need to learn on your own. If I told you, I would become your crutch, and when you left after next year, what would you do? So yes, I suppose . . . I care."

"How did you know I was a telepath the day we met?" The last time he'd asked me that, the only response I'd given was, *I'm observant.*

"Your eyes," I answered begrudgingly.

"What about them?" He was completely clueless.

"You glazed over and didn't watch my hands. When I saw that, I knew immediately what you were. I blocked you, and you were stunned. I beat you that day because you've allowed yourself to be crippled by your ability." I took a seat on the edge of the marble fountain and looked up into the sky.

"Crippled by my ability . . . " he murmured the words aloud to himself.

I kept my eyes on the sky, watching the stars, even when Lucas sat next to me.

"Thank you. I still wish you'd trusted me, but thank you," he said.

"It didn't have to do with trust. It had to do with what I thought was best." I was amazed by how far I'd come. How much I'd done. I couldn't help the unease when it came to Lily and how far she'd fallen.

"I wish my sisters were as understanding as you." We'd had so many arguments in the last year alone, and things just kept getting worse with Lily.

"You worry too much." His shoulder bumped mine, and I laughed once.

"You sound like Alexandra," I glanced at him, grinning.

"She must be pretty smart, then," he laughed.

"Shut up." I elbowed him, laughing. I lost my balance,

and before I realized it, I was falling backward into the fountain.

Just when I knew I was going to hit the water, he wrapped a strong arm around my waist, pulling me back up. We were close. Very close. I kept my gaze on his chest, broad arms, and full lips. I couldn't look at his eyes. I shouldn't look at his lips either because then I was tempted to do something I shouldn't. It was just so much, too much . . . him. His smell, his warmth, the callouses on his hands—I felt it all. Again, I reminded myself of the line. I waited for him to move back, but he didn't. My heart pounded in my ears, and when I heard another heartbeat match it, I looked up, finally, into his eyes. I wasn't ready for what I saw there. He stepped back, and I took an unsteady breath.

"You're welcome," he tried to joke, but there was a strain behind it.

"I was going to say thank you until you said that," I said.

"I could have let you fall."

"A little water never hurt anyone." I smiled, more comfortable with the easy banter than the proximity that was screwing with my mind.

"Really?" His smile was smug.

"Really," I challenged.

When he came at me like I'd expected, I jumped to my feet while pushing back on his shoulder. He hit the water with a crash, and I covered my mouth as I laughed.

"I thought a little water never hurt anyone?" He got to his feet, drenched from head to toe.

"What are you looking at me for? You had it coming."

He cocked his head to the side as if he couldn't believe

I'd just said that. He climbed out of the fountain and walked toward me.

"What are you doing?" I asked sharply. I backed up as he got closer.

"Nothing," he lied. Grinning, he darted forward to grab me. I was trapped between him and the bush as he snatched me up, cradling me in his arms while I squirmed.

"Let me go. You're all wet!" I complained, trying to push him away. The water soaked through my black dress, turning the pleasant breeze chilly.

He finally let me go—in the fountain. I went under and squeezed my eyes shut, holding my breath. Gasping for air when I reached the surface, I tried to stand, but my dress seemed to weigh a hundred pounds.

"Need help?" Lucas snickered at me.

"Sure," I agreed, taking his hand. As he pulled me up, I pulled him down, and he went over the edge. I stepped carefully over the side, trying not to slip in my heels.

Lucas had tugged his jacket off and was unbuttoning his shirt. Water droplets clung to his tanned skin, and he shook his hair like a wet dog.

"That's the last time I help you," he said and laughed, running a hand through his wet hair.

"I didn't need your help." I pulled my shoulders back and held my head higher in a show of dignity.

"I'll remember that." He clambered out of the pool.

"We should start heading back," I said. We walked in silence until I reached my door.

"I had a good time tonight," Lucas said.

"Me too." My voice had lost all its playfulness in the five-minute walk as cold and fatigue took its place.

"You look beautiful," he said.

"Thank you." My hair was a soaked mess, my dress ruined, and my makeup smeared, so clearly he was just being kind. I needed to get inside before he realized I'd crossed that invisible barrier.

"Selena." He paused.

"Hmm?" I asked, without even looking at him.

"Thank you."

"For what?"

"Caring."

I stayed silent for a moment before turning to him. "Goodnight, Lucas," I whispered as I closed the door behind me.

His whisper followed me all the way to bed that night. "Goodnight, Selena."

CHAPTER 48

After the dinner party, it was four days of fighting filled with sweat and blood. I would finish one match only to have another opponent ten minutes later. I was tired and sore, but I'd fought my way to the top through forty-eight men. Now, as I stood in the Gathering Hall, I had one final opponent. One person stood between me and victory. Had this been a team-based sport, this wouldn't have been possible, but it wasn't. No matter which team won, someone had to be crowned the victor. The champion.

It just so happened that my opponent was the one person who knew me better than anybody, and the only person who actually had a chance of winning against me. Lucas didn't underestimate me. I could see it in his green eyes as I watched him now.

His shirt was off, and his muscles looked tight. Already sweating, his skin gleamed and you could see the defined ridges of his abs. He had complete focus on sparring, but I was sure he knew I was watching.

I turned away to stretch. The cheering of the crowd was

deafening. Thousands of Supernaturals had come to see who would win. On the second floor, there were balconies where only members of the Council and their friends sat. Every seat was filled.

Someone told Coach Avery that it was time. Standing, I blocked out the noise and walked toward my coach, awaiting whatever advice he had to give.

"I don't know what to tell either of you. This has never happened before. No matter who wins and loses in that ring, I'm proud of both of you and how far you've come, and I'm proud to be your coach." His words were touching but lost effect when a buzzer rang to hurry us along. "Good luck, both of you."

Lucas and I turned away, getting into the ring for the last time this year. How fitting that both my first and last fight of the year were with him, my best friend.

"I haven't actually fought you in almost a year. I hope you're ready."

"You're a sophomore, girl, what makes you think I'll lose so easily? I'm a year older than you and twice as big."

I laughed. We both knew that meant nothing with me. "Remember that when you're looking up at me from the mat," I called across the ring.

"We'll see about that," he said in a teasing voice, turning to wrap his hands.

This was it. Boxing was the only thing I was passionate about. I didn't know what I would do in the future, but right now this was what kept me going. My earlier fights had left me feeling rejuvenated and in control. I had the killing gene locked down. He would walk away when this was done, and nothing would change. We would not change.

The crowd went silent as an announcer came on to introduce us one last time. I took a deep breath, and closed my eyes. A buzzer sounded, and they snapped open.

Good timing too, because Lucas had already crossed the space and thrown a punch at me, which I narrowly dodged. We continued to exchange punches for what seemed like hours, but neither of us could get a leg up. After the last year of training together, we knew each other's moves as well as our own. We were equals, and whoever won this fight wasn't necessarily better. Just the one who didn't make a mistake first. It would be me.

As time went on, I noticed that he was falling back on his only flaw: telepathy. It was his gift and his curse; that much we had in common. His eyes started to glaze over, and he was losing focus. He was intent on not only winning this, but also getting in my head.

How many times do I have to tell him?

Not this time. We were in the middle of the most important fight of the year.

I would wait until he was completely under before striking. I had to do something different. He knew my usual targets: face, throat, gut. I needed a different target, one that was unexpected but could take him down.

Then it hit me, and I knew exactly what to do. Without wasting any more time, I put my plan into action. I stepped in closer to him and—for a fraction of a second—dropped all my shields as I aimed for his face. His eyes narrowed, and he went to block my hand. While he was focusing on the expected, I threw my shields back up and changed direction, right into his sternum. As my fist made contact, the urge to hurl hit me; he'd punched me in the stomach. Before the pain could consume me, I managed to put everything I had into that one punch.

He stared, eyes open, as he fell. I was clutching my stomach as if it would hold back the unbearable pain. Around me, the crowd erupted into applause. I looked down at Lucas. He wasn't moving. How could that be? Shock filled me, and I dropped to my knees next to him.

"Lucas," I managed to say despite the throbbing.

He didn't respond and his face was starting to turn blue.

"Lucas." I hit him in the arm, but there was no reaction.

"Lucas," I yelled and slapped him in the face. His eyes were vacant, wide and staring, unseeing.

"No," I whispered, shaking my head. "No. No. Not you too."

Others were entering the ring now, and I tried one last time, slamming my hand down on his chest. I opened my mouth to call for help, but he jerked. He blinked once, and there was recognition in his eyes when he looked at me. He sucked in a breath of air and slowly exhaled. He was all right. I hadn't killed him.

I took a deep breath and sank onto the floor. "Are you okay?" I whispered.

"Fine," he grunted, sitting up.

"Why did you look like you were dead, then?" I stuttered on the word *dead*.

"You stopped my heart when you punched me, and you started it when you hit me again." His words were husky, and he was breathing harder than normal.

"Oh . . ." I said, not able to find the words.

"Selena! Ms. Foster!" People were calling as they crowded around me, completely oblivious to what had just happened. I pulled my knees up and wrapped my arms around them. I really did not want to deal with all of this right now.

"Hey, y'all need to leave. You're not supposed to be up here," Lucas spoke up, noticing my discomfort.

As the crowd cleared from the ring, others entered, replacing them, and these people couldn't be sent away.

"Ms. Foster, that was quite a fight. One hour, thirteen minutes, and fifty-two seconds," Aldric Fortescue said as he approached me with his arrogant granddaughter. He stared at me with peculiar fascination.

"It felt longer," I said. I was tired, physically and mentally.

This was the Council, and appearance was everything. Despite the nausea and stomach cramps, I got to my feet and faced them like the champion I was.

"I imagine it did. That reminds me." He looked at Lucas. "How is your . . . " He motioned to his chest.

"Fine." Lucas's voice was deep and unemotional. I could tell he didn't want to talk about it.

"Good, good . . . " Aldric murmured. "Well, I just wanted to congratulate you on your victory. We will see you both tomorrow at the awards banquet." He turned to leave along with Anastasia, who'd stayed unnaturally quiet throughout the conversation.

I glanced over at Lucas, who was looking away, and sighed.

"You used telepathy to beat me," he said. I was expecting that.

"Yes."

"I knew you would do that. That's why I hit you in the stomach. I just didn't expect to have the wind knocked out of me." He chuckled, and his deep voice rumbled around me.

"What's funny?"

"You. You beguile me. You fascinate me. You're beautiful, and yet you have a brain. You're not afraid to think for yourself, and your smart mouth gets you into trouble more often than not. You're not a stupid teenage girl with her head stuck in the clouds. You see things how they are." He turned to me, staring into my eyes with such conviction. "There are just so many things about you that you wouldn't expect. You're perfect. I don't know how you do it." His voice was distant, as if he were talking to himself. He was looking at me in a way that demanded a response. I couldn't ignore him.

The sincerity behind his statement rocked me to my core. Not because he actually thought this about me, but because he saw what no one else could see. I wouldn't let them, and yet, he saw it. I'd given him the only thing I had left to give, and he knew it. This moment was so intense and so fleeting. My fight or flight instincts kicked in, but I was done fighting him.

"You're wrong. I'm far from perfect." That was all I could say as thoughts of my constant struggle for sanity surfaced . . . and my failing grades, Lily, my parents, the *other me* . . .

As we stood there in silence, I became aware of my

surroundings. The crowd was cheering ecstatically, and reporters were calling out my name in hopes of getting an interview. Outside the ring, Coach Avery was beaming as he spoke with Aldric. In all this chaos, I was standing silently with Lucas, and the conversation had taken an awkward turn.

"You should go," he said, motioning to the reporters.

"Yeah . . . " I walked over to the edge of the ring and ducked under one of the ropes. After slipping through, I jumped off the edge and hit the floor with a thud.

"Selena! Ms. Foster! Could you please answer a few questions?" People shouted to me from across the single rope that separated us.

I looked back at Lucas once before turning to the reporters. He was watching me with his usual mysterious half-smile, and for once, I found myself wondering what he was thinking.

CHAPTER 49

Today was my last day at the Council, and as beautiful as it was, I hoped not to be back anytime soon. I took my time admiring the garden as I made my way to the Gathering Hall for the ceremony. I strode in through the double doors and was pleasantly surprised that the paparazzi and most of the fans were gone, as was the ring, and everything else boxing-related. Instead, they'd been replaced by the finer things in life—classical musicians, tablecloths, and silver cutlery. There were only a few hundred people here today, and I instantly felt more at ease away from prying eyes.

"Ah, Ms. Foster, just the girl I was looking for. Please, join us." Mr. Fortescue's voice was just audible above the music and I turned to the group of people. "Dimitri tells me that you're moving into an Advanced Battle Simulation class." I turned and saw that Dimitri was my very own Professor Vonlowsky. I still didn't know why he was here, but it wasn't my place to ask.

"Yes, and both her sisters as well. They are all very gifted." There was a sarcastic note in his voice, but Aldric appeared not to have noticed.

"Really? Is that so? What are their gifts?" he turned to ask me.

"Alexandra's a fire user, and Lily . . . she was a healer until recently. We're not entirely sure what she is at the moment." I didn't want to go into Lily's condition. Even thinking of Lily now made me get the *feeling* like something was going to happen.

"That's quite interesting—" Aldric started, but a servant carrying champagne interrupted.

"Sir, it's six o'clock," he reported.

I reached over and took a glass of champagne, sipping it.

"Thank you for reminding me, Henri." He paused and turned to the rest of us. "You must excuse me. Awards do have to be given. We can continue this conversation another time." He walked away.

The music stopped as he went to stand behind a podium. "Good evening, everyone . . . "

I didn't pay attention to the rest because my cellphone vibrated. I quickly reached down my dress and pulled it out. Lily. I glanced up to see everyone engrossed in whatever Aldric was saying, except for Lucas. He was watching me.

"What are you doing?" he mouthed.

"I need to take this. I'll be right back," I whispered and walked out the door. "Hey," I answered the phone once I was outside.

"Selena?" she whispered, and there was fear in her voice.

"Lily, what's wrong?" Panic instantly struck me.

"I'm so sorry, Selena. I didn't mean to— I didn't realize —" She broke into a sob.

"What are you talking about?" Something had happened.

"Their eyes are so black," she continued. "Elizabeth, she didn't know . . . they took us." There was a long silence. "I'm scared, Selena." This girl was nothing like the power-hungry killer I'd seen three weeks ago.

"Lily! Focus. What's wrong? What happened?" I could hear the desperation in my own voice as I paced back and forth. When I turned, I came face-to-face with Lucas.

"What's going on?" There was a spark in his eyes. He knew something was up.

Over the phone, Lily was whimpering. Then, so quietly I could barely hear it, she spoke one word. "*Demons.*"

The line went dead.

My stomach dropped. The blood drained from my face. My phone slipped from my hand, but I didn't care.

"What is it? What happened?" Grabbing my upper arms, he took my weight to keep me from crashing to the ground.

"Lily. She's in trouble . . . " I reached down and grabbed my phone from the pavement. "I have to go."

"What?" He shook me, making me focus on his face. "Go where? You're almost seven thousand miles away from school. How are you going to get there?" He undoubtedly thought he was being reasonable, but all I saw was someone standing in my way.

They come first.

"The jet. It's already waiting for us." A plan was coming together in my head.

"That's insane, Selena. What will I tell Coach Avery? And when you get there, what are you going to be able to do? Do you even know what kind of trouble she's in?"

They come first.

"Lucas, I have to go. Lily needs me, and you are not going to stop me. Nobody is. You and I both know those are all trivial things, so are you going to help me or not?" I demanded.

The look on his face told me I'd won this fight. "Fine," he agreed.

"I need you to go back in there and pretend like nothing's wrong while I get on that plane back to Daizlei. Can you do that?" I knew this went against every fiber of his being. He wanted to be there. He wanted to go with me or stop me, but letting me go by myself was not on his agenda.

Please don't make this any harder, I begged silently.

He didn't hear me. I couldn't let him, because if he heard me, Anastasia probably would too.

"What are you going to do when you get back to Daizlei?"

"Find Lily."

"Do you even know what kind of trouble she's in, Selena?"

I studied his eyes for a moment, deciding whether or not to tell him the truth. "No." I looked away.

"Goddammit, Selena, I heard her on the phone. You just lied to my face."

I flinched, but he didn't move.

"How can I trust you're not just going to do something stupid when you do find her?"

Truthfully, it was smarter for him to come with me; to

fight with me. I knew the real reason I didn't want him with me. It was selfish, so selfish when it was Lily's life on the line.

"I guess you'll have to trust me." I returned the glare. I needed to go.

"You just lied to me," he repeated.

"Because I'm trying to protect you!" I needed to keep my voice down. This was wasting time.

His eyes softened, and I turned away. "Wait." He grabbed my arm.

"Lucas, I have to go. My sister needs me. You're going to help me, or you aren't, but I don't have time to console you and make you feel better about this. Are you with me?" I looked into his eyes, not knowing how to say goodbye.

He was with me. He always had been, and he always would be. This hurt him, and if I came out of this, we were going to have a lot to talk about.

"Yes," he whispered.

I pulled away from his grasp and started walking.

They come first.

"Selena!"

"What?"

"What am I going to tell Avery?" He was stalling, and we both knew it.

"You'll figure it out," I said flatly and started walking again.

"Selena," he called again.

"What?" I growled. I turned one last time; this was his last chance to say whatever he had to say. This was it.

"Come back to me."

His voice was soft and enticing. Oh, how I wished things were different.

They come first.

I nodded once because it was all I could do. I'd never understood goodbyes. I'd never liked them. So much easier to just disappear and be a ghost. As I turned my back on him, I saw his final resigned look, and the way his bright green eyes became guarded once again.

I will come back and fix things, I promise.

Lily had called me three minutes ago. The clock was ticking. I didn't have any more time to waste.

CHAPTER 50

Power coursed through my veins, just waiting to be released. The day was coming when I wouldn't be able to be dormant anymore, and I was fighting it, though my body screamed to let it go. After twelve years, my walls were about to fall—the only question was when.

I glanced out of the window and saw nothing but white clouds.

How much longer?

The question nagged at me, and it was taking all my will not to ask the pilot every ten minutes. I'd basically threatened to kill him if he didn't take me back to Daizlei. I'd been expecting a fight, but he knew who I was. After the plane left, I'd tried to call Lily back, but I'd only gotten her usual happy-go-lucky voicemail telling me to leave a message and have a great day. After leaving five of them with no response, it was clear I was just wasting my time. Then I'd tried to call Alexandra, but got her voicemail too.

Now I was staring down at the same picture I'd been looking at for the last nine hours. *Demons.* Attractive men and women with raven hair and eyes so dark and cruel that only fire from the pits of hell could match them. I looked at the words I'd already read twenty times and read them again.

DEMONS ARE creatures that come straight from Hell itself. They are here to collect souls and wreak havoc. As creatures of fire, they cannot conjure it, but are not affected by it either. They travel in shadows with inhuman speed and strength. They are nearly indestructible. There are only three ways to kill a demon, each as effective as the last. The first is decapitation—the head must be removed completely, or they will heal. The second method, and usually the easiest, is to stab them in the heart. The last way to kill one is to drown them. This last is said to be the most difficult, but all require you to get close enough; a rather tricky feat to pull off without dying.

RIGHT AS I was finishing the paragraph, the pilot came on to tell me we were landing in five minutes. I hurriedly stashed the book in my bag. Soon the school came into view, getting closer every second. When we were only feet from the ground, I got up and walked to the door. I had no time to spare.

It was already dusk here. I took off down the pathway in search of Alexandra. If Lily was missing, she was my best chance of finding her. The wind whipped my hair around, and I shivered, wishing I'd changed out of the dress I wore for the banquet.

I opened Alexandra's door, hoping by some miracle Lily was here and this was a joke.

Alexandra was sitting cross-legged on the bed, painting her nails, and there was confusion in her brown eyes. "I thought I wasn't going to see you until tomorrow—"

"Where's Lily?"

"I don't know. Why?" I saw red. She was supposed to be watching her. She'd promised.

"Have you seen her since you got back to Daizlei?" I gritted my teeth and fought the heat that wanted to consume me—and what was left of my heart.

She's your sister. They both are. Calm yourself.

"No . . . she's probably with Bella. Selena, what's going on?" She stood and capped the nail polish, but I was already on my way out the door.

"Selena!" She ran after me.

"She's missing, Alexandra. Gone. I got a call from her ten hours ago, and she's in trouble. I have to find her."

"But I saw her yesterday," Alexandra said in disbelief.

"Well, she's gone. I knew I shouldn't have left," I muttered grimly as I barged into Lily's room. Both her roommates were talking and laughing, but she wasn't there.

"Bella," I barked.

The girl with big, brown, Bambi eyes jumped. "Yes?"

"Where's Lily?"

"I . . . I don't know." She looked away; her discomfort was obvious.

"Where did you see her last?" I demanded, my patience running thin.

"In California." She stared at her hands, unmoving. She was hiding something.

I wasn't afraid to resort to more effective, and less humane, methods if need be. "Was she with anyone?"

"Blair and another girl. She was tall with brown hair and really gray eyes."

I knew exactly who she was describing. "Elizabeth," I muttered. Lily had mentioned her on the phone in the middle of her hysterical babble.

"Where were they going?"

"Toward some . . . warehouse, I think," she said meekly.

"What did it look like?" I was starting to crack, but I had to keep myself from lashing out.

"Big and metal, with sliding doors and graffiti painted on it." Her eyebrows bunched together as she tried to remember.

"What color was it?"

"Black," she answered, nodding as if to reassure herself.

"Do you know what they were doing there?" It was my final question, and by the way she stared at everything but me, this was what she was lying about.

"No . . . " she said, her voice unsteady.

"Are you sure you have no idea?" *Last chance.* I had to go whether she told me the truth or not.

"All I know is that the brown-haired girl was leading them, but I think she's in trouble."

Without another word, I turned and left the room with Alexandra on my heels. I didn't have time to hear more.

"So Elizabeth took her and Blair into a warehouse, but we don't know what for. Okay, and you know that Lily's in trouble because she called you, but you don't know where from. This makes no sense." Alexandra frowned in frustration.

"Maybe not, but I still have to find her." I stopped at my door.

"I'm going too," she declared.

How did I know this would happen? "No."

"Why not?"

"Because it's dangerous, Alexandra. I already have to save her, and I don't need you there getting in the way." It sounded harsh, but it was the truth. Alexandra was a liability, and I didn't need another one.

"I can take care of myself," she said, clearly offended.

I shook my head. "No, I need you to stay here. Please, Alexandra. I might already be too late, but I don't want to put you in danger too." I wanted her to understand, but if she didn't give soon, it really didn't matter. I wasn't taking her, no matter what.

"I can help you, though."

"Not this time." I shook my head.

"You know what kind of trouble she's in, don't you?" Her eyes were as accusing as her voice.

"Yes." I didn't even bother lying.

"Then why can't I go? It won't be like we're going in blind, okay? We can, like, make a plan and—"

I held up my hand to silence her. "No. End of story." I went into my room and closed the door, not even waiting for a response.

My roommates were plopped on Tori's bed, watching a movie. I flipped on the light, ignoring their protests as I rummaged through my suitcase for clothes.

"Selena, we weren't expectin' you back till tomorrow!" Tori exclaimed, getting up.

"Change of plans," I muttered, stripping off my dress. Modesty wasn't exactly my priority.

"Why are you back so early?" she asked, throwing herself on my bed.

"Lily's missing." I tugged on black skinny jeans.

"What? How? I saw her—"

"Yesterday," I finished for her. I yanked my black tank top over my head and shimmied into it.

"What happened?"

"Not entirely sure, but she's in trouble. I need your help." Flopping down next to her, I picked up my black boots and hurriedly jammed my feet into them.

"Of course! Anythin'—"

"I need you to teleport me to California."

After a moment of silence, she said, "I've never done it over such a big distance before, and I'm not the prodigy Lucas is—"

"Please, Tori. I could already be too late," I begged, lacing my boots up.

"I guess I can try . . ." She nodded. She wanted to do this, and I needed her to.

"Thank you," I said while I grabbed my leather jacket. I reached into my nightstand and pulled out a six-inch knife wrapped in a leather case.

"Is that what I think it is?" Amber demanded.

"Yep." I slid it down my pants in the middle of my back.

"How long have you had a knife—" she yelled.

"I have several, and I've had them all year." I quickly ducked under my bed and pulled out another two. The longer one with the armband, I strapped to my left arm and put my jacket on to cover it.

"Exactly what kind of trouble is your sister in?" Tori asked with a nervous waver in her voice.

"Demons," I answered, sliding the last knife into my boot. There was no point trying to keep it from them—and it wasn't like they would try to stop me.

The room went silent, apart from the movie still playing. I unclipped the barrette in my hair and let it fall, only to pull it back into a tight ponytail.

"Ready?" I asked, breaking the silence. I looked expectantly at Tori, and she nodded, feebly holding her hands out. I took them in mine and held my breath.

"Close your eyes, and don't hold your breath," she warned.

I took one breath, and the feeling of being sucked through a vortex returned. This time it was longer. When I felt the ground beneath my feet again, I cautiously opened one eye.

We weren't in the room anymore, but it definitely wasn't California.

"Where are we?" I asked.

"Idaho," she breathed. "We're goin' to have to do this in smaller distances. I can't make it all the way to California in one shot."

My stomach dropped, but I didn't protest. This was still a million times faster than a plane. I closed my eyes and slowed my breathing.

In an instant, the feeling returned. Her hands tightened on mine, and I knew she was struggling. I hit the ground hard. Tori landed on top of me in a tangle of limbs. This was hell on both of us, but we were closer.

"Where are we now?" I grunted, and she rolled off me.

"Border between California and Nevada . . . I've only got energy left for one more, Selena. Where exactly are you tryin' to go?" She wheezed, trying to sit up.

"A warehouse. You guys were near it yesterday when Lily disappeared. Do you remember anything like that?" I should've cleared this up before we left Montana.

"There was a big black one near the coast," she said.

"Was it metal with a lot of graffiti?"

"Yeah."

"That's it," I said, getting to my feet.

Tori's knees were shaking, and I offered her a hand to help her up. Under other circumstances I wouldn't have asked her to keep going, but I had no choice. I closed my eyes one last time and took a deep breath. Tori squeezed my hands, and the feeling of teleportation kicked in.

I opened my eyes, just for a second. Blackness swirled around us like a tornado enclosing us. My claustrophobia reared its ugly head, and nausea came in waves. Tori's face was tight with tension, and her tan had disappeared, leaving her skin unnaturally white. Her eyes were closed, and dark circles surrounded them. Her energy was dwindling.

We hit the ground with a bang, but luckily we landed in the grass. I opened my eyes to see a dark sky with the lights of L.A. twinkling beautifully in the distance. Music boomed out of a building down the street. The place was alive.

Next to me, Tori moaned, and I looked over to see her scrunched in a ball.

"Tori?"

When her green eyes opened, the whites were marred by several burst veins. She needed sleep.

"I'm fine. Go to your sister," she insisted weakly.

I wasn't going to leave her in the middle of L.A in this condition. I scooped her into my arms and cradled her. Across the street, there was a little diner with a sign reading *24-hour-service*. I walked in and laid her in a booth, setting my cellphone on her lap.

"Excuse me—" A waitress tapped me on the shoulder.

I dug through my pocket, pulled out a fifty, and put it in her hand. "Let her sleep, and when she wakes up, give her food. You can keep the change."

She nodded once, and I walked out onto the sidewalk. Not even a hundred yards from where we'd landed was a warehouse, just like the one Bella had described.

CHAPTER 51

The metal was cold as ice. I placed my hands on the edge and pulled, and the door creaked open. I stepped into the warehouse. Darkness enveloped me, apart from a lamp in the corner.

"Lily," I called out. I knew that wasn't the best idea, but how else was I going to find her?

I took another step into the warehouse before I saw them. The picture in the book didn't do them justice. Their hair was just as black, and they were every bit as attractive as the picture showed, but their beauty was cruel *and* seductive; their eyes fathomless.

I pulled my shoulders back, narrowing my eyes. I never got the chance to get closer. Pain exploded in my head, and my vision faded as I fell to the ground. I never found out if I hit it because the blackness closed in.

Well, damn.

~.~.~

When I woke, images were blurry, and I could only vaguely hear voices. After a few seconds, things became clearer, and I remembered what had happened. Without thinking, I shot up, only to hit something. I rubbed my forehead and bit back the urge to hurl as the nausea overwhelmed me.

"Ow," Lily complained, clutching her head.

"You're alive," I breathed and crushed her to me. Her face was smeared with grime, and her brown eyes were exhausted, but she seemed unharmed. "What's going on?"

"Shhh," someone else whispered.

I looked across the small room to see Elizabeth sitting against the wall.

"They can hear us," Lily whispered very quietly in my ear.

I nodded slowly then looked around the room. If it weren't for my Supernatural vision, I wouldn't have been able to see anything. The room was small and dark, with no windows and only the shattered remnants of a light bulb above. On the far side, Elizabeth sat next to the metal door. A wooden desk was pushed up against the wall where Blair sat, watching. It was unnaturally warm—the only thing even vaguely cool was the concrete floor. We were trapped.

"I need you to explain what's going on," I whispered against her ear.

She nodded, trying to hold back tears. When she leaned close and tried to talk, mainly sobs came out, and the few words she managed were far too loud.

I quickly placed a hand over her mouth. "Shhh . . . shhh . . . it's okay now. I'm here. I won't let anything happen to you, I promise," I whispered. She clung to me like a frightened child, and I held her, rocking back and forth until she fell asleep.

I slowly removed my arms from around her and unclasped her hands from my waist. Without waking her, I leaned her against the wall and silently slipped over to Blair, who looked the most stable of the three.

I bent my head and whispered to her, "How long have you guys been in here?"

"Almost fifteen hours," she rattled off without glancing at her watch.

"Do you have any idea what they plan on doing with us?" I asked.

"Nope. We can't hear anything through the door," she answered.

"Well, whatever it is, it's going to happen soon," I said.

"How do you know?" She shot me a sideways glance.

"Just a feeling," I muttered, rubbing my stomach to keep the nausea down.

She looked skeptical.

"Look, I'm not your favorite person. I get it. The feeling's mutual. But we're trapped in a warehouse with some of the most dangerous creatures known to our world. If we want to get out alive, I'm going to need your help, so you can drop the tough girl act because this isn't a movie. This is real, and our lives are at stake." I laid it out for her because I didn't have time for bullshit. "Do you want to die?"

"No," she murmured, her icy composure breaking just enough to let me in.

"Okay, so work with me," I said.

She thought for a second before nodding.

"I need to know everything you know," I whispered.

"There are seven demons, all male. The leader's the tallest, and the other six do everything he says." She spoke so softly that I had to read her lips.

"Is that all?" I mouthed.

She shook her head. "I don't know if this helps, but they were looking for someone. A girl. I don't know who."

Interesting.

"How did you guys even get here?" Their story was choppy. Someone was lying, and I had a feeling it was going to get a lot worse.

Just as Blair was starting to answer, the door unlocked with a quiet click. Before they opened it, I shot across the room to Lily. I didn't know what to expect at this point, but I was not leaving her on her own.

The door flew open, and one of them strode in. He glanced around the room, then his eyes rested on me.

"Get up." His voice was deep and far too lovely.

I started to get to my feet, but Lily tugged at me.

"Don't go," she cried. The sound of the door hitting the wall must've woken her.

"I have to," I told her, pulling away as she screamed at me to stay.

I pulled my hand free, but that didn't stop the demon from slapping her.

"Stop," I yelled at him.

He laughed wickedly. "Come with me," he said with a sadistic smile. He wrapped a strong hand around my arm and dragged me out of the room. I went freely, not wanting them to hurt Lily anymore.

Wooden crates were scattered randomly throughout

the room, and a single oil lamp sat on a crate near the metal door I'd come through. Blair was right; there were seven. Most of them were shirtless, sporting scars and tattoos, and the smile they wore told me what was coming would not be pleasant. The tallest one wore black slacks and a white button-down shirt. His hair, long by modern standards, was worn in a low ponytail. He watched me with interest.

The demon gripping my arm stopped a short distance in front of their leader. The others closed in as well, ruling out escape as an option. The leader walked toward me and took my chin, moving my face from one side to the other while he examined me. I kept my eyes on his every second. I would not show fear. I would not bow to these beings. I would conquer.

"What's your name?" His voice was deep with a slight accent I couldn't place.

I didn't answer.

"What is your name?" He studied me.

Again, I didn't answer, and his eyes flicked to the side for a second.

The demon behind me removed his hand from my arm and pulled off my jacket. I tried to stop him, but he was much stronger than me.

"Interesting," the leader murmured, eyeing the long knife strapped to my arm. "I'm only going to ask you one more time. If you don't answer, there will be consequences."

Behind him, one of the demons held up something shiny. A knife.

"What is your name?"

"What's yours?" I spat. He was going to threaten me

with knives? Please. He wouldn't do it. He wanted something from me.

That didn't stop the demon from walking up to him and offering him one. Instead of taking it, he reached up and slid the one on my arm out of its sheath. He stepped closer until I could feel his breath on my face. Then, in a gentle, almost caressing way, he ran the tip of the knife over my skin.

"Do not test me, child. I have been around far longer than you." He whispered the words in my ear so tenderly, like a kiss. His closeness scared me more than the blade.

"Selena Foster," I said. My voice was calm and gave away nothing.

"Good." I could hear the smile in his voice. He moved his face back so that he could see my eyes. "What are you doing here, Selena?" He said my name lovingly, like a term of endearment. What was he playing at?

"I don't know. Why don't you tell me?" I answered sarcastically.

He smiled slightly, clearly amused by my defiance. He took a step back and grasped my hand as if he was going to hold it. Instead, he buried the knifepoint in my skin. Starting at my shoulder, he dragged the knife down my arm. When he got to my bicep, he let it wind around my skin, encircling it down to my wrist. It hurt, but I'd endured worse over the years.

"Now, what are you doing here?" he repeated calmly as though we were friends and he wasn't torturing me.

I didn't give in.

He ran his fingers across my skin and down to my other hand then repeated the carving with perfect precision on my other arm. The pain was excruciating, and he wasn't going to stop. I had to drag this out and hope that Lucas was coming for me.

"For Lily," I said through gritted teeth, still refusing to show weakness.

"Lily? Who is Lily?" He ran the knife across my throat, barely touching my skin.

I didn't answer. Unfortunately, someone else did. "One of the blondes begged me not to take this one. That must be the girl," he supplied, far too proud of himself.

I will kill you.

"Is that true, Selena?" the leader asked me.

I refused to look at him.

"Ahh, yes. So, who is this Lily?" He pressed the knife to my throat.

"My sister," I answered icily.

"Sister . . . interesting. That would make you the brunette's cousin. You're the one . . ." he announced with obvious delight.

"What do you know about that?" I said, stalling for time.

He laughed cruelly. "So you know? Then tell me, why do they want you?"

"Why does who want me?" I demanded, but he only laughed.

"I'm the one asking questions here. What makes you so special? You're beautiful, yes, but that's not a reason. You must be a Supernatural, which makes me wonder if they want you for what you can do . . ." He pondered this, examining my face. "What's your gift?"

This time there was no budging. I didn't have room to haggle.

"No answer? Fine, let me show you something." He unbuttoned his shirt and dropped it to the floor. "Many years ago, when the world was still very aware of our existence, I was hunted. They caught me once. They trapped me and tortured me for information, trying to break me. One of the many things they did was this."

He turned and showed me his back. In between his shoulder blades, a giant six-pointed star had been carved into his skin.

"I never gave in. When I escaped, I murdered every single one of them. We're going to see just how strong you are, little one, and I can promise you that when I'm done, you will wish you were dead."

He snapped his fingers once, and someone lifted my shirt. I watched him walk behind me, and in seconds, the blade of my own knife was pressed against my skin. Slowly, oh so slowly, he carved, and I was his canvas.

There has to be a way out of here.

The thought vanished as he continued. The pain was so acute, so raw … and blood ran down my back and arms. I wanted to scream, but I wouldn't give in. I went to a place in my mind where there was nothing but rage. Nothing but power. He was going to pay for this. I focused on that power until he stopped carving into me and walked back around to face me.

"My dear, are you ready to talk now?" His voice was gentle, but the threat behind it was clear.

I didn't say a word.

He took my hand and carved another hexagram on my

palm, connecting the tip of the star to the cuts on my already bleeding arms. When he finished it, instead of asking me again, he just began on my other palm.

I tried to fight it, but his grip was so strong.

"There's fire in you, Selena. I like that. It's a shame I have to kill you." He ran his fingertips down my cheek. "You really are lovely."

I didn't flinch. I held my ground. I refused to let him see fear.

"Just answer me, little one. What are you? Why do they want you?" His voice caressed my bleeding skin, the tingle of his breath soft on the wounds.

"Bite me," I spat.

Flames consumed his eyes, and he wrapped his fingers around my throat. He tilted my head back and sliced through the skin just below the hollow of my throat. When he was finished, he released me, but the anger hadn't left him.

"You will tell me, Selena, even if others have to suffer. I'm going to make you beg. I'm going to break you. And before you die, you're going to watch me kill the others one by one, starting with you sister."

"No," I gasped, but they were already dragging them out.

"Selena," Lily whimpered.

"So, you weren't lying . . . good to know," he murmured. He left me to examine Lily. "No knives. Not for this one." I saw the wheels turning behind his devil eyes. He grinned at me. No, he had a whole other method of torture for her. He set the bloody knife on the crate.

"Hold her." He pointed at me.

Two of the demons moved forward, each taking an arm.

Slowly, he ran his fingers along her arms and neck like he was looking for something. Then—faster than I would've thought possible—he struck. Grabbing her hand, he extended her arm and used his palm to snap it in half at the elbow.

Her scream pierced my ears. It was the same arm I'd broken three weeks ago.

"No," I shouted, anger rolling off me in waves. My heartbeat had skyrocketed. Heat. I felt heat, as if I were standing on the surface of the sun.

He picked her up by the hair and threw her against the wall. Her body crumpled, and she moaned. I had to stop this.

"Last time. Why do they want you?" he demanded.

"I don't know," I answered in truth.

He laughed wickedly, but I had no idea whether he believed me.

"This is it, Selena, and I want you to know that I've enjoyed every second of this." His voice echoed in the warehouse. He picked her up by the neck. "I'm getting excited just thinking of the reward I'll get for her soul. She's going to burn for all eternity. Because of you." He laughed.

I snapped.

CHAPTER 52

My control was gone in an instant, replaced by cold fury. Power exploded from me, and I let my wrath rain down on them. The warehouse shook as everything was thrown away from me. Glass shattered. The door ripped off the hinges, revealing the lights of L.A. It didn't take me time to recover. I had the upper hand now.

I pulled the knife that was tucked into my waistband and stabbed the demon closest to me. He hissed and his eyes flared before he dissipated into black smoke. I turned to see another approaching me. His eyes were wicked, and he smiled cruelly. Death was too kind for them, but my body was not strong enough to take my time. I needed to kill them before I passed out from blood loss.

The knife from my boot came to my hand with a thought. Letting my instincts take over, I threw. It landed with deadly accuracy, and he disappeared.

Three others were closing in on me. I slammed two back against the wall and faced the remaining one. He went for my neck with his hand, and I slit his wrist. He hissed in pain, but didn't back down. He grabbed at me with the other hand, and I sidestepped so that I could snap his arm. The wound only distracted him for a moment, but it was all I needed to decapitate him with one swipe.

As he disappeared, the other two were already on me. I wasn't as quick this time. The blood loss was weighing on me; my energy was waning with every passing minute. There was a sharp pain in my thigh, and I glanced down to see a knife planted in it. One of them had thrown it. I swore under my breath and wrenched it from my leg as it bled profusely.

Bad idea.

I needed to end this soon.

I summoned another dagger to my hand and threw both of them at once. Before I saw if they'd hit their targets, another five knives were flying at me. I dropped onto all fours, and they narrowly missed me. When I looked up, the black smoke told me that my attackers were dead.

I turned on the last two demons, immediately going after the lesser—I was saving the leader for last. The demon grabbed me around the neck in an attempt to suffocate me but realized too late that he'd gotten too close. I lunged and bit his nose, clawing into his eyes. He tried to push me away, and I took his eyeballs out altogether. Stumbling, I kicked him in the sternum hard enough to send him flying back, and a knife appeared in his chest. Ash. His skin turned gray and dry as he left the world. The body hit the wall, leaving only smoke.

The leader watched me at a distance as I killed all six of his companions in my rage. There was more than just interest in his eyes—but no fear.

"Telekinesis," he said.

This was the first time someone outside the family had named my gift. It was telekinesis, in a way. I could move things with my mind, but at its core, I could do so much more. I could control matter itself, manipulating anything and everything to my will.

"Yes."

"I understand now. Yes . . . you are far more special than I thought." He smiled.

"What are you talking about?" I demanded, closing the distance between us. He couldn't move; I had ensured that. But did he have to look so fucking cocky?

"I'm curious to see how this plays out. You're the first telekinetic in a thousand years. Of course, that's why they want you."

A thousand years . . . why did that ring a bell? I shook my head, dismissing the thought. He was screwing with me.

"Who wants me?" I demanded. I needed to make sure this never happened again. No one was ever taken again.

"You really don't know. Hmmm . . . everything will become clear in due time." He cackled, and the wicked gleam in his eye was both knowing and insane. I couldn't trust a word he said.

"You're crazy. And you know what else? You won't be keeping your promise because I have several of my own to keep. Starting with your death." I aimed for his heart.

His hand closed around the knife. "You are strong, like me. You are beautiful and clever, yet you have no idea what you are capable of." He motioned to the ash that covered the floor with a lazy grin. "I bet you struggle with your sanity, don't you?"

He shouldn't have known that. Maybe he wasn't so insane . . . My vision was getting blurrier by the second. The fatigue weighed on me.

End this, my mind whispered.

I threw him back against the wall with my mind. Bending down, I picked up the fallen blade and stepped closer to him.

"Last chance. Who's after me?"

There was silence in the room. With his assailants dead and my companions unconscious from the blast of my reawakening, that left only us.

"Everything will become clear very soon; that I can guarantee."

I was sick of the riddles and games. His time was up.

With my last bit of strength, I beheaded the bastard.

I was going to end this—even if it killed me.

CHAPTER 53

Pain consumed me. It covered me with its bloodstained hands. My bloodstained hands. My cuts were still bleeding, and my head throbbed. Someone was carrying me. With a jolt, I managed to pry my eyes open.

Lucas. The sun was shining, and he was carrying me. But where? How? I tried to say something. Anything. I couldn't find the words. Couldn't find the strength.

The sunlight disappeared as he hurried me somewhere . . . but Lily . . . I had to know what had happened to her. I had to know. Somewhere in me, I found my voice, but only one word would come out.

"Lily," I whispered.

He looked down at me, and the world went still. His eyes—always so careful, so guarded—were filled with emotions that swirled and raged. He said something, but the blackness was already closing in. And then I was gone . . .

.

~.~.~

First, death claimed my vision, and then my body, and finally my mind. For once, I knew true pain and fear. I saw my parents, and I knew I would never see my sisters again.

My parents were dressed the same as they'd been the night they died, and I couldn't help but try to run to them. Something held me back. I tore my eyes away from them and looked behind me. A hole appeared in the blackness. Beautiful, brilliant white light flooded in, filled with images of the living. Images of people I cared about.

I turned back and looked at my parents. They were reaching for me. My father called my name, and I ran toward them, but my feet were slow and dragging.

Something tugged at me. Something I had to remember. These were my parents. My parents needed me. They'd always needed me. It was my fault they were dead . . .

Dead.

I was . . . dead. Dying. It was my fault they'd died, and now they'd come to claim me in return. If I had to go, it was only right. Only fair for taking their lives.

I felt another tug.

When I turned around, my heart broke. My sisters were standing over me. Alexandra was screaming and crying, and Lily . . . white glowed from her hands. She was trying to heal me.

"It won't work," the shadows whispered in my subconscious.

They were right. She could try all she wanted, but Lily wasn't strong enough. Even with all her power, she couldn't bring me back. The world of the dead was here to claim me. It was my fault my parents had died, and now I'd stolen Lily's life right out from under them when I'd rescued her and the others at the warehouse, and they were not happy.

My sisters faded as the dark closed around me.

"This is it," I whispered.

Only blackness remained. My parents welcomed me with open arms, but they were different. They were laughing—cackling. My resolve faltered.

It wasn't them. It was the world of the dead trying to trick me into not fighting. Into giving up.

"You're not a quitter, Selena. Keep fighting. For me," Lucas said softly.

His voice was the only thing that made sense here. When another tug came, I turned around before the world of the shadows consumed me. One image had remained when the rest faded. Lucas stood over me, and I could see it in his eyes. He *knew* I was looking at him.

I had to leave. Run. This was a trick. It all was a trick.

I ran, trying to flee the darkness, but it followed me. It grabbed my arms and legs so that I couldn't move. I struggled, trying anything to get away. But he was fading. His voice was fading. I was going to die.

I lashed out with everything I had. My final shot at escape. Everything disappeared.

My eyes flew open.

I was in a white room. It was chaos. My sisters were there with Coach Avery, Professor Vonlowsky, and Lucas. When I'd lashed out, I must've thrown them, because bodies littered the floor. Heavy leather restraints bit into my wrists and ankles, but I wasn't lying on the bed—I was suspended a few feet over it. Purple-black energy surrounded around me. Encased me. My arms swayed at my sides, and my black hair swirled around me like the sticky tendrils of death.

I took in a single breath of air, and fell. Everything was black.

~.~.~

This time when the darkness came for me, it wasn't death, but a dreamless sleep. For that I was thankful. I didn't have it in me to fight death again. My body pieced itself back together ever-so-slowly as the darkness kept me safe. I didn't want to go back. I needed to go back. Death was easy, and life would be hard, but I had promises to keep, and miles to go before I could sleep . . .

~.~.~

My eyes fluttered open. The white room was in darkness. Nighttime. I was alone, apart from Ms. Love, the school's resident healer. She was standing next to me, taking my temperature.

I looked up at her with questioning eyes.

She sighed. "Welcome back to the world of the living," she said.

I stayed quiet, not knowing where to start. What questions to ask first.

"You gave us all quite a scare, you know . . ."

I looked down at my wrists, remembering the last time I awoke. The restraints had been removed, leaving them red and raw.

"You look confused. Would you like to talk?" she asked, offering me the little push I needed.

"Where is everyone?" I stumbled over the words. After not talking for so long, my voice was scratchy and broken.

"Your sisters went back to their rooms about an hour ago. I agreed to get them if you woke up." She started changing the IV bags filled with mysterious liquid I could only assume were keeping me both hydrated and alive.

"What about—" I tried to ask.

"Lucas?" she guessed. A knowing smile ghosted across her face. "He left a few moments ago. I told him to get some fresh air. He'll be back soon, I'm sure," she said.

I nodded. "What happened?"

"Well, three days ago, they rushed you out of the plane and into here. For a while you seemed to be doing better, but then you suddenly crashed. None of us thought you'd make it. Lily tried healing you, but you started fighting back. We tried to restrain you, but it became so bad that you broke away. That was when you woke up the first time."

Her gaze avoided mine. I could guess what was troubling her.

"You fainted, but we kept you hooked up in case you had a relapse. You continued sleeping peacefully for the rest of the day. Professor Vonlowsky left with Headmaster Daizlei after I told them you were stable. You're going to be okay."

That probably would've been reassuring to any other patient. For me, it meant only one thing. My secret was out.

I was back.

"I shouldn't be alive," I whispered.

"No, you shouldn't. Your cuts were too deep, and you'd lost so much blood before they even got you back here. If it weren't for your sister, I don't know if you'd be here right now."

I sighed. We sat in silence for a while. She didn't know the real reason I'd lived, but I did. Lily couldn't have saved me on her own. It was because of Lucas that I was here.

"What's going to happen?" I asked her. My voice was getting stronger by the minute.

"I don't know, my dear." We stayed silent for a few more minutes before there was a knock at the door.

"Come in," she called.

I knew who it was before he opened the door.

"I'll leave you two to talk." She gathered her things and left the room.

He walked toward me, almost hesitantly. I gave him a weak smile and he took a seat in the chair next to mine. We didn't speak, but I could see the questions in his eyes. I was on shaky ground.

"Ask," I said. Not that I was in any place to be telling him what to do.

"I don't know where to start," he murmured.

"I lied to you, I'm telekinetic, I'm dangerous . . . the list goes on and on. Take your pick," I said, feeling hopeless. I couldn't hold his gaze anymore. I had to look away. This was the thing I'd been so scared of, right here in this room. I would lose my best friend because of what I was.

"Yes, you lied to me, but I'm not angry. I know you're telekinetic, but I'm not scared. And you've always been dangerous, but not to me." His voice was gentle, and he took my chin, turning my face back toward him so that I had to look. "Those weren't my questions; they were your fears." He spoke so quietly, yet he was the only thing I could hear.

"What's going to happen now?" I whispered.

"I can't tell you for sure, but they're probably going to have questions only you can answer. There's going to be a lot happening here in the next few days while they try to straighten this out." He sighed, and ran his thumb over my cheek ever so softly.

"Lily!" I exclaimed in a panic, ashamed that I'd only just remembered to ask about her.

"She's fine. They fixed her arm, and her concussion wasn't that bad. She's even back in school," he assured me.

Silence filled the room, but it wasn't awkward or strange. We understood each other, and he knew the truth now. Strangely enough, he didn't hate me. I was relieved; a weight was lifted from my shoulders that had been there too long.

My eyes watered, and for the first time in over six years, a single tear ran down my cheek.

"It's okay. Everything has a way of working itself out," he whispered, wiping away the tear and taking my hand. He trailed his fingers lightly across my scars, and I released his hand. I'd forgotten about those.

"What is it?" He sounded concerned.

"I need a mirror. I have to see something," I insisted as I slipped out of bed.

Once I was on my feet, I stumbled and started falling into the IV stand. He came around and grabbed my arm, keeping me steady. I started to walk toward the bathroom, wheeling the stand with me. When I flipped the light on, I sucked in a breath.

My hair and face were pretty normal, and someone had wiped the blood and grime from me. For whatever reason, they'd kept me in the same clothes they'd found me in. I was going to need a shower ASAP. My scars stood out stark against my skin. A sickly red line wound around my arms. When I held my palms out, they sported identical hexagrams. I turned to see my back and swept my hair aside. The tank top had been cut off and now hung from my arms by the tiny straps, leaving my back bare. In between my shoulder blades was a giant, red, six-pointed star that matched the ones on my palms. If it hadn't been so gruesome, it would've been beautiful—in a cruel way. I turned around to see the smallest star just below the hollow of my throat. These scars . . . they were the markings of a warrior. I flinched when remembering how I'd gotten them, but I wasn't going to live in fear of my own body. Things were changing, and these were just the start of it. Someone was after me. Let these scars serve as a reminder of what happened to those who crossed me.

"Lily was able to take you out of danger, but she wasn't strong enough to heal it all the way." His eyes didn't leave the scars.

"Do they bother you?" I asked.

"No. They make you look . . . exotic." He ran his hands lightly over my arms, following the scars. I shivered under his touch, but it wasn't from pain.

"How'd you get them?" He must've heard about the demons from the others, but they'd missed a lot of it. That was a question I wasn't ready to go into detail over, not yet.

But I owed him an explanation for giving me more kindness than I'd deserved.

"They questioned me, and when I wouldn't give them any answers, they used other means to get them. The pain was excruciating." I flinched, remembering. It would take a long time to dull the pain of that knife in my memory. "I didn't give in; not until I had no other choice."

I saw the leader who'd marked me; the malice in his smile. He'd been smiling even as his head fell to the floor and turned to ash. I would never forget.

"Lily told me they took her and forced you to watch while they tried to kill her." He grimaced.

"Yes, that came after these. When I didn't give in, they tried to kill her, and I lost it. There were seven, and then there was just me. I killed them all."

"Does it bother you?" I could tell he wanted to say more, to know more, but I was only willing to share so much. I had changed. I was tortured. Now, I was different.

"No, it only made me stronger."

I wasn't dormant anymore, and my power was returning at an alarming rate. I not only had my curse back, but I was stronger, faster, sharper. Whether I liked it or not, my ability was a part of me. I had forced it away for years, but even if I'd wanted to, I wouldn't be able to do it again. Besides, everyone already knew about it now. The damage was done.

"You gave up being dormant to save your sister."

"Yes."

I looked at his eyes, the very essence that had brought me to life a year ago when I first saw them. I'd given up being dormant for my sister. Only he knew that even for saving her I wouldn't endanger him. I hadn't let him come because I cared too much. If I'd given up being dormant for her, I didn't want to think about what I would do for him.

"Now what are you going to do?"

"I'm going to deal with it. Whatever happens from here, I'll take care of it. I'm not hiding anymore. That didn't get me very far last time," I said.

Only then did I realize he hadn't spoken. My shield was in tatters, and despite that, I sighed in contentment, leaning against him. He was safe, my sisters were safe, and I was alive. For the first time since my parents died, I was glad of it.

In fighting death, I'd realized how much I wanted to live.

CHAPTER 54

"Ms. Foster, we would like to have a chat with you." Vonlowsky barged into the room without even knocking, and Headmaster Daizlei followed. This must be the backlash I was waiting for.

"What do you want?" I sighed.

For some reason, Vonlowsky always put me on edge. Perhaps because he'd known long before anyone else that I wasn't using my true ability. Aside from that, the man lacked manners. I didn't understand how he was able to get along with members of the Council.

"You recently hijacked a jet from the Council without permission, threatened its pilot, left campus to hunt down demons, and only narrowly escaped with your life. I don't believe you're in a position to have an attitude, Ms. Foster," he snarled.

"And I don't believe you're in a position to be questioning me, but here you are," I said icily.

His gaze narrowed.

"We're not here to question you, Ms. Foster, we would

just like to talk," Headmaster Daizlei said as he tried to smooth things over. The man was several hundred years old and had mastered the act of choosing one's battles wisely.

"About?" I asked.

"A number of things . . . " He glanced around the room as if he were interested in it, but I knew the meaning behind his words.

"My ability," I summed up for them.

"Of course—"

"Among other things," Daizlei assured me, cutting Vonlowsky off.

"Well, can you cut to the chase? My sisters are going to be here soon," I said with a certain distaste.

"It's been brought to my attention that we have a prodigy in our midst. I've been asked to move you up to a senior Advanced Battle Simulation class. How do you feel about this?"

I considered his proposition. With my ability back, I was even further above my peers. My sisters were also being moved up, which would allow me to keep an eye on them, and I was going to need to perfect my self-control and learn how to use my ability. If there was one thing I'd learned from the demons, it was that this was only the beginning. Someone was looking for me. Someone knew the truth. I needed to be able to protect my sisters—and myself—until I could hunt them down.

"I'll do it, but with the understanding that you don't control me. If I say no, I mean it."

Vonlowsky's face flamed with outrage. "Why, you insolent—"

"Understood." Daizlei again overrode Vonlowsky's insult and agreed to my condition.

"She is a child! I will not take commands from children, no matter how gifted they may be!" His gaze went between the headmaster and me.

"I haven't been a child in a long time. I grew up. Maybe you should do the same." I shifted out of bed so that I was standing. Without the IVs, the process was so much easier. "I've been taking care of my sisters since I was ten years old. I got them through everything. Where were you guys when we manifested? When I had to cover up our abilities over and over again? When we moved from house to house because we weren't wanted, and trouble followed us everywhere we went? My point: you weren't there. None of you were, and now you suddenly think you're in a position to make demands?"

I didn't raise my voice as I strode up to him. In the bare hospital gown I wore, my scars were very visible. His eyes went to my arms as I advanced.

"In fact, where were you when three students disappeared on a trip you people took them on? I've been watching them for six years on my own, and I never once let them get into danger like that. You weren't there. I had time to leave the Council—halfway across the world, let me remind you—and I still got there before anyone knew what had happened. I was the one who took the risk." I paused, looking at my palms. "I was the one who was tortured." His eyes flashed to my open palms as I ran my fingers over the scars. "I was the one who killed every single one of them. And I lived." I clenched my hands into fists, and turned a hard glare on him. "Not you. We were surviving without you, so before you go assuming yourself superior to me just because of your age, think again." I was directly in front of him now, and out of breath.

He looked down at me, a ghost of a smirk crossed his lips, and I waited for the fire and brimstone. "I'm sorry. I owe you an apology." There was no trace of mockery on his face.

"What?" I stammered.

"You're right. You've been through more than the rest of your peers. You're not naïve, and you're not a little girl. You did take care of your sisters all those years, and you did save your sister—killing a number of demons in the process, not only dangerous but a nearly impossible feat." He looked at Headmaster Daizlei before continuing. "I owe you an apology because you're not a child, and though your actions were impulsive—and quite frankly, stupid—you still did what no one else could've done."

I stared at him, not able to make sense of the words coming out of his mouth. This arrogant asshole actually knew when someone had bested him. Who would've thought?

"This doesn't change anything."

"No, it doesn't," he agreed. "But I respect you, Selena, despite your flaws and insufferable attitude."

There was a knock at the door that had to be my sisters. I went and sat back on the metal hospital bed I was growing to hate.

"Ms. Foster, I know there've been problems in the past, and that you don't agree with everything that goes on here, but you've become part of this school. I don't know if this counts for anything, but we're proud to have you. You've exhibited courage I haven't seen in a very long time, and I've been around a while." He paused when there was another knock at the door.

"Come in," I called.

The latch opened, and Alexandra peeked around the door.

"We were just finishing up," I told her.

The door opened the rest of the way, and she and Lily walked in. Vonlowsky left silently with the headmaster following him once again. He paused at the door.

"Have a good summer, ladies. I look forward to seeing *all* of you next year."

He was right. We would be back next year, because oddly enough, Daizlei Academy had become home.

CHAPTER 55

"I'm sorry, Selena. This is my fault." Lily ran her fingers
over my scars.

I shrugged. "You didn't take the knife to me. Besides,
they've kind of grown on me." I attempted the half-smile
that Lucas always made look so easy. When Lily cracked a
smile at me, I knew I'd failed. Alexandra laughed tightly; it
was too strained. As much as I wanted to ease Lily's burden,
it was hers to bear.

"I know you're trying to make me feel better."

"Is it working?" I smiled.

She tried to laugh, but there was sadness in it. "I need to
tell you something," she said.

"I'm listening."

"Do you remember back when I asked you to teach me
how to fight?"

I nodded.

"When you two refused to teach me, I was mad. So mad
that I went to Elizabeth, and she agreed. All the bruises and
times I was missing were because she was teaching me how

to fight. She always said, 'be aggressive,' and, 'pain is for wimps.' I thought about backing out and quitting a couple times, but she always talked me back into it." Tears slowly streamed down her face. The guilt was consuming her. Someone had to pay.

"Somewhere along the way, I changed. My powers changed. I was always so angry and exhausted. One day when I was fighting her, it happened. I learned that I could take energy just like I could give it. After that, I started to get power hungry." The killing gene . . . I was going to need to address that with her very soon. The sooner she knew, the sooner she would realize there was hope—in self-control.

"When we were in California, she told me to go with her. I didn't really question it because it was Elizabeth, and we'd been fighting for months and never got caught. I didn't think anything bad would happen, and then . . . and then it did. She told me she just had to take care of something, and that she needed my help. Then the demons came, and I panicked. I called you when they threw us in the room, but they caught me and smashed my phone. I'm so sorry . . . " She broke down into sobs, and I held her.

"It's okay now. It's all over, Lily," I whispered.

One thing had become very clear: Elizabeth had betrayed my trust, and that was *not* okay.

CHAPTER 56

I knocked lightly on her door.

"It's open," her sharp voice said.

I clicked the latch and walked in, closing the door behind me. In an all-too-familiar metal bed was my blond-haired, gray-eyed cousin, Blair. When I'd lost it on the demons in the warehouse, they hadn't been the only ones affected. Blair had been thrown through a double-paned window and landed on the glass. Now her body was covered in scars, and although they hadn't been inflicted the same way as mine, she too wore hers with pride. We had survived.

"How are you feeling?"

"Could be worse," she said. She eyed my bare arms, but I didn't flinch or move to cover myself.

"When are they going to release you?" I walked around her bed to sit in the vacant chair.

"Three days. Love says my ribs should be healed enough to walk by then." She groaned, and the words "I'm sorry" came to my lips. It was my fault, after all, but it was also my doing that we were alive, and for that alone I think she forgave me.

"I have to ask you about someone," I said seriously, ditching the idle chitchat.

"Elizabeth."

"Yes, I need to know exactly how you ended up in that warehouse." I didn't say it, but in the last week, these two sisters had switched in mind. For once, I actually admired Blair; the girl not only had strength, but spirit. The spirit of a survivor. Elizabeth, however, had made my shit list.

"If I tell you, I want you to do me a favor because I can't do it myself right now." There was anger in her voice—a deadly anger that held promise.

"Agreed." I didn't bother to ask. I had to know, and whatever her condition, it was worth it.

"A while back, my dearly beloved sister went on a trip to the black market in Vegas. Where she happened to run into some very wicked people."

"Demons." Realization dawned on me—the book from all those months ago; the first sign of her betrayal.

A shadow of rage moved behind her eyes, but the physical pain she was in kept it at bay. While her wounds might not have been quite as severe as my own, I was much stronger. I healed faster, and I had Lily. No one had healed Blair because they'd had me to deal with. Now I could walk, and probably even run, but she was confined to this metal prison. I understood the frustration.

"She stumbled onto a conversation, and even though she didn't understand what she'd overheard, they said all knowledge has a price. Her price was her life. So she made a deal with them to save her own ass. Three souls for hers.

Instead of doing the right thing and telling someone, she decided to handle it by herself. She claimed it was because they said they'd kill her if she went to anyone. The catch is that you can only trade blood relatives."

"Lily . . ." I murmured.

"Oh, I'm not even at the good part yet. She'd already agreed to train your sister to fight, but she needed two others." She paused as if considering how to say the next thing.

"Wait . . . if Lily was the first—"

"During your final match before the championships, she started the fight between Lily and April. Then she told Tori about it, because she knew you would come if there was any chance Lily was in trouble, and you would forfeit. Meaning you wouldn't go to the championships and you'd be in California with the rest of us."

Oh my god.

"How did she know you would go?" I whispered.

"I'm her sister, for god's sake, Selena. Do you really think I'm so apathetic that when my sister told me she needed me that I wouldn't go? She's my sister . . . and she's a coward. She told us she needed our help and to go with her. She tried to get Alexandra to go, but your sister was smarter than the rest of us. The second we were inside the warehouse, they grabbed us and threw us into the room. All of us. She knew she needed one more person, so she told Lily to call you, that you were the only one who could help."

I had trusted her, and she'd not only betrayed my trust but also tried to kill me.

"She took us there to die." Her voice was stone-cold.

"Who told you this?" I asked, getting up.

"The infamous Elizabeth herself." She smiled a bitter smile.

"Why would she tell you all this?"

It couldn't be true . . . she wasn't that stupid.

"Because when she found out you were alive, she knew you would start asking questions and eventually come for her. She came to me for advice because she thought I would forgive her, and protect her."

I stared, openmouthed, but only for a moment.

I was pissed.

I was at the door, ready to leave. "Selena," she said, stopping me.

"What?"

"My favor . . ." she murmured. "I didn't forgive her, and I never will. I want revenge, and I know you can take it for me even when I can't." She spoke so softly, and her words sealed Elizabeth's death warrant.

I turned to her. "Consider it done. You didn't even have to ask."

Blair and I understood each other. We'd never been friends, but she was my equal. One of the few.

When I got to elevator, I mashed the button over and over. I couldn't get up to the ground level fast enough. As the doors opened, I slipped out silently and walked down the hall to the double doors that led outside.

Above me, the giant glass clock chimed, and I headed for the cafeteria. Dinner was over, and Elizabeth was there.

People stared openly as I passed. I still technically hadn't been released by Ms. Love, and this was the first time anyone had seen me in while. I was faintly aware that my scars tingled in the fresh air, but all thoughts disappeared as Elizabeth came strolling out of the cafeteria. I stopped and let her keep walking for a few feet. She was playing on her phone and didn't notice me. Until she ran smack into me.

"Excuse you—" She glanced up. Her eyes widened, and I heard that coward heart skip a beat as it drummed in her chest. I grabbed her cell and tossed it over my shoulder. She took a step back, but I advanced on her.

"You stupid, lying bitch!" I swung at her face, and red clouded my vision. She didn't have time to react. "You didn't actually think you'd get away with it, did you?"

"I'm sorry!" she screamed. Blood, snot, and tears ran down her face.

"Liar," I shouted. Using my mind, I threw her back thirty feet and straight through the glass doors of the cafeteria. It was only fitting she had scars to match ours—her victims.

I mentally dragged her back across the concrete to me. Bloody scrapes and gashes covered her body, and she was trembling.

I picked her up by her hair. "This is for lying to me." I punched her.

She dropped to the ground, unconscious, but I picked her up again—this time by her neck.

"This is for Blair." I hit her again.

I threw her down with a thud and kicked her mercilessly. A crowd had gathered around me, and people were trying to pull me off her. No one was strong enough.

"And this, this is for what you did to Lily!" I dropped on top of her. I punched her again, and again, and again. My anger refused to fade.

"Selena!" Alexandra yelled in the distance.

Someone else was trying to pull me off her—and they were succeeding.

That can't be right . . .

"Selena, stop this," Lucas murmured in my ear.

I ignored him.

"Selena, you're killing her." His voice was urgent, and he placed his hands over mine, pulling me back.

"Get her out of here," Alexandra instructed from somewhere, but my head was spinning with rage.

I fought and struggled with him as he dragged me into a building and then a room. I wanted to kill her, and the rage within was urging me on. It told me it wouldn't be satisfied until she was dead. I was more than willing to comply, except that Lucas had me pinned to a wall inside a dorm room I'd never seen before.

CHAPTER 57

"Selena, stop it."

"No." I grunted, trying to shove him off me and get to the door.

"Selena." He shook me, hard enough to rattle my teeth.

"Stop. Why do you even care? Stay out of it." I lashed out, struggling with him.

"This isn't you. Snap out of it." He shook me harder.

"Stop!" I pushed him without lifting a finger. He flew across the room and hit the opposite wall with a thud, falling to the floor.

Silence suspended for a half-second as shock threatened to set in.

I blinked, and my heart sank. "No . . ." I whispered and ran to him, only to stop a foot away. I started to reach for his hand, but stopped myself. I'd done enough.

Lucas groaned and started to get to his feet.

I backed away.

This is what I was worried about.

My temper and my ability were a deadly combination. They made me unstable. Powerful to the point that I was a danger to everyone.

"Are you okay now?" He sounded concerned. He shouldn't be.

I shook my head, still fuming. Power bubbled just beneath the surface, wanting to go off like an atomic bomb.

He walked toward me.

"Don't," I said, holding my hands up.

"I'm not afraid of you, Selena."

"Well, you should be. I'm not safe yet. Stay back." I was somewhere between arguing and pleading. I turned away from him to the wall and slammed my fist against it. A sound like thunder shot through the room, and a crack appeared in the wall. My throat closed as I tried to keep my panic under control.

My strength . . .

"You should go," I said between ragged breaths. I wasn't sure of myself, even with him . . . I had to get things under control.

"I'm not leaving you."

Hands settled on my shoulders. Rough but gentle. He was trying to soothe me, but there was no calming the hurricane that brewed inside.

He was too close.

"I can help you, if you'll let me," Lucas whispered.

"I can't." My hands shook and I squeezed them into fists. "I can't control it."

"Let me show you . . . " Something had changed in his eyes, as if he'd made up his mind.

He brushed his lips over mine, unsure. A spark inside

me caught, and the burning spread. I reached for him, running my fingers through his raven hair as I reeled him in. Nothing could have prepared me for the feel of his mouth, hot and ready against my own. There was no hesitation, and all the pressure I'd felt just . . . vanished. He slipped his tongue between my lips, tasting me, testing the boundary. If I thought I'd crossed the line in the past, I'd obliterated it completely this time. I let my tongue meet his, stroke for stroke, as he slid a hand into my hair, gently knotting his fingers through, tilting my head back.

He wanted more.

I let him take it.

I hit the wall roughly, and a groan escaped my lips. His scent. His touch. I couldn't get enough. I inhaled him greedily. God, did he smell good. He broke free, only to run his lips up my jaw. I tilted back, giving him better access. His kisses weren't sweet, and I gasped when he nipped my ear. A shudder ran through me as I surrendered to him.

"Selena." He murmured my name like a prayer. A question.

Yes. Yes. Yes.

He groaned, pressing me into him. He moved his hands to my hips and brushed his fingers against the skin just beneath my shirt. My back arched, and his hands slipped lower, lifting me as he pinned me to the wall. I wrapped my legs around his waist, and my blood heated when I felt him pressed against me.

Oh god, yes.

"Say it, Selena. Say you want me." His voice was rough. His breath made me shiver. He wanted this.

My eyes opened.

But it wasn't his eyes I saw first.

My gaze drifted over the room, which was destroyed. That pressure hadn't disappeared; it had exploded. I just hadn't realized it. Everything had been thrown away from me—the door wasn't even on its hinges.

I cringed. The heat left me as realization set in.

I'd never consciously made the decision to be with him. I didn't know if I wanted this, but I didn't know if I didn't want it either.

"Selena," he murmured. He sensed it; the change in me. His voice was almost a growl as it brought my attention back to him. To us.

This had to stop.

I pulled away, pushing him back.

My feet hit the ground with a thud, and he stumbled.

Lucas was gorgeous. Six-foot-two with a tan and smoldering green eyes. There was no denying it. He was smart. Athletic. Kind. Understanding. He knew me. Lucas knew everything about me, and he was perfect.

But I couldn't. Too much could happen when I lost control, and I now knew just how easy that would be with him. No, Lucas and I could never be anything.

It was too dangerous.

Relationships were messy. They required commitments. People were expected to act a certain way. Being more than friends would just mess everything up, and I *did not* want that. It was perfect like this; as friends. Nothing more, because then I'd lose him forever.

"We can't do this."

"Yes, we can. Listen to me, Selena." There was a hint of desperation to his voice.

No. I shook my head.

"You think this is going to get any easier? You think people are going to forget about you? Nothing is going to be the same again. I can be there for you. I can be your rock. Stop backing away from me." He reached out, but I was already too far gone.

"You have to stop this, Lucas. You have to forget it ever happened." I was guarded, already closed off from the possibility of anything with him.

"What are you so scared of?" he asked in disbelief. Hadn't he looked around?

I wasn't a damsel in distress.

I was the dragon.

"Everything," I whispered.

Without looking at him, I walked straight to the door. Just when I thought I had everything figured out, he came along and sprang this on me.

How dare he?

"Don't walk away from me, Selena. You can't just ignore me like you do everyone else." Oh, he was angry. I couldn't tell if it was at me, or himself. He should've actually considered what I might've felt before he did this. This was not on me.

"But I can," I said, kicking the fragments of wood out of my way as I stepped through the door.

"Where are you going?" I could hear the hurt in his voice as he tried to come after me. He was scrambling, looking for anything to say to keep me with him.

"I'm leaving." Despite myself, I couldn't walk away without taking one last look at him. I had to stop this. I only knew one way to do that, and he wasn't going to like it. My gaze was cold, stopping him in his tracks.

He searched my eyes, looking for any sign of warmth, but all he found was indifference. The only thing worse than hate was never caring at all. He had to believe I'd never cared. More than that, I had to believe it.

CHAPTER 58

"WHEN DO YOU LEAVE?"

"Lucas told me he'd come get me when it was time to go." Tori shrugged.

I hadn't seen Lucas since we'd kissed. It wasn't like it was his fault. I was the one avoiding him. Of course, he would come by to get her. I had no time to avoid him now.

"You have to come visit me in Tennessee this summer," she insisted.

"I will," I agreed, zipping my bag shut. Finally, I had everything packed.

"You know, if you wanted, you could come in a few weeks and stay all summer. Since Elizabeth's goin' to be at your aunt's and all," she suggested.

"I might take you up on that. Is that okay with your parents?"

"Yeah . . . they won't mind—I'm sure." She smiled, and I couldn't help laughing. "I'm goin' to miss you, Selena," she said suddenly, hugging me goodbye.

"I'm going to miss you too." I hugged her back.

I looked over Tori's shoulder to see the one person I couldn't stop thinking about. His eyes locked with mine, and I looked away. He sighed, confirming my suspicions. He was here to see me, and getting Tori was just the excuse.

"Your brother's here."

"My brother . . . you make it sound so formal, Selena. Like you don't know him." She laughed, but then, she didn't know how close to the mark she was.

"Ready to go?" he asked her, but his eyes were on me.

"Almost," she said, running to the bathroom, leaving us alone.

I crossed my arms, keeping my demeanor cold.

"Selena . . ." he murmured.

I shook my head without glancing at him, and walked to the bathroom. "You need any help?" I offered.

"Nah, I got it." She walked out of the bathroom with a single toothbrush. If it weren't for the tension I couldn't push away, I would've laughed.

"Bye, I'll text you."

"Bye." I looked up as she left.

Lucas just stood there, and for a second he caught my gaze again before following her. I sat in silence looking over my now empty room for I don't know how long. Eventually, I couldn't take it anymore. I had to do something to keep my mind off him. Off whatever this was.

I started walking, intending to let my mind wander over anything but him. When I ended up next to the boxing gym, I knew my mind had plans of its own. I was turning to walk away when voices caught my ear.

"Are you certain Selena's the one?" Headmaster Daizlei's voice drifted to me.

"Yes. She looks just like him. I'm certain it's her," Vonlowsky said.

"This is one of the biggest secrets in our history, Vonlowsky. I'm going to need more than looks."

"I've talked to him. We're certain it's her. The age is right, the look, her personality . . . if you look at her past, the timeline adds up."

What the hell? The demon had said I was the one too. *But what does it mean?*

That was the only thing I'd left out in my retelling of what happened—the real reason they'd tortured me.

My phone buzzed, and I jumped. Alexandra's name lit up the screen.

"Hey," I answered in a hushed tone.

"The plane's leaving. Like, where are you?"

"Coming." I dropped the call.

I didn't have any more time to listen to their conversation. I sprinted out the door without looking back and was at the jet in seconds.

"Nice of you to make it," Alexandra said sarcastically.

I ignored her and took a seat next to the window. As we left the ground behind, I thought about what they could've meant. As Daizlei disappeared, and thoughts of Lucas, Elizabeth, and the summer ahead took its place, I decided it could wait. After all, we would have next year, and the year after . . .

Then again, everything could wait. For once, I was going to enjoy this small peace of mind—because as soon as this plane landed, the reality was going to set in. I would have to sit next to the girl who'd agreed to trade my soul to demons—and try not to kill her.

Again.

Acknowledgments

There are so many people I'd like to thank for making this dream come true. I've aspired to be a writer since I was fourteen, when the first thoughts of the Daizlei Academy series were developing. Now, seven years later, I'm turning that dream into a reality. Being a writer can put you on a long road, and sometimes it's easy to lose sight of where you're going. It's the people who've stuck with me through it, and gave me the courage possible to publish, that have my thanks.

First, to all my readers for buying and reading *Heir of Shadows,* you have my thanks most of all. Without you, this wouldn't be possible. I hope you love this book as much as I do, and continue reading to see where Selena's story goes.

To Matt, you've been my rock through everything, and I don't think I could've gotten here without you. You are a wonderful boyfriend, and have encouraged my writing every step of the way. You took every insecurity and gave me hope. Without that hope, I would never have found the courage to pursue self-publishing. Thank you.

To Courtney, my best friend, you've been here with me through every late night phone call and text at 3am. This has become our norm, and I wouldn't have it any other way.

To all the wonderful people I've worked with along the way, I don't have the words to express my appreciation for you. Thank you for everything you have done in helping me become the author I am today.